DOORS

By Penelope Dyan

DOORS

By Penelope Dyan

Bellissima Publishing
Jamul, California

This Book is dedicated to my friend and mentor, the late Robert Donald Deems whose art for practicing law like a gentleman was unsurpassed, and for most attorneys is a lost art. Although I never got the chance to write your life story, I hope I captured the essence of who you were.

Doors

CHAPTER ONE

THE END OF A RELATIONSHIP

She stared down at the bloody butcher knife in her hand. Her hands were covered with blood. There was blood on the walls and floor. There was blood everywhere. The body at her feet held his hands outstretched, and he was flat on his back where he had suddenly fallen like a great and strong old tree. A gurgling sound came from his throat, and his mouth and eyes were opened wide.

"I didn't mean to kill him," she thought, paralyzed for a moment at the reality of it all. "If only he'd just left us alone."

The faint sound of her child crying interrupted her thoughts abruptly.

"What happened to Daddy?" her child asked. "Is Daddy dead? I hope Daddy's dead," the child said, "Daddy was mean to us. Did you kill Daddy, Mommy?" the child asked full of innocence.

"I don't know."

"Shall I call 911, Mommy? Is this an emergency?"

"Yes, it is, honey. Call 911 just like Mommy showed you . . . Call 911. "

"O.K., Mommy," the child said as she went to the telephone in the living room.

Doors

"My Mommy killed my Daddy," the child said into the telephone. "Please come and help us. There's blood all over. Mommy needs help. Daddy was bad, so she killed him."

It seemed like only moments thereafter when the sound of sirens filled the air.

The butcher knife was dropped next to the body, and the child began screaming as the policeman pulled the child unrelentlessly from the arms of her mother. The child had blood on her dress.

"I want my Mommy! I want my Mommy!" she screamed as she watched another policeman handcuff her mother's hands behind her.

Someone else read the woman her rights.

"Your Mommy will be all right," a matron policewoman told the child.

Somehow the child knew that her mother would never be all right again.

"Daddy was bad," the child said . . . "Daddy hurt Mommy and me . . . real bad . . . "the child explained. "Mommy had to kill Daddy. I wanted to kill him when he hurt me, but I was too little . . . "

"How old are you, honey?" the Matron asked.

"Three," came the reply. "I'm three years old. I had my birthday, and now I'm almost four. I'm getting bigger and stronger every day," she said, "Do you want to see my muscle?" the child asked flexing her arm and pointing at the place where her small muscle was.

"Wow!" the Matron told her, "You certainly do have a big muscle, and you are very a big and brave little girl. Can you tell me what happened to

Doors

your Daddy?"

"I was sleeping," the child explained and I heard screaming. "My Daddy was hitting my Mommy again, and she said, 'Please stop! Please stop! You are hurting me!' and then my Daddy was screaming and then I heard a big noise and it got quiet and I was afraid, so I went to the kitchen to look, and I saw a lot of blood and my Daddy was dead because my Mommy killed him with a big knife. Then I was happy because he couldn't hurt us anymore."

"Oh," said the Matron wondering at the stoic composure of this young child.

"Is that Daddy?" asked the child as she observed the cloth-covered stretcher being placed in the ambulance by the paramedics.

"Got one for the morgue," the paramedic reported on his two-way radio as he entered the vehicle.

"What a shame," his partner said. "He was in the prime of his life . . . killed by a stinkin' bitch!"

The matron turned the child from them.

"Daddy won't be hurting you or Mommy anymore," she said, "But you must continue to be a brave little girl, O.K.?"

"O.K.," came the reply, "I'll be brave, but I need my Mommy," the child begged as she started to cry.

"Your Mommy can't see you now," the matron explained. "You must be brave. Do you have a Grandma and Grandpa?" the matron asked.

"Yes," the child told her through her tears.

Doors

"Well," the matron said, "As soon as we tell them what happened, I am sure they will want to come and take care of you . . . O.K.? Is that O.K.? Just until Mommy feels better and can come back . . . "

"That's O.K. I would like that," the child said. "I like staying with Grandma and Grandpa. I feel safe with Grandma and Grandpa," the child said.

"Come with me then," the Matron told her as she escorted the child to a police car, "We'll see about finding them . . . "

"Can I hear the siren?" asked the little girl.

"Not now," replied the Matron, "Later . . . We don't want to disturb Mommy, do we?"

"No," said the child, "We don't want to disturb Mommy," she said as her seatbelt was fastened and they drove away.

"Mommy says that if you don't wear a seatbelt you can get a ticket," the child said.

"We wouldn't want that to happen, would we?" replied the Matron.

"No," said the child. "We need to obey the law. It's very important to obey the law."

Doors

CHAPTER TWO

THE BOOKING

"I'm sorry, Mrs. Mason," the policeman said, "We have to book you."

"...But I didn't do anything wrong," came the protest, "I told you it was self defense and he was going to kill me . . . he was going to kill me," came the words in a flood of tears brought on by fear of the unknown . . . "

"You need to talk to your lawyer, Mrs. Mason . . . I'm only following orders . . . I have to book you . . . "

"Do you always book self-defense killings?"

"I don't know . . . I'm strictly the booking officer . . . I don't know the particulars of the people I book . . . but I do think you need to talk to a lawyer, Mrs. Mason . . . You really need to talk to a lawyer . . . after all, you husband was an important man, being the police chief and all . . . "

"Are you saying they don't believe me?"

"I don't know, Mrs. Mason . . . but you really need to talk to a lawyer. "

"How am I going to afford a lawyer now?"

"If you can't afford an attorney one will be appointed for you . . . didn't they tell you that when they read you your rights, Mrs. Mason?"

Doors

"I suppose so . . . I can't remember . . . Everything is so unclear . . . and I'm so tired."

"You can rest soon, Mrs. Mason, as soon as I'm finished booking you. "

"What about my daughter?"

"Your parents picked her up at the station over an hour ago . . . She's doing fine . . . just fine . . . "

"That's good," came the reply.

Let's take your picture now, Mrs. Mason . . . "

"You mean the mug shots?"

"Yes. "

"Will I have to be strip searched?"

" . . . with a cavity search," he told her.

 "But I didn't do anything wrong . . . "

"It's standard procedure, Mrs. Mason . . . After all, you did kill the police chief . . . "

"But I told you, it was self defense . . . How can they send me to jail when it was self- defense . . .?"

"That will be up to the District Attorney's office, Mrs. Mason . . . It's not up to me,"

"And if it was up to you, you'd fry me, wouldn't you, you son of a bitch?"

"The point is, it's not up to me, Mrs. Mason . . . It's not up to me . . . "

"The hell it isn't," came the reply. "It's up to you and the whole damn city . . . when it's really your fault that this happened in the first place. "

"What do you mean?"

Doors

"What do I mean . . . ? I could have stopped him if any of you would have believed me . . . I could have stopped him before it came to this . . . but, oh no, a pillar of the community could never be a wife beater . . . forget the hospital stays and medical bills he caused me . . . I just happen to be accident prone, right? Accident prone, my eye . . . Or is it that all you cops are wife beaters . . . ?"

"Look, Mrs. Mason," the booking officer said becoming agitated, "I told you, I am only the booking officer . . . I don't have any control over that. I am not responsible for anything else other than for booking you . . . "

"Then book me," came the curt reply.

"Full name?"

"Mary Margaret Mason. "

"Address?"

"1567 Larkspur Drive. "

"Phone number?"

"559-6784. "

"Give me your right hand first, then your left," said the booking officer, "We're going to do some prints before we take the pictures . . . "

"Just like a common criminal, huh?"

"Just like a common criminal," said the booking officer shaking his head with impatience at his prisoner.

"Can I post bail?"

"Not until Monday, Mrs. Mason . . . not on a capital offense . . . "

"Find me a lawyer," came the reply.

Doors

"When we're all done here, you can call your parents. They can get a lawyer for you."

"I guess I need a lawyer," said Mrs. Mason.

"That's what I've been trying to tell you," replied the booking officer.

"This is a hell of a state of affairs, isn't it?" she asked.

"It certainly is, Mrs. Mason . . . It certainly is . . . "

"We'll then," she said, "Better get on with it . . . "

CHAPTER THREE

PROSECUTION OR DEFENSE

"Mary Mason's parents called me today, Nick," April said as she rolled away from him in their bed and stared up at the ceiling.

"So...?" he said as he fondled her breast.

"This is serious, Nick...Mary's in a lot of trouble..."

"What do you mean?" he said as he rolled over and bit her shoulder.

"Cut it out, Nick . . . I need to talk to someone . . . " April explained.

"Go ahead . . . talk . . . " Nick said rolling away from her.

"Mary Mason's in a lot of trouble, she killed her husband . . . "

"What!?!" Nick said raising his voice and sitting straight up in the bed. April sat up next to him.

"You know how I couldn't get that restraining order that I had against him for beating her enforced . . . ? How the police ignored it as if it didn't exist . . . ?"

"Yeah . . .?"

"Well, it finally became too much for Mary. Apparently she grabbed a butcher Knife last night and did him in . . . "

Doors

"Why didn't you tell me earlier?"

"I didn't want to create a conflict of interest for you, you working for the District Attorney's office and all . . . I figured you'd hear about it on Monday when you got to work . . . "

"Oh my God . . . " said Nick sadly, shaking his head . . . "Oh my God!"

"If I only could have gotten that restraining order enforced," said April, "None of this ever would have happened."

"Well," said Nick, "He was a powerful man . . . "

"*Was* is the Key word here, Nick . . . *was*"

"It's a shame," said Nick.

"It's more than a shame, Nick. It's a travesty . . . "

"Do you think they will put her on trial for murder?" April asked.

"Probably . . . " replied Nick.

"Why? It was self defense . . . " explained April.

"Mary will have to prove that . . . " Nick said quite simply.

"I thought you were innocent until proven guilty in this country, Nick."

"You know better than that, April. You know that might makes right."

"I'm so tired of this," said April. "Can't you do something? Can't you call in a favor or pull some strings, or something?"

"You know better than to even ask me that, April. I Thought you would be used to it by now, darling, you've been practicing law quite a while now."

"And I'm sick to my stomach of the whole damn thing, just sick of it because none of it makes any sense . . . and I've tried it all...The law certainly isn't about justice, that's for sure . . . "

"That all depends," said Nick.

"Depends on what?"

"That all depends on your view of justice.   It all depends on how you look at it . . ."

 "I would like to think that right would make right," said April.

"Everyone has their own moral standards," said Nick.

"You mean for some evil becomes good, and wrong becomes right?"

"Like I said, it all depends on how you look at it."

"But it's not fair . . . "

"You mean that Mary might have to go to trial?" Nick asked.

"That Mary *will* have to go to trial," said April.

"How do you figure . . . ?"

"The law is illogical . . . What other result . . . ?"

"The law is *not* illogical," argued Nick.

"No, perhaps not, but people are and the way people apply the law is, and nothing will ever change that, nothing at all, Nick. . . "

"You're probably right . . . "

"Mary's daughter was taking a nap and woke up and heard the whole thing . . . Do you think that will prove self defense?"

"A jury might buy it . . . but she's *only* three . . . "

"You mean she'll have to go to trial, Mr. Assistant District Attorney?"

"It's not up to me," said Nick.

"Who is it up to, then . . . ?"

Doors

"Not me . . . It's not my responsibility . . . "

"You're the head of the office, Nick . . . "

"Now you are creating a conflict of interest . . . "

"Promise me you won't be the one to take it to trial," begged April.

"I can't promise you that, Sweetheart," came the reply.

"Why not?"

"Because it's not up to me . . . "

"What if I defend her?"

"You wouldn't do that."

"I might."

" . . . but you said you were retiring from the practice of law . . . "

"Mary's my best friend. I may have no choice."

"I'd rather you didn't."

"Will you promise not to be the one to take it to trial?"

"I can't promise you that. It's not up to me . . ."

"Even if I'm defense counsel?"

"That's blackmail . . . I don't want you to do it . . . that <u>will</u> create a conflict of interest for me . . . Mr. and Mrs. Wilcox, attorneys for the prosecution and the defense, respectively . . . the press will have a field day . . . "

"Can you take the heat?"

"I don't think so . . . "

"Me neither . . . "

"What will we do?"

Doors

"I have no idea."

"We'll decide later, O.K.?"

"Good idea," said April.

Then they rolled away from one another and instead of making love, they went to sleep.

CHAPTER FOUR

THE UNEVEN HAND OF JUSTICE

Mary sat quietly in her jail cell. Someone had come by to see if she would like to attend Sunday Chapel, but she refused. Her mother sent a priest over to see her to get her confession, but she told him she had nothing to confess. The priest tried to convince her otherwise, but Mary turned away from him. He finally left.

Mary had a cellmate.

"What's your name?" the cellmate asked, breaking the silence that filled the cell.

"Mary," came the reply.

"I'm Marsha...What are you in for..."

"Killing a son of a bitch..." Mary said without remorse.

"What do you mean?" asked her cellmate.

"My husband was beating me for the millionth time and I took a butcher knife and..."

"Self defense, huh?" Marsha interrupted. "I got you beat...they put me

Doors

in here because my boyfriend killed my baby..." Marsha began to cry.

Mary got up from where she was, forgetting about herself for a moment and sat next to Marsha on the cot. She lovingly put her arms around the woman letting her cry. When the tears subsided Mary continued to hold Marsha in her arms. She finally let go.

"How could they put *you* in jail for that?" she asked.

"They said I should have stopped it...they said it was my fault for not stopping *him* from hurting the baby...I tried to stop him...God knows I tried...he just kept hitting her and hitting her; and she was crying, 'Mommy! Mommy! Help me Mommy!' over and over again...then he threw her against the wall and the crying stopped...and there was a streak of blood on the wall where her head had hit...he ran out the door; and I picked up my baby and I said, 'It's all right now, he can't hurt you now,' and I called 911. Then they came and arrested me and booked me on accessory to murder...and I guess I should have done something before he killed her, but I was afraid he would kill us both...they found him and arrested him too, but he got out on bail. I can't afford to post bail...but what do I have to go home to...a blood streaked wall? The lawyers said I'd get credit for time served if I'm convicted...I don't understand it...I didn't kill my baby...he did...but they said I had a duty to protect her, so I was guilty too..1 .Does that make sense?" Marsha asked as tears streamed down her face.

"No," Mary replied stoically, "It doesn't make any sense at all...None of this makes any sense to me at all...I tried to protect my child and me and I'm in jail...You were afraid to protect yourself and your child and you're in jail...You just can't win, can you?"

"I guess not came the reply...I guess not..."

"Do you have a lawyer?"

"One was appointed for me..."

"That's good," Mary said moving over to her own cot.

"When I get out I think I'll become a prostitute," said Marsha as she lay down on her cot, "...at least that way I can finally screw 'em.'

"You mean men?" asked Mary.

"Yeah," came the reply.

Mary started to laugh. "I think I'll join you," she said as she lay down and tried to close her eyes.

"You'll get used to it here," Marsha said knowingly.

"All I want it a good night's sleep," said Mary.

"Don't count on it," said Marsha.

"I won't," came the reply.

"I'll pray for you," said Marsha.

"Thanks," said Mary. "I'll pray for you too...I have a feeling God's the only one who can help us now..."

"Yeah," said Marsha, "And he's probably the only one who believes us..."

Mary crossed herself and somehow managed to fall asleep. Marsha lay awake all night trying to think of the manner in which she might be able to end the life that she believed she could no longer endure.

"Perhaps I should raise bail..." she thought.

CHAPTER FIVE

THE MOTHER IN LAW

She was very old. She sat with the blinds drawn dreaming of days past.
The lace curtains that covered the blinds needed to be taken down and
cleaned, but her eyesight was so poor, she didn't notice. The house
smelled of musk and mothballs. Old and faded pictures were displayed
everywhere among the chipped porcelain nick-knacks. Two elegant
Victorian style Tiffany lamps sat on the old French provincial end tables
that sided the dusty antique couch which bore underneath it the white
house seal indicating this once fine piece of furniture had long ago graced
the living room or sitting room of a first lady or two. The other furniture
in the room was equally interesting, or not so interesting, depending on
how you looked at it. The old woman was certain the couch with the white
house seal was worth a fortune...and it probably was...it was, after all *her*
most prized possession...!

The doorbell rang.

The old woman got up from the rocking chair and walked to the door.

Doors

Two policemen stood in the doorway.

"May we come in, Mrs. Mason?" one of them asked.

"Certainly," the old woman said ushering them in the door, for she was both proud and happy to have some company for a change.

"I get lonely, you know..." she said as she directed the men to sit on her prized sofa and she returned to her old wooden rocker next to the spinning wheel full of cobwebs.

"We have some bad news for you..." one of the men began...

"Did you know that I knew Clara Bow?" the old woman interrupted..."Why she had a white dog, a Pekingese, I think...or maybe it was a toy poodle...anyway..."the old woman continued, "She had a very small white dog...and she dyed its hair pink to match the furnishings of her house...everything in her house was pink, you know. Pink was her favorite color..."

"No..." I didn't know that came the uninterested reply.

"Of course, that was a long time ago...long before Sonny came along, you know...We never expected to have a child since we had tried for so long without success...then just as we were giving up on the family idea...along came little Sonny, much to our surprise...Do you know Sonny?" she asked.

"That's what we came to talk to you about..." the second policeman interjected.

"The mister was a merchant, you know. There a lot of money in being a merchant...after the mister died, we sold the store, you know...but he left me with enough...he's done well by me, the mister...The mister was a lot older than I, you know..."

"...As we were saying," the second policeman continued, "We came to talk to you about your son..."

The old woman rose and went to the mantle and picked up a dusty picture.

"He's quite handsome in his uniform, isn't he?" she said, wiping away the dust because she could see the dust at close range. "I always loved a man in uniform, although we weren't too happy at the prospect of Sonny becoming a policeman, you know...far too dangerous...far too dangerous..."she said shaking her head..."He should have gone into the family business," added the old woman, "...There's a lot of money to be made if you're a merchant, you know..."

"We understand that," the first policeman said, "But that's not why we are here," he said. "I'm afraid we have some bad news for you...It's about your son..."

"About Sonny?" the old woman asked. "Is Sonny hurt?"

"I'm afraid so, Ma'am"

"Where is he? I need to go to him."

"Calm down Ma'am," the first policeman said. "We'll take you to him, but we have to explain something to you first..."

"...What?" asked the old woman inquisitively, not dreaming that anything could really be wrong with her beloved Sonny, "...Sonny was always such a good boy," she said. "Is Sonny in some kind of trouble?"

Doors

"I'm afraid that Sonny has been killed, Ma'am," she first policeman blurted out, growing impatient with the old woman.

"This is a joke, right?" the old woman retorted.

"I'm afraid it's true," the second policeman said.

"How did it happen?" asked the old woman shedding no tears, "Was it in the line of duty?" she bravely and proudly asked as she sat up straight and shook her shoulders once from side to side.

"No," the second impatient policeman said as the first policeman starred down at the floor, "I'm afraid there was a domestic squabble...It involved his estranged wife..."

"How did it happen?" asked the old woman again, repeating herself.

"The ex-wife says it was self defense," came the reply.

"That bitch!" said the old woman. "Women these days just don't know their place," she said. "The mister used to keep me in line just fine. I never complained," she said.

"We need you to make an identification of the body," the first policeman said. "Do you think you can come with us?"

"Of course," said the old woman, rising from her chair and looking around the room as the second policeman helped her to the door. "Do you think I'll need a wrap," she said.

"I don't think so. It's a warm day today."

"Did I tell you that I knew Clara Bow?" asked the old woman. "I knew Mary Pickford too! Clara Bow was the 'It ' girl, you know..." she said as she left the old house.

CHAPTER SIX

OUT ON BAIL

"I'm getting out on bail," Mary said, "My parents put up their house...After thirty years they finally burned the mortgage, now they have to put up their house as collateral to get me out of prison because I killed that Son of a Bitch..."

"Better not talk that way, Mary," Marsha said. "It shows lack of remorse...they'll fry you for that..."

"He deserved to die..."

"Say that to yourself, but show remorse to the rest of the world..."

"How do you know so much?"

"I have a good lawyer."

"What's your lawyer's name?"

"Bob Grant. He was appointed for me."

"Isn't he the old blind guy?"

"Yeah, but he can see a lot more than you think," Marsha said. "He's really smart."

Doors

"But is he good in court?" asked Mary.

"He got me out O.R.," said Marsha.

"What's O.R.?"

"It means I get out without paying until trial...on my own recognisince."

"Oh Yeah...What are you going to do when you get out?" asked Mary.

"Not much," came the reply. "What are you going to do."

"Well, I can't go home because they have the house all marked for evidence. I can't even get my clothes out of there...So I'm moving home, so to speak, and staying with my parents...with my little girl...God knows how I miss that little pumpkin..."

"You really love her, don't you?" Marsha said more than questioned.

"I don't know what I'd do without her," came the reply.

Marsha started to cry.

"Oh..." said Mary, "...I'm so sorry...I shouldn't have talked about her, you losing your baby and all..."

Gaining her composure Marsha said, "Don't worry about it. At least my baby is safe at last. No one can hurt her now."

Attempting to change the subject Mary said, "What did you say you were going to do when you get out..."

"I didn't say," Marsha said turning her back to Mary.

"I'm sorry," Mary said, "I didn't mean to pry..."

"Do you really want to know what I'm going to do?" Marsha asked as she turned to face Mary.

"Only if you want to tell me," came the reply. "I don't want to know if you don't want to tell me."

"Well," Marsha said, "I have a little money in the bank that I managed to keep from that jerk that killed my little baby; and I'm going to get it out and bury her. Then I'm going to take the rest of it and go downtown and buy a Saturday night special, put it to my head and play Russian roulette..."

"You're kidding..." Mary said with her eyes wide.

"Do I sound like I'm kidding?" came the reply.

"Don't you want to see that boyfriend of yours get what he deserves?"

"Sure," said Marsha, "Maybe I'll kill him *before* I pull the trigger on myself.

"Don't do that," said Mary. "Don't do that...You have your whole life ahead of you..."

"Look," said Marsha, "I have nobody to live for or to answer to in this life. I've been alone a long time. My father deserted me when I was ten, and my stepfather raped me over and over again when I was eleven. I went to a priest for help and all he did was pray for me. Even my own mother wouldn't believe me, and she kicked me out of her home when I was sixteen accusing *me* of seducing *her* husband. I've received nothing but abuse my entire life. Now the system is abusing me. I've never done drugs. I tried to be a good mother, but I was a failure. I lost my baby, and maybe it *was* my own fault. I don't know anymore. I'm tired. I'm so very tired. I just can't stand it anymore... and when I close my eyes to sleep all I can see is my limp little baby in my arms and the blood streaked wall where that jerk threw her and killed her..."

"Will you promise me one thing?" Mary asked.

"Sure. Why not?" came the reply.

"Will you call me at my parents home before you do anything? Will you let me help you get some help?"

"Why should you want to help me?" Marsha asked. "I'm nothing to you."

"That's where you're wrong," Mary said. "Don't you see? the system is screwed...It's not about justice anymore, it's about political empowerment. The people say they want the system to get tough on crime, and the system just takes off its blindfold making an example of innocent people. It's easy to throw defenseless women in jail. They can't get the crime king heads, so they make an example of us and throw us to the dogs. We can't give up. The people are fooled by the convictions of the innocent, and then they believe that their politicians have actually gotten tough on crime. Then the politicians get re-elected and the system gets worse and worse, and we serve as the example...Don't you get it...?

"I don't care anymore," Marsha said. "I'm too tired to fight...It's been too many years..."

"So you're going to give up?"

"I didn't say that," said Marsha.

"What *are* you saying then?"

"I guess I'm saying I'll think about it."

"Then you'll call me before you do anything?"

"I didn't say that either."

Doors

"Then what are you saying...?"

"I'm saying, 'I'll think about it' and that's all. I'm just saying that I'll think about it."

"I guess that's better than nothing," said Mary. "Do you mind if I pray for you?"

"Sure. Why not? I believe in God."

"Then *how* can you do away with yourself?" Mary asked.

"The question *is*," Marsha replied, "How can I *not* do away with myself?"

Doors

CHAPTER SEVEN

THE IDENTIFICATION

"Just follow me," the policeman said as he directed her into the building.   "I'll get someone to take you to the morgue for the identification."

"Who am I identifying?" the old woman asked.

"Don't you remember, Mrs. Mason?" came the reply.   "You came to identify your son."

"You mean Sonny?" she asked.   "Where is Sonny?"

"Better get a Matron down here," the other policeman said, "I think we have a problem."

"I'll get the acting chief," came the reply.   "He'll know what to do," he said as he directed Mrs. Mason to a lobby chair.

"I like what you people have done with this place," Mrs. Mason said observing the mauve interior walls and the beige and oak accent furniture. "This is much better than the old stuff," she said as her hand ran across the fabric-covered arm of the chair. "I really like those mauve blinds," she said. "Maybe I should redecorate my place...Sonny's been after me to do that for years," she said as she began to cry.

"Is everything all right?" the assistant chief said as he scurried around the corner at break neck speed.

"I'm all right," Mrs. Mason replied reaching for the lace and linen handkerchief inside the purse she had quickly grabbed as she was escorted out the door of her home. "I just remembered about Sonny, that's all," she said dabbing the handkerchief to her eyes. "Can I see him now? I want to see him now. I know it isn't very ladylike to say this..." she continued, "...but I want to see for myself what that bitch did to kill him...I never did like that bitch, you know...Sonny was always such a good boy..." she said.

"Take her to the morgue," the acting chief said. "If she identifies the body it will save us all a lot of time and trouble...We won't have to I.D. him by his dental work...it'll save us a hell of a lot of time..."

"But the old lady's a little off her rocker..." one of the policemen whispered to him.

"I don't care," came the reply. "Get him identified and do it now!" he ordered sternly as he turned and walked away. "It will save the taxpayers a hell of a lot of money," he said not turning around, "Besides, it will make my budget look good."

"Budget...? What's he talking about?" one of the policemen said, "He's only the *acting* chief..."

"Not for long...Not if he can help it..." came the reply. "Let's take her down to the morgue before she forgets who she is or something..."

"Don't you want to wait for a matron?"

"Why?"

"I need to use the restroom," Mrs. Mason interjected at that moment.

"That's why," came the reply.

Just then a female officer appeared.

"Take Mrs. Mason to the restroom and then down to the morgue," one of the men ordered.

"I'd be happy to," the female officer said as she approached Mrs. Mason and held out a hand of assistance. "My name is Dottie," she said. "Let me help you to the restroom."

"Thank you very much dear," Mrs. Mason said as the two male officers disappeared down the hall.

After the restroom they took the elevator down to the basement.

As they stood at the door labeled 'Morgue' Mrs. Mason said, "I can't go in there. If I go in there it will mean Sonny is dead."

Dottie put her arm around Mrs. Mason's shoulders and squeezed her gently.

"You don't *have* to go in there," she said. "There are other ways we can identify the body. It will just take more time, that's all..."

"No...Let's go in," said Mrs. Mason raising her chin high. "I need to take care of this right now," she said. "It's just that I always thought I would go first and he would bury me," she explained, "And now I'm having to bury him...my little Sonny...my poor little Sonny..." she shook her head as the

Doors

door was opened.

"Are you all right? Dottie asked as they walked inside the room.

"It's cold in here," said Mrs. Mason. "It smells like death."

"Everything will be fine," Dottie told her as the coroner entered the room.

"Can I help you?" the Coroner asked.

"Yes you can, Frank," came the reply. "This is Mrs. Mason. We're here to identify the chief..."

"How do you do Mrs. Mason..." came the reply, "Please follow me..."

"How about lunch today?" he asked Dottie.

"That all depends..."

"On what?"

"On whether I have an appetite after this," came the reply.

"Is this your first identification assignment, Dottie?"

"No," came the reply, "But I always hope it's my last."

The coroner laughed as he pulled out the drawer. A white plastic material covered the body.

"Is this your son?" asked the coroner looking at Mrs. Mason as he pulled back the covering.

"That's Sonny," she said starring down at the bloodied corpse. "When can I bury him?" she asked as if in a trance.

"Have your mortuary contact me," the coroner said. "We need him out of here as soon as possible. We're short on space..."

Dottie looked away.

Doors

"That's disgusting," she said.

"It's just the facts. Ma'am...just the facts..." came the reply jokingly.

"You can forget about lunch," said Dottie. "I'd rather dine with Dracula."

They walked toward the door.

"I feel funny," said Mrs. Mason as she slumped to the floor.

Dottie tried to steady her as she fell.

The coroner took her pulse.

"She's dead," he said quite simply shrugging his shoulders and closing her eyes as she lay there in front of the door. "Can you help me get her to a table?"

"Oh my God!" said Dottie in panic. "Oh my God!"

"She's dead. Big deal! Get control! Be a professional and help me get her to a table."

"Aren't you going to try to revive her?"

"I'm a coroner," he said. "I'm not that kind of a doctor. Besides, she's old..."

"You are Dracula," said Dottie as she lifted Mrs. Mason's head and began C.P.R.. After ten minutes she said, "It's no use."

"I could have told you that," came the reply.

"I'm putting you on report," Dottie told him.

"Go ahead. See if I care? Makes no difference to me. I hate this job. It's a thankless job. No one ever thanks me. Everyone is dead," he said, "So there's no one to thank me!"

Doors

"What did I ever see in you?" Dottie asked him.

"My personality?" came the reply.

"You are sick..." she said. "You are really sick..."   "It's this job," came the reply. "It's enough to make anyone sick."

"Who will bury her now?" asked Dottie.

"Probably the daughter-in-law..."came the reply. "She'll have to bury them both. It's only fitting. Of course, she won't be able to attend the funerals...that wouldn't be right, since she killed them and all..."

"You are really sick, Frank."

"No," Frank interjected, "I've been in this business for ten years now, and I'm realistic.

"I hope I never become as realistic as you, Frank."

"You will...you will..." came the reply. "...How about lunch?"

"As soon as we get this body to a table," Dottie told him, "Then we'll go to lunch, and *you'll* pay this time."

"It's a date," said Frank. "We'll do the paperwork later."

CHAPTER EIGHT

THE ARRANGEMENTS FOR BURIAL

"Life is being real good to us," the funeral director told his wife as they sat down to dinner.

"What do you mean?" she asked.

"Pass the peas..." he said. "What I mean is, we're getting a whole bunch of business these days..."

"This is a small town," his wife said. "How much business can we get?"

"There's an epidemic..." her husband explained.

"Of death?" she asked.

"Of murder," he replied.

"Thank God it's not the bubonic plague," his wife said. "I'd hate to think that we have a whole bunch of diseased bodies downstairs..."

"This pot roast is delicious," the mortician told her.

"Thank-you, darling," came the reply.

Doors

"You know why we're so lucky?" asked the mortician.

"Why?" his wife asked.

"I've been making deals," he said.

"Is that legal?"

"Better me that Clarks' Mortuary," the mortician said.

His wife poured him a glass of wine.

"What kind of deals are you talking about?" she asked.

"It's simple," the mortician explained to his wife, "I pay the acting police chief five hundred dollars per body; and he sends me all the unclaimed bodies for which the state pays *me* three thousand dollars each to bury in a state plot. It's pure profit. No make-up on the body, no special care, just stick 'em in a pine box, put 'em in the ground and take the profit to the bank."

"You're a mercenary," his wife said.

"Can I have more mashed potatoes and gravy?" the mortician asked her.

As she put the potatoes on his plate she said, "So when are these bodies coming?"

"I've got three coming tomorrow," he said. "It's a family, so to speak...Apparently he killed the child and she went to jail for not stopping him, he was out on bail, and then she got out O.R., bought a gun somewhere and killed him and then herself in a murder-suicide thing...the irony of it is that I'm getting paid double for her and the baby..." the mortician said.

"What do you mean?" his wife asked.

Doors

"Well..." the mortician said talking with his mouth full of mashed potatoes, "She came in last week and paid for her and the child to be buried..."

"Then how can the state pay you?" his wife asked.

"She paid me in cash," he said. "No written contract. I tore it up. She left her copy on the child's casket she picked out."

"You are going to give her what she picked out, aren't you?" his wife asked him.

"I haven't decided. Maybe," he said.

"I think you better," she said.

"What do you mean?" he asked.

"Look," she told him, "It's bad enough living in a place above a mortuary with all those dead bodies downstairs, I don't care to be haunted by ghosts who have been put in the wrong caskets..."

"You're being silly," he said as he took another bite of mashed potatoes. "It's from dust to dust, you know..."

"Do you want to sleep alone tonight?" she asked.

"No," came the reply.

"Then promise me you will put the girl and her child in the caskets she chose."

"Why should you care?" he asked.

"I don't know," she said, "But I do. Maybe it's because I don't think you should screw anyone who is dead and can't defend themselves..."

"To please you," he said, "I'll do it. I'll bury them in the caskets she chose next to each other."

"Thank-you," she said.

Then he reached inside his jacket pocket and took out a small box.

"This is for you," he said.

Inside was a two-carat diamond ring.

"It's the engagement ring I always wanted to give you," he said. "We can afford it now."

She looked at him in surprise.

"It's beautiful," she said as she put it on her finger. "You didn't have to do this, you know."

"It's an investment in our future," he said. "Besides, you deserve something special for living here above all those dead bodies..."

"I'm sorry I've been so rough on you," she said, admiring the ring.

"That's all right," he replied. "Did I tell you that I'm also burying the police chief and his mother?" he asked.

"How did you get that job?"

"I've been friends with the wife's father for years," he said. "...through the Masonic Lodge...I get a lot of lodge business... Most of those Masons are over the hill, you know...It's good for business to belong to the Masonic Lodge."

The mortician's wife began clearing the table.

"I guess there's always work for a mortician," she said thoughtlessly.

"There are two things you can count on in this life," the mortician said, "And that's that you will be born and you will die...and I just happen to be in the business of death...the harder times get for others, the better business gets for me," he said.

"You're so sexy when you talk like that," his wife told him looking into his dark eyes.

"I guess that's why you married me," he said. "Do you want to have sex on the table downstairs?" he asked her.

"You mean the body table?" she asked getting excited.

"You can pretend you're dead," he said.

"All right," came the reply, "But if I like it can we make a habit of it?"

"I don't see any reason why not?" he said, shrugging his shoulders as he headed for the stairs. "...bring a bowl of ice and some candles," he said, "...for effect...I'll get everything else ready..."

She did as she was told and he made love to her by candlelight on the table of death...she lay very still...her body cold from ice...her face made up like a mask of death.

She found it quite provocative.

"Don't *ever* do this with a real corpse," she said when they were finished. "I'll get jealous."

"Don't worry," he told her. "It wouldn't be the same."

"Are you ready for desert?" she asked.

"What do you have in mind?"

"The fires of hell," she replied, "But would you settle for peach cobbler?"

"Sounds delicious," he said kissing her.

Doors

An hour later they went upstairs, showered together, and ate peach cobbler in front of the fireplace. They fell asleep in each other's arms. She wore nothing but her wedding band and her new two-carat diamond engagement ring, and he wore nothing at all.

CHAPTER NINE

NO MORE CONFLICT OF INTERESTS

April sat in the restaurant booth waiting for Nick. He was late again for lunch. In fact, April hoped Nick wasn't going to be a no show, because she had something important to tell him.

She took a sip of her margarita and smoothed her wrinkled skirt.

"God, I'm so sick of wearing these monkey suits," she thought. "It's like wearing a uniform," she thought at she straightened up, "I'm beginning to hate pin stripes, navy blue and gray..."

April felt defiant today. She wore a red blouse to court as a statement of power. It looked great with her navy pin striped suit. She couldn't wait to get home, let down her long blond hair and slip into a pair of cut off jeans and a tee shirt. She couldn't wait to get out of her high heels and run barefoot through the house.

"My feet are killing me," she thought as she slipped off her shoes under the table and wiggled her toes.

"A penny for your thoughts..." Nick said as he sat down across from her in the booth. "...Sorry I'm late," he apologized.

Doors

April took the hairpin from her hair and let her long blond hair fall to her shoulders.

"I think I'll go home early today," she said. "My feet are killing me. Besides I've had quite a morning in court..."

"One of those days, huh?" Nick asked her.

"Yes, *another* one of those days where I stood in court making my motion for summary judgment before Judge Cole and suddenly looked up at the judge and realized, 'she doesn't understand a damn thing I'm saying'..." April sighed.

"I take it you lost..."

"You got that one right. The bad thing is my client just won't understand. How could he understand. When you're right, you're right...that's all...you should win when you're right, especially when the law is behind you..."

"At least you got to make your record for appeal..."

"Oh sure, big deal!" April said emphatically. "Don't these judges realize that the little guy can't afford an appeal? Don't they realize that this is the only opportunity that the little guy has to have his day in court? People can't afford appeals unless they have lots of money or an attorney who will work for nothing and foot all the costs...I just can't do that anymore. I'm getting too tired...too burned out..."

"Well, you know what the trouble is, don't you?" Nick asked.

"What?" April questioned.

"The superior court judges don't want to be appealed. They think it

Doors

makes them look bad. They *know positively* that the big guys, the corporations and the like, *will* appeal right or wrong. The big guys want the costs to go as high as they can go. They'll spend any amount over or under the table to make sure they win so that the little guys will never try to stand up for themselves again; and the judges want to please the big guys because they pull all the political strings and judges are, after all, political appointees..."

"Well," said April, "That's basically what the opposition said to me. The attorney looked at me and said, 'I don't know who's funding this lawsuit, you or your client, but I'm here to tell you that my client will spend any amount and we will fight this all the way up to the United States Supreme Court if we have to...and if we have to we'll break you and your client.' and the funny thing is that he said it right in front of the judge in chambers and she did nothing, nothing at all..."

"That's unethical," Nick said, "To say something like that to you and to threaten you that way; but in actuality, he was telling the truth...How did you end up in the judge's chambers, anyway?" Nick asked.

"The judge said she wanted to discuss settlement, and she wanted to discuss it now..." April explained. "Basically, she ordered us into chambers. She probably was embarrassing herself with her stupid ruling..."

"Is she for real?" Nick asked.

"Apparently," replied April, "But I'm still mad that I lost my motion for summary judgment.

"Those are difficult to win, April. You know that. If you win a judgment in summary, the opposition loses his day in court..."

"I know that," April said, "But the judge said it looked like I had a prima facie case of fraud. She agreed with me that the actions of opposing counsel bordered on being in contempt of court; but she said that even though the actions smelled, even though the facts smelled fishy and that she basically agreed with me, that didn't do it...that didn't overcome my burden of proof... She was *not* going to grant me my motion...God! What does a person have to do!?!"

"Did you ask the judge?"

"Of course...and on the record...She said, 'I can't tell you that, all I can tell you is you have to have more to meet the burden of proof' and that she sympathized with me that my client had a tough row to hoe. Can you believe it? We're talking about a fraud committed by an insurance company that is so horrendous it's unreal, and the judge agrees with me; and I *still* lose!"

"Remember what I told you," Nick said. "It's about power. It's about political clout; and the sad part is, the little guy only has one vote at the polls and very little to contribute financially to the politicians who just happen to be the ones who really make the rules...the ones *who*, in fact, appoint judges like Judge Cole and all the others. Judge Cole knew exactly what you were talking about...that's why she said she agreed with you...the only burden of proof you didn't meet was the proof of your political power..."

"But what the defense attorneys for the big guys don't realize," April said, "Is that when they've killed off all the little guys and their attorneys, there won't be any work left for them...nobody will need a defense...they are killing the goose that lays their golden egg, so to speak..."

"They're only in this for the short term, April," Nick told her, "It's like the corporations themselves. They want quick profit; and they want it now, so they open their factories abroad, close down factories at home, and wonder why their sales end up going down when there are no working Americans to buy their goods. We Americans are the big consumers after all...They don't pay the foreign workers enough to take up the slack of the American consumer's buying power."

"I think you're off the subject," April told him.

"Where's that waitress?" Nick asked, "I'm starved," he said opening up his menu.

"Let's have sizzling fajitas for two," April said. "I'm starving too!"

"Sounds good," Nick told her. "Beef or chicken?"

"How about beef and chicken?" April asked.

"Sounds fine," came the reply. "Want another margarita?"

"I'm driving, remember?"

"I could always be your designated driver," he said. "Remember, we did car pool today..."

"You'll call in sick?"

"I'll tell them I had something at lunch that upset me and I need to go home..."

"What upset you?"

Doors

"Our conversation," Nick said looking over his menu at her. "Something tells me you need a shoulder to cry on and about a million hugs..."

"You right," said April. "Thank-you. I really love you, you know."

"I know."

"By the way," April told him, "We don't have that conflict of interest problem with the Mary Mason case anymore?"

"Oh yeah? Why's that?"

"Mary's parents hired Bob Grant to defend Mary."

"The blind guy?" Nick asked.

"The very one..."

"An excellent choice," Nick said.

"I couldn't agree more," April replied.

"I'll have my work cut out for me," Nick said.

"What do you mean?"

"I got the assignment today. I'm Mary's prosecutor. They didn't give me a choice."

"Mind if I don't wish you luck?" April asked.

"Not at all," came the reply. "It's just business...business as usual..."

CHAPTER TEN

"THANK-YOU MR. GRANT"

Mary approached the office door. She stopped for a moment before she knocked.

"God! I'm nervous," she thought. "I guess I'm afraid of what I might be told."

Suddenly, the door opened, startling her. It was Mr. Grant's secretary.

"Can I help you?" she asked, equally surprised to find someone standing at the door.

"I'm here to see Mr. Grant," Mary said.

"You must be Mary," came the reply. "Go on in and sit down. I have a quick errand to run," she said as she held open the door for Mary.

Mary went inside and sat down on an old worn couch.

"Mr. Grant's not much on office furnishings," the secretary explained, "Especially since he can't see them." The secretary laughed jokingly.

Mary was taken aback. She didn't think blindness was something to be laughed about. The truth was that the secretary didn't think of Mr. Grant as blind in the handicapped sense of the word. Sometimes she even

Doors

forgot he couldn't see.

The secretary left with a bundle of clothes under her arm.

Mr. Grant came out of an outer office.

"We'll have to make this quick," he said. "My dog is sick and just had diarrhea all over my office and me," he explained. I had to cancel all my court hearings because I had to change my clothes," he explained. "The funny part about it is I couldn't smell it, and because I couldn't see it either, I was really glad my secretary, Sandra, told me it was there."

Bob Grant stood before her in a blue plaid shirt, jeans, red suspenders and cowboy boots.

"These are my riding clothes," he explained.

Mary sat quietly for a moment.

"I thought blind people had an enhanced sense of smell," she said.

"That's a myth," Mr. Grant explained. "I don't hear too well either. People who see invented that myth so they wouldn't feel so guilty about us blind folks," he explained laughing heartily out loud.

"Oh," Mary said simply.

"Do you mind if we talk out here, rather than in my office?" asked Mr. Grant. "Under the circumstances, I think you'd appreciate it more," he said.

"Where's your dog?" asked Mary looking around.

"He's in my office," explained Mr. Grant. "Sandra's taking us to the vet right after this..." he said as he sat opposite her in a large overstuffed armchair that did not match the fabric of the worn couch.

Doors

"I hope I'm not inconveniencing you too much," Mary said.

"Not at all," came the reply. "...Now tell me, tell me everything...tell me how and why you killed your husband..."

Mary related the story.

"It's self defense, pure and simple," Bob told her, "But it still won't be easy..."

"What do you mean?" Mary asked.

"It's politics, my dear, pure and simple. Why do you think I'm not a judge? I could be a judge all right, but I'd have to play politics..."

"I don't understand," Mary said.

"Your husband was a big shot in this town. It's pure and simple. Everyone in this town wants to know what happened. They don't want to know that their chief of police was a wife beating maniac...besides that there is going to be some fear downtown that if they let you 'get away with it' that a floodgate of murders will occur against all those men who have been abusing their wives for years...not to mention lawsuits against the police departments for not enforcing the too numerous to mention restraining orders against those maniacs..."

"What are you saying?" Mary asked.

"I'm saying that after we win this criminal case, we are going to sue the pants off city hall for not enforcing that retraining order," said Mr. Grant. "I'm saying that the blame will be where the blame should go, not on you...City hall and the police department are the true culprits in this matter...not you..."

Doors

Mary smiled.

"Do you understand what I'm saying?" Mr. Grant asked not being able to see her face.

"Yes," Mary replied.

"Do you understand that there is going to be a lot of work ahead of us...not just from me, but from you? Do you understand that?"

"What do you mean?" Mary asked him starring in his sightless white eyes, forgetting that this man could not see.

"I mean that you are going to have to get active in this community. I want you to go to church and to join the P.T.A. and to assist elderly groups and to feed the hungry...You must become an active vital community force. You must not act like you have done anything wrong. You must not hide yourself in your home behind closed doors," he said. "You must let this town know exactly who you are and that you are not a murderess. You must gain political clout! Now do you get it?"

"Yes," said Mary, "and I thank God he put you on this earth," she said.

"Don't thank God for anything," Mr. Grant said. "I don't believe in God."

"You don't?" Mary asked in surprise.

"More trouble is caused in the name of religion and God in this world than by anything else," he explained. "I can't believe in a God like that."

"Oh," Mary said simply as Mr. Grant's dog began to howl from the other room.

"Be quiet, Duke!" Mr. Grant shouted and the dog was silent.

"He's very obedient," Mary said.

"Most of the time," came the reply.

"But doesn't he have to be perfect being a Seeing Eye dog and all..."

"He's my eyes," explained Mr. Grant, "But he's still a dog..."

Just then Sandra entered the room.

"I'll have that paperwork out for you to sign in a jiffy," she told Mary.

"Thank-you, Sandra," said Mr. Grant.

There was a brief silence.

"I understand you represent a friend of mine?" Mary asked.

"What friend?" asked Mr. Grant.

"Marsha Collins?" asked Mary, "She was my cell mate."

"Not anymore," came the reply.

"What do you mean?" Mary asked. "She thought you were wonderful," Mary said.

"I should have left her in jail," Mr. Grant said.

"...but why?" asked Mary. "She didn't do anything wrong..."

"Because if I had left her in jail, I would still be representing her," said Mr. Grant tossing his head into the air, his white eyes gazing nowhere.

"Ms. Collins killed herself and her boyfriend," Sandra interjected.

Mary looked away.

"She promised me she wouldn't do that," said Mary. "She promised me she would let me get her help..."

"She's beyond help now," said Mr. Grant.

"I have your papers ready," said Sandra.

Mary signed the papers.

Doors

As she left the office she said, "I hope your dog gets well soon..."

"He will," said Mr. Grant.

"And...Oh yes," Mary added. "Thank-you, Mr. Grant. Thank you so much..."

"I'm only sorry I couldn't help your friend," he said.

"God is with her now," Mary said.

"I told you I don't believe in God," said Mr. Grant as she walked out the door and he rose from his chair, the sunlight bouncing off his thick white hair.

"I forgot," said Mary, "Sorry."

"Think nothing of it," said Mr. Grant. "Maybe someday I'll explain it to you..." he said.

"Well, thank-you, Mr. Grant. Thank-you so much," Mary said as she continued to leave.

"I'll call you tomorrow and let you know when Mr. Grant wants to see you again," Sandra called after her as the door closed.

Outside the door, Mary breathed a sigh of relief.

CHAPTER ELEVEN
THE ARRAIGNMENT

"All rise, the Honorable Judge Leslie Cole, presiding over the Superior Court of the County of Larkin, the City of Central City in the State of California..." the bailiff said..."All face the flag..." he continued as the judge entered the courtroom and took her place before them.

"I'm nervous," whispered Mary.

"Don't worry about a thing. It's just the arraignment and bail review," Bob Grant explained. "It's nothing to worry about..." he said as he reached down to pat his dog, Duke."

"Mr. Grant," the judge said, "Are you appearing before this court today?"

"Robert Donald Grant appearing for Ms. Mary Mason," came the reply as the attorney and his dog stood up to face in the direction of the voice.

"Well, then," she said, "Let's take Mr. Grant first and not keep him waiting, shall we?" the judge said more than asked. "Clerk, get me Ms. Mason's file," she directed as Mr. Grant, his dog and Mary all walked past the court gate and up to the podium.

Doors

"Please state your appearances for the record," the judge said as the clerk handed her the file...Is the prosecution ready?" she asked.

"Ready, your Honor," came the reply from the prosecution table set up just behind them.

Mary turned around for a moment and noticed that the table was covered with rows of well-organized files.

"Please state your appearances for the record..." the judge repeated as the court reporter to her right took down the information methodically.

"Robert Donald Grant, appearing for Ms. Mary Mason," Mr. Grant stated boldly, "Ms. Mary Mason is in the courtroom with me at my side, your Honor," he said.

"Thank-you, Mr. Grant," said the judge. "Ms. Mason, how do you Plea to count one of Murder in the First Degree?"

"Not guilty," came the whispered reply.

"Mr. Grant, will you direct your client to speak louder?" the judge asked.

"Speak louder," Mr. Grant whispered to Mary.

"Not guilty," Mary said loudly.

"That's better," said the judge. We can hear you now. How do you plea to count two of the complaint, child endangerment?"

"Not guilty," came the reply just as loudly as before.

"How do you plea, Ms. Mason, to the third count of the complaint, possession of a deadly weapon?" the judge continued.

"Not guilty," came the reply again loudly and clearly stated.

Doors

"The defendant Ms. Mason has pled 'not guilty' to all three counts of the State's complaint against her," the judge announced. "Did your attorney advise you of your constitutional rights?" asked the judge.

"Yes, he did," came the reply.

"Do you understand that you have the right to a speedy trial, that you have the right to a trial by jury, that you have the right not to speak unless your attorney is present, that anything you say can and will be used against you in a court of law...Do you understand that Ms. Mason?"

"I understand," came the reply.

"Then let the pleas be entered," ordered the judge as she sounded the gavel.

"Mr. Grant, you will file the appropriate paperwork with the clerk," she said.

"We have one more matter," interjected Mr. Grant, "Bail review..."

"Oh yes," said the judge rather absent-mindedly, "Bail has been set at twenty thousand dollars," she said and the defendant is now free on bail. Does the prosecution have any objection?"

"The prosecution objects," came the reply. "Twenty thousand dollars is not a sufficient amount of bail in light of the crimes against the state committed by Ms. Mason."

Mary felt her knees failing. Instinctively or out of his vast experience, Mr. Grant took her arm with his free hand and steadied her. His other hand controlled his dog, Duke.

"Ms. Mason is of no danger to the state," Mr. Grant explained. "She has no criminal record. There is no evidence that she will go out and commit these crimes or any others. Most respectfully," he continued, "I would also like to point out that Ms. Mason has not been found guilty of committing any crimes against the state and she is innocent until proven guilty..."

The prosecution rose.

"I apologize," he said, "I should have said that the bail of Ms. Mason should be higher in light of the crimes she allegedly committed against the state," he said...but he had already lost a bit of his credibility before the judge so it didn't seem to matter.

"I agree with Mr. Grant," the judge said. "There is indeed no evidence before this court that Ms. Mason will be a danger to herself or others, and unless you are prepared to offer me this evidence," she said, looking at the prosecutor, "then I will leave bail as it stands and Ms. Mason will be free on bail as posted."

"I have no evidence to offer at this time," the prosecutor stood and said, "But I would like to reserve the right to present such evidence at future hearing."

"I'm not going to give you that right, Sir," came the reply from the judge. "You need to be prepared when you come into my courtroom, and I do not intend to leave Mr. Grant hanging in mid air over this matter. It isn't fair to him or his client," the judge said.

Mary relaxed and Mr. Grant let go of her arm.

"Thank-you, your honor," he said.

"The order is that bail will remain at twenty thousand dollars," the judge said as the gavel sounded again.

Mr. Grant, Mary and Duke turned to leave.

"There's Sandra," Mary said as Sandra entered the courtroom door and walked up to them.

"Take care of the paperwork," Mr. Grant told her.

"O.K. boss," she said as she approached the bailiff for direction.

Mr. Grant, Mary and Duke left the courtroom. The doors swung closed behind them.

"That's it for round one," Mr. Grant said. "The rest won't be quite so easy."

"Thank-you, Mr. Grant," was all Mary could say.

Mr. Grant bent over to pet Duke.

"We're going to be working very closely together," he said, "So from now on I want you to call me Bob."

Mary was surprised.

"You see, I'm going to be delving into the most intimate moments of your life and you have to think of me as a friend, or this won't work...it won't work at all," he explained.

"All right," Mary said. "If you think it will help, I'll call you 'Bob'."

"Trust me," he told her. "It will help. I've been doing this a long time, and it will help. You must think of me as your attorney; and you must do exactly as I say," he explained, "But you must also think of me as a friend and trust in me as you have never trusted in any friend before...Do you understand...?"

Doors

"I think so," came the reply.

"Well, at any rate you will understand later," he said, "So from mow on I'm 'Bob', your friend and attorney, 'Bob'."

"All right, Bob," came the reply, rather forced.

"Now you go home and get some rest," he said as Sandra appeared at the courtroom doors with the papers in her hands. "I have paper work to sign," he said as Duke took him to sit on a bench just outside the courtroom doors.

"See you later, Mary," Sandra said as Mary walked down the hall.

"See you later," Mary repeated back.

"I think we're going to be all right," Bob said as Mary walked out of sight.

"Do you think you'll get her off?" Sandra asked.

"A piece of cake..." Bob said patting Duke on the head. "I can't lose this one..."

"I'm not so sure the prosecution will agree with you," said Sandra laughing.

"To hell with the prosecution!" Bob said tossing his head back, his sightless eyes gazing aimlessly. "If they can't see the truth...to hell with them!"

"Sometimes the blind see, don't they Bob?" Sandra asked him.

"Yes," Bob replied, "And sometimes only the blind see," he said laughing, "Do you see what I mean?"

"Sign here," Sandra said directing Bob's hand to the paper and pen.

Doors

"Read it to me first, Sandra..."

"Don't you trust me?" she asked.

"I don't trust anyone," he said.

Sandra laughed and read the papers to Bob. When she was finished he signed them.

"Trust me now?" she said laughing.

"No," came the reply.

"Let's get out of here," she said, "I'll take you to lunch."

"You know I don't eat lunch," he said.

"Then have a cigarette and a cup of coffee," came the reply. "Kill yourself...I'm eating...it's lunchtime and I'm eating," Sandra told him. "We can work over my lunch and your cigarette and coffee."

"Sounds good," Bob said.

"Smoking is bad for you," Sandra told him as they left the building.

"Then why do you smoke?" Bob asked.

"Because you got me into a bad habit," Sandra replied laughing, "But I'm going to quit before it ruins my health."

"You'll gain weight if you quit," Bob told her.

"Look at me! I'm overweight already! Does it look like I care about how much I weigh?" Sandra asked.

"How should I know?" Bob asked her. "I can't see you!"

"That's right," Sandra told him. "I told you I was tall and thin and looked like a fashion model didn't I?" she said laughing again. "...Well, I lied."

"I know that," Bob said, "Why do you think I don't trust you?"

CHAPTER TWELVE

BY THE POOL

April and Nick lay in the sun dripping wet after their swim. Sounds of the children playing in the pool made an annoying background noise. April grimaced.

"I wish they had a separate pool for children," she said.

"That's the problem with condominium life," Nick replied. Maybe we should sell this place and buy a house..."

"Can we afford it?" April asked, "I mean with me quitting my law practice and all...Can we afford it?"

"I think so," Nick said. "We have enough for a down payment saved, and homes are going for a premium now with the economy being so bad. We can probably buy a government foreclosure, or better yet, a government seizure, for pennies on the dollar, so to speak..."

"How can we find out about those?" April asked.

"I'm the head of the District Attorney's office, remember? I deal in crime, remember? The war on drugs and the forfeiture laws have yielded guys like us a windfall, of sorts."

"What about this place?" April asked. "How can we sell this place if the economy is so bad?"

"We'll rent it," came the reply.

"Will we have our dream home?" April asked.

"Some of the forfeiture places are pretty nice," Nick told her.

"Why didn't we do this sooner?" April asked him as she wrapped her long wet blond hair in a towel and leaned back on the pool chair, eyes closed to the sun.

"I didn't want to compromise my values," Nick said quite simply.

"What do you mean?" April asked.

"It means that I'll have to pull a few political strings which I didn't want to pull before," he said.

"What made you change your mind?" April asked him. "I'm not so sure I want you to compromise your values."

"Well..." Nick began, "...everyone is doing it. I mean everyone is cashing in on the drug war right now. I keep hearing, 'We work hard for our money. We may as well get a few deals...You know that boat Jake has?" Nick asked her.

"Yeah..?.."

"Well, that's a government seizure...You don't think Jake could afford that on a police officer's salary, do you? He got that cabin cruiser for peanuts...for peanuts...And the guys keep asking me if I want to check the list...Is there anything I want to buy..."

"Sounds illegal," April said. "Don't those things have to go to public auction?" she asked.

"You would logically think so," came the reply, "But that's not the way it works anymore...The new law isn't clear on how these things are to be disposed of, besides...all you have to do is advertise the public auction in fine print in some little newspaper nobody reads, don't shout the news too loudly to the general public...and you're home free...You have to have cash to purchase so very few people show up at those auctions anyway..." he explained.

"We don't have that Kind of cash," April said.

"That's no problem," Nick explained, "The bank will work with me. I'll have a cashiers check in hand."

"I don't know," April said. "I want a house, but I want my principals too..."

"You'll just have to change your principals," Nick explained.

"Are you willing to do that?" April asked him.

"I don't know," came the reply, "Maybe...to some extent," he said. "I'll have to think about it. Everyone's doing it, after all...Why should the drug dealers be the only ones to profit from the drug wars?"

"We'd be cashing in on someone else's misery," April said. "I don't know if I like that idea."

"We're taking away from the dealers and pimps who addicted, maybe millions of kids..." said Nick. "Someone is going to get the forfeiture bounty. It may as well be us."

"Shouldn't the forfeiture money and property go to rehabilitation centers?" April asked him. "That makes more sense."

"Maybe it should, but the facts are that it doesn't. It goes to buy police helicopters, to fund special investigative troops, to buy guns and equipment that the police can use to get more forfeiture property and so on and so forth at nauseam..." Nick explained. "So we may as well get in on the deal."

"You sound like you've already made up your mind," April said.

"I'm sick of thinking about it," Nick told her. "I'm sick of seeing it happen. I just thought that if I got in on it, maybe I'd understand. Maybe it wouldn't make me so sick anymore...but I don't know. I mean, I'm fighting like hell in the courtroom to get these guys put away and I barely get a thank-you..."

"It's your job," April said.

"I know it's my job," Nick explained as he picked up the sunscreen and smoothed some over his muscles arms and chest, "But it's such a thankless job. This could be my way of saying thank-you to myself," he said.

"I don't know," April told him. "It's tempting..."

"There's nothing wrong with it. It is all quite legal," Nick told her.

"I know, but is it morally correct?" April asked him.

"Look, why don't I look into it and see what's available...No harm in that is there? Then if there's something we like, we can decide then, all right?"

Doors

"All right," April said. "No harm in that, I guess."

The compromise had begun. There was no going back.

"Let's go inside," April said. "It's getting hot out here in the sun."

"Don't you want a tan?" Nick asked.

"Tans are out," April said. "They're bad for your skin," she explained. "And I don't want a burn."

"Let me put some sunscreen on you," Nick said leaning toward her with the bottle of sunscreen.

"No thanks," came the reply. "I really want to go in. I have something to tell you."

"What's that?"

"Can't I tell you over a nice steak and glass of champagne over lunch?" she asked.

"We're having champagne for lunch?" he asked. "What's the occasion?"

"Correction, counselor," came the reply, "...You're having champagne, I'm having a sparkling water..."

"But you love champagne..."

"Precisely..." she said.

"Are you trying to tell me something?" he asked.

April looked at him.

"Precisely," she replied with a smile.

"What are you trying to tell me?" he asked her.

"Objection. Vague, ambiguous, unintelligible. Counsel must rephrase the question..." April said laughing again and unwrapping her long damp blond hair.

"Are you having a baby?" Nick asked her. "We've been wanting a baby for so long."

"Can we afford a baby?" April asked him.

"I have insurance, remember?"

"Do you want a baby?" April teased him knowing full well they had been trying for months.

"You're having a baby, aren't you?" Nick asked excitedly.

"Correction, counselor," came the reply. "We're having a baby, a June baby."

Nick looked at her wide-eyed.

"If it's a girl we'll call her June," he said.

"Why June?" April asked.

"Well, you were born in April and you're named April..."

"And what if it's a boy..."

"We'll call him Nicholas, of course," said Nick. "And if it's a girl and she comes early we'll call her May, or April after you, or whatever the case might be..." he said excitedly.

"You're a nut!" said April as she got up and dove into the pool."

"And you are wonderful," Nick said as he dove in after her.

Then they paid in the pool like a couple of children.

Later, they went upstairs and made mad and passionate love.

CHAPTER THIRTEEN

THE WORK BEGINS

"Hi boss!" Sandra said looking up from her computer as Bob Grant entered his office with Duke.

"How are you this morning?" Bob asked.

"Couldn't be better. Started a diet..." she answered.

"You don't need to diet," Bob told her. "You never looked better to me!" he said as he walked to his office door.

Sandra laughed.

Bob sat at his office desk. Duke lay next to him. A few minutes later, Sandra entered his office.

"Bob Reed called just before you came in," Sandra said.

"Did he leave a message?"

"Yup," came the reply. "He said, 'it worked! Thank-you!' and that's all..." said Sandra, "...so it looks like your little scheme worked again..."

"It never fails," Bob told her.

"How do people become such animals?" Sandra asked.

"If I had the answer to that question," Bob told her, "I could make an end of the war on drugs."

Doors

"Well, at least the kids are all right," Sandra said.

"Yes. I told Mr. Reed that all we had to do was get custody of those kids so that Mom could no longer collect welfare payments on them, then she and the boyfriend would give them up for sure. I've seen it over and over again. Mom and the boyfriend live in deplorable conditions, take the welfare money and buy drugs instead of milk and baby food. Remove the ability to collect that money, and the kids are no longer wanted."

"It's sad," said Sandra, "I mean, the kids had to go hungry before Dad could even get them. Then they were dropped off at his house like so much useless baggage."

"Mom is not always the best parent," Bob said. "Mrs. Reed had no business collecting welfare on the kids anyway because Dad was employed and had been sending her support all along until he found out how the kids were living with pornographic pictures covering the walls and filth all over. Then he said he wanted the kids, and she refused because she was double dipping on the State of California by collecting welfare payments and buying drugs. The kids had been eating nothing but dry cereal and toast made from day old bread for days, other than the occasional trip to the Salvation Army for a plate of hot food. I still say its simple...take away the money, and you get back the kids..."

"Well," said Sandra. "It certainly worked!"

"Yes, it did," said Bob. "Any other calls today?"

"Jack Morgan called," she said. "He wants to discuss settlement."

"Let him sweat a few days," Bob said.

Doors

"Rachel Goldstein called. She wants to meet and confer on your motion to compel discovery."

"Call her back and tell her we *have* met and conferred. What did she think that two-page letter I wrote explaining the law was anyway? Tell her if she has any additional authority to write me and let me know...back it up with a confirming letter. Tell her I'm going forward with my motion unless she complies with discovery and answers my interrogatories and requests for admissions. I want sanctions."

All right, Boss," Sandra said. "That's it. Anything else you want me to do today."

"Yes," came the reply. "I want you to go in my library and pull the penal code sections on the Mary Mason charges, then I want you to cross reference that with the digest and pull up all the cases on the California Reporter books. Then I want you to go to Westlaw and use Shepherds Citations and update the cases and look for corresponding cases on the subject. Print out any cases we don't have in our library. When you're done, let me know...and we'll start reading them."

"What are you looking for, Boss?" Sandra asked him.

"I want abuse cases where the abused finally kills or maims the abuser," he said. "And I want examples of children that were inadvertently killed as a result of getting between the abuser and the victim."

"What about that case last month in San Diego?" Sandra asked. A two year old was shot by a rifle Mom and Dad were fighting over..."

"It's not authority because it wasn't published," Bob said, "But it will be

Doors

persuasive to a jury. Go to the library and get me the articles on that."

"You're the boss!" Sandra said.

"You better believe it..."

"Well, I better get to work," Sandra told him.

"Thank-you Sandra," he said. "Can I take you to lunch?"

"You don't eat lunch, Boss...Remember?"

"Today I'll eat lunch," he said.

"I'm on a diet, remember?"

"It's a working lunch," Bob explained.

"In that case I'd better start my diet tomorrow...huh?"

"Good idea," Bob said. "We'll go to lunch at one o'clock...miss the crowds...you drive..."

"Are you sure you don't want to drive?" Sandra asked him.

"Don't get cute," he replied.

Sandra laughed.

"You're funny, boss," she said.

"I have a new joke to tell you," he replied.

"Tell me at lunch," Sandra told him as she left his office laughing. "I've got work to do..."

"It's a good thing she has a sense of humor," Bob thought as Sandra left the room. "That's the only way you can tolerate this business."

Meanwhile, at her parent's home, Mary sat on the bed in the room where she had spent her childhood with a loaded and cocked revolver held in her mouth.

Doors

CHAPTER FOURTEEN
THE GUN

Mary put the cocked gun in her mouth and prepared herself to draw the trigger.

"That son of a bitch," she thought. "I'm about to commit the ultimate sin..."

Suddenly, her mother entered the room. Mom had a terrible habit of not knocking.

"What are you doing she screamed!?!"

Ironically, Mary took the gun out of her mouth to say, "What does it look like I'm doing?"

"It looks like you're trying to kill yourself," her mother said sarcastically.

Mary looked at her mother, stunned.

"Aren't you going to try and stop me?" Mary asked.

"What for?" came the reply. "So you can take a bottle of pills tomorrow?"

"That's a poor attitude," Mary said putting down the gun.

"Poor attitude!?!" her mother questioned, angrily. "I'd say you're the one with the poor attitude...selfish...I'd say, plain and simple...just selfish..."

"How do you figure?" Mary asked.

"Suicide is the easy way out. It's the way to escape all your problems all right, but it doesn't consider the lives of the ones who love you...It doesn't consider them at all..." she explained putting her arms around her daughter.

Mary began to cry.

"What if Quinn had walked in just now instead of me?" her mother asked. "How would Quinn feel if she had walked in <u>after</u> you pulled that trigger...or while the gun was going off? Did you even stop and think about Quinn?"

"You know I love Quinn. You know I wouldn't do anything to hurt her...but I just can't take it anymore...I just can't stand it..."

"Quinn thinks you're brave," Mary's mother told her.

"Brave?" Mary asked. "Why Brave?"

"Why because you stood up to that no good jerk of a husband...that's why..."

"I killed him," came the reply.

"You protected your home and daughter," her mother said. "Quinn sees that as heroic."

"But what if I'm found guilty of murder?" Mary asked. "How will Quinn feel then?"

"She'll think you're a hero," her mother said. "She'll love you and never see you any differently than that. Domestic violence is a terrible thing," her mother said. "You can turn this around by sharing your experiences with others," she said.

"You mean tell other women to kill their husbands?" Mary asked, wiping away her tears with a tissue her mother handed her from the nightstand.

Mary's mother took the gun and put it in her apron pocket.

"Of course not," she explained. "But others may benefit by your experiences as well as your mistakes."

"Are you saying that killing Garth was a mistake?" Mary asked.

"I'm not saying that at all," Mary's mother said. "I'm saying that you are not alone in this thing. There are thousands, no millions of women in this country who are getting abused and raped by men every day; and they feel like they are the only ones in the world having this experience, and it's just not true."

"I wonder if it's my fault," Mary said. "If I had been a better wife..."

"That's the kind of thinking that let this thing get out of hand," her mother said. "That's what I was talking about when I said others could learn from your mistakes."

"How do you know so much?" Mary asked.

"I never told you this, but before I married your father I dated a man who abused me...even stalked me...he wouldn't leave me alone...I thought I loved him, and then he raped me; and then somebody told me what I'm telling you now and I had the courage to turn him in to the police."

"Did they take you seriously?"

"No, of course not. They said I asked for it."

Doors

"Are you kidding me?"

"No."

"Why didn't you tell me this before?"

"I was embarrassed to tell you. Why didn't you tell me Garth was abusing you? I know he was terribly cruel in a verbal sense, but I had no idea he was beating you..."

"That's because he always hit me where it wouldn't show, or he used a rubber hose so there would be no marks," Mary explained. "He broke my ribs a couple of times and I tried to make him leave the house, even got a restraining order to make him leave, but I couldn't get it enforced. Finally, he left one night in a rage and stayed away for a couple of weeks. Then he started coming back and...Well, you know the ultimate outcome...I killed him. I just didn't tell you about the mergency room visits, that's all."

"Did he ever hurt Quinn?" Mary's mother asked.

"I don't think so," came the reply.

"Would it surprise you if I told you that he may have been sexually abusing Quinn?"

"Oh my God!" said Mary turning away.

"You see," her mother said lovingly, "You can't leave Quinn now. She needs you more than ever. Promise me you'll let me get you and Quinn help," her mother begged.

Mary began to cry.

"I promise," she said looking through her tears at the kind and understanding face of her mother.

Doors

Mary's mother patted her apron pocket.

"I'm going to dispose of this thing," she said. "I never wanted your Dad to have one of these things...and of all the insane things to do...he puts it in the nightstand...Why what if you had pulled the trigger just now? Worse yet...what if Quinn had found the gun and hurt or accidentally killed herself with it?" her mother asked.

"Then Dad would go to jail," Mary said.

"He'd deserve it too," came the reply. "People have no business with loaded guns sitting in nightstand drawers."

"What are you going to do with the gun?" Mary asked.

"I'm taking out the bullets and putting it in a safety deposit box and throwing the key off the end of the pier into the ocean," she said. "Then we'll all go down to the beach and have a picnic."

"Can we have fish and chips?" Mary asked.

"Fish and chips and ice-cream and cake," Mary's Mom said. "After all, we'll be celebrating a life!"

"Who's?" Mary asked.

"Your's," her mother replied. "It's just about ready to begin all over again, and that's an *excellent* reason to celebrate."

"I agree!" Mary said.

"Then go out back and get Quinn out of the sandbox and tell her we are getting ready for a party!" her mother said.

"Do you think the press will have a field day with that?" Mary asked.

"To hell with the press!" her mother replied.

Doors

"You're right!" Mary said, "To hell with them all!"

Doors

CHAPTER FIFTEEN

THE NEW HOUSE

"How do you like the place?" Nick asked as he and April drove up to a house in an exclusive neighborhood.

"Wow!" was all April could reply.

"It's great, isn't it?"

"How could we possibly afford a place like this?" April asked.

"We can afford it because the government owns it," came the reply. "There's no outstanding mortgage on it because it was originally built and purchased with drug cash," Nick told her.

"Are there drugs hidden in the walls?" April asked as they drove through the open gate and up the long driveway.

"We had a dog check for that," Nick said. "The place is clean, and nobody will be coming back."

"Are you sure?" April asked.

"Sure...I'm sure..." Nick replied hesitantly.

"Why are you hesitating?" April asked him.

"Well," came the reply. "It was a good question," Nick replied, "I mean it never crossed my mind, but I suppose someone might come back...or something...I mean I'm not a cop...I'm just a D.A....But those guys could come after me anyway...!" he said. "After all, I'm the guy that put most of them away, so what difference would it make, huh?"

"None," said April, "Except that it would amount to the same thing as hanging a sign around your neck saying 'Here I am! Come and get me!'" April said as Nick helped her out of the car.

"It's a beautiful place. Isn't it?" said Nick.

"Yes it is," came the reply as the two of them walked to the front door.

Nick took the key out of his pocket and opened the door. He reached inside as they entered and turned on a beautiful glass chandelier hanging above the entranceway.

April stepped inside the door and looked around and said quite simply, "This is too much house for me, Nick. Let's go."

"Come on," Nick urged. "The place is beautiful! You'll love it!"

"I could never live here," April told him.

"Come and see the kitchen," he urged as he led the way. "It's like being in a dream. And the best part is that this whole place is furnished. We get the furniture and everything!"

"I hate this place, Nick," April said. "All I want is a simple cottage with a white picket fence around it and a nice little nursery tucked next to the master bedroom."

"This place has a huge nursery," Nick told her.

They stood in the kitchen looking around.

"It has a walk-in pantry that's temperature controlled," Nick told her.

Doors

"This place is gross," April said. "It has everything in it that some poor white trash would want, and it's all put together in one place. It doesn't match. It's ugly!" April added.

"We can always re-decorate," Nick pleaded.

"Are you trying to tell me something?" April asked him.

"I was going to surprise you," Nick said.

"Oh my God!" gasped April, "You didn't. Please tell me you didn't."

"O.k.," said Nick, "I didn't...but I did."

"You already bought this place?"

"I bought this place," Nick said looking down at his feet.

"How could you do something like this without asking me first?"

"I wanted to surprise you."

"You certainly did that," April said. "Now the problem is, how do we get rid of it?"

"We could try living here just for a little while," Nick said. "It has an indoor lap pool, a weight room, and a sauna...?"

April smiled.

"You're getting to me, Nick."

"We can refurnish," Nick said.

"How much is this place setting us back?" April asked him.

"We got it for under the county appraised value," Nick said as he whispered the amount in her ear.

"You're kidding?" April said. "They practically gave this place to you."

"To us," Nick said. "It's a present for you."

Doors

"Keep me out of this, "April told him. "I still have my values."

"I've got values," Nick said.

"Sure you do, Nick," came the reply.

"Do you still love me?" he asked.

"You know I do," April told him. "I just think you did a stupid thing, that's all," she said.

"You'll get used to it," Nick laughed. "I'm a stupid guy."

"No argument there," April said.

"Let's go home," she begged.

"Don't you want to see the master bedroom?" he asked.

"All right," April sighed.

Nick led the way. The room was done beautifully in black and gold with a black spa tub sitting on a pedestal in one corner of the room and a beautiful black marble fireplace on the wall opposite the foot for the four poster black lacquer bed.

April was taken back by the beauty of it all as Nick picked her up in his arms and carried her to their new bed. There on the black satin coverings and among the many colored throw pillows they made love, sweetly and tenderly.

After they were finished April asked, "Where is the nursery?"

"I'll show you later," Nick said as he kissed her all over her naked body.

"I love you more than any man loved any woman," he said.

"I love you too, Nick," April whispered.

"I promise that I'll love and take care of you for the rest of my life," he

Doors

said. Then he kissed her belly and whispered, "I love you little baby...Daddy loves you..."

April began to cry.

"Why are you crying?" Nick asked her. "You never cry."

"I guess it's the pregnancy," she lied. "You know what they say about pregnant women," she said.

April was crying because she loved Nick and because she was afraid of this house. She was afraid the house would simply consume them, and she feared that she was right.

"I hate this house," she thought as she starred up at the ceiling while Nick kept on caressing her.

Then Nick made love to her again, and she forgot about the house.

CHAPTER SIXTEEN

GROUP THERAPY

Mary approached the door of the ranch style home.

"I'm nervous," she thought. Her hands felt damp. She wiped them on her skirt before ringing the bell.

"Come in," said Dr. Brewster. "A few of the women have already arrived," she said.

"Thank-you," was all Mary could muster. Her mouth felt dry.

"Would you like some lemonade?" Dr. Brewster asked as if she knew about the dryness in Mary's mouth.

"I'd love some!" Mary said, starting to relax a little.

One of the women sat on the couch wringing a handkerchief in her hands.

"Hello," she said. "I'm Amy."

"I'm Mary," Mary said as Dr. Brewster left to get her some lemonade.

"The lemonade is delicious," Amy said. "Dr. Brewster makes it herself from lemons she grows on the tree out back...Try a cookie," she added holding up a plate of sugar cookies that had been sitting on the coffee table. "It was my turn to bring cookies this week," she said. "You'll like Dr.

Doors

Brewster," she added. "She's different from other therapists..."

"How do you mean?" Mary asked.

"She helps you," came the reply. "She *really* helps you..."

"I'm glad to hear that," said Mary as she sat down on the couch next to Amy who had momentarily stopped wringing her handkerchief.

"Here's your lemonade," Dr. Brewster said as she re-entered the room and handed a glass of cold lemonade to Mary whose mouth now didn't seem quite so dry. "I see you've met Amy," she said. "Good! That's what it's all about. We're going to work out our problems together," she explained as if addressing the room as well as Mary.

Mary looked around the room noticing that several new women had entered the house. There were about twelve of them now. Mary wondered why she hadn't noticed the women before.

"I was nervous my first time too," said Amy.

"Let's talk," said Dr. Brewster as she sat in the rocking chair across from the couch.

Some of the women sat in chairs from the dining room table. Others sat on the living room chairs, a few on the floor and another woman sat next to Mary on the couch.

"We have a new member in our group," Dr. Brewster began. "Maybe you've heard about her," she said. "Her name is Mary Mason."

Mary looked away.

"It's all right Mary," someone said. "We understand."

"Mary," began Dr. Brewster, "Each one of us her has been abused by a

Doors

husband, father, brother or lover, some sexually, some physically, some verbally and emotionally, some a combination of all three...including me...We have all thought about what you have done...that is we have all thought about doing what you did to your husband, so we understand...You can be free here to say exactly what you think and feel; and hopefully, we can help each other."

"Was it worth it, Mary?" one of the women asked.

Mary started to answer but before she could reply Dr. Brewster interrupted, "...Before we begin," she said, "I think it would be helpful if we went around the room and introduced ourselves one at a time," she said.

The names whirled around the room. Mary knew that in the end she would only remember Amy and Dr. Brewster, but she smiled at each woman as they introduced themselves to her anyway, and tried to memorize their faces in case they should meet later in the supermarket or something. After all, they were about to get intimate with one another.

The question that was first asked eventually was voiced again.

"Was it worth it, Mary?" a woman named Ann asked.

"I don't know yet," Mary told them. "I mean I didn't think about it when I was doing it. It was like a reflex. I was scared. It was like I was watching myself out of my own body doing this terrible thing, and I couldn't stop. Once I started I couldn't stop!" Mary started to cry.

"Why do you think it was such a terrible thing?" the doctor asked her.

Mary wiped her face with her hand, and the doctor handed her a tissue from a box on a table next to her. Mary blew her nose. After that, she wiped her eyes once more with the tissue.

"I don't know," Mary said.

"Is it because you don't think you are worth fighting for?" asked the doctor.

"I don't know," Mary repeated.

"If the tables had been turned," the doctor asked, "What would he have done?"

"...Killed me..." came the reply.

"With regret?"

"No," Mary answered.

"Mary," Dr. Brewster told her, "We are here to tell you that you have worth. You have self-worth and are entitled to defend yourself, no matter what anyone else tries to tell you."

"That's what my attorney told me," Mary said, "But then why am I going through all of this?"

"Someday," Dr. Brewster explained, "Maybe women won't have to get into these kinds of situations. Someday society may step in and help us, but right now we have to help ourselves. We simply have to help one another until society catches up with us."

"Mary," Ann said, "I wish I had the courage to do what you did. It took me years to stand up to my husband. I felt financially trapped; and while I stood by and did nothing, he raped my child, he raped our son! God! It makes me sick," she said. "I ran, Mary...and he just kept coming after me and finding me...and I was uprooting this little boy and I just kept running and running...I was scared, Mary...really, really scared!"

"What did you do?" Mary asked.

"I finally went to legal aid and got help. Child protective services stepped into the picture and got his parental rights terminated until he got some help."

"Did he get some help?"

"No," came the reply. "But I'm not running anymore. I call the police when he comes within a hundred yards of me or the kid."

"I tried that," said Mary, "But it didn't work. I couldn't even get the son of a bitch out of my house with a notice to quit. I mean he finally left for a few months, but then he came back and...well...you know the rest...I killed him..." Mary began to cry.

"Did you have a choice, Mary?" the doctor asked.

"No," came the reply. "Not really...I had to protect my daughter, Quinn...Someone had to protect her...and that was me...if I let him kill me then who would protect Quinn?" she asked.

"We understand, Mary," Dr. Brewster said, "We really do understand."

"I also just found out that he was sexually abusing my daughter," Mary confessed. "I suppose I had suspected it, but I never really wanted to believe it."

"I know," Ann said nodding her head. "It's terrible. It's just terrible..."

"And the problem was that my husband was the chief of police and *his boys* wouldn't help me because they were all too busy kissing his butt...to hell with me and Quinn...to hell with the fact the chief of police was a sicko!" Mary said emphatically with anger in her voice.

"Good, Mary," the doctor encouraged her. "Get it out. Let that anger out..." she said. "It's good for you and it's all right to be angry. It really is all right to be angry. Life has dealt you a bad deck of cards, Mary; and you didn't deserve it."

"Did my mother tell you I tried to kill myself?"

"We do that, Mary," the doctor said not acting the least bit surprised, "because we don't have self esteem. Somehow we don't think we're good enough to live. We blame ourselves for the failings and flaws of those who have abused us. We say, 'if only I had been a better mother...a better wife...a better little girl...person...or whatever...then maybe he wouldn't beat me, or abuse me...but it just doesn't work that way, Mary. That's just not the way it works. You see, we enable them to continue being sick by our lack of self esteem, but we do not make them sick; and their sickness is not our fault."

"We're victims, Mary," someone in the room said.

"When we get well, when we stand up for ourselves, or try to leave or stop the abuse, they don't know what to do. We get well, but they stay sick," another woman said. "They don't want to let us go because we feed their sickness."

"You see, Mary," yet another woman said, "When you went to court and got the notice to quit the premises and told him to leave, you were doing a healthy thing. He was still sick, so he couldn't see that. He didn't understand that it was time for <u>him</u> to get out and to get help."

"I tried to tell him that," Mary said, "But he wouldn't listen."

"We've all been there," Ann said.

"I loved him once," Mary said. "I did love him...once...and I wanted desperately to love him again...I really tried desperately...It's terrible to live together without love..."

"And it's worse when it's replaced by fear," Dr. Brewster interjected.

Mary nodded her head in agreement.

"How many of you have been beaten by your husband, boyfriend or other significant person?" the doctor asked.

Three quarters of the room raised their hands.

"How may have had their children abused?" she asked.

Half the room raised their hands.

"How many of you have been raped?" she asked.

One quarter of the room raised their hands.

"How many of you are healing?" the doctor asked.

Everyone raised a hand except Mary.

"Don't worry, Mary. You're not alone," Dr. Brewster told her.

Then they went around the room and each and every woman there told Mary how they had been abused. When they were all done, Mary did not feel quite so alone. She had begun the process of healing.

CHAPTER SEVENTEEN

THE PRESS

A group of reporters gathered around Mary as she ladled the gravy and mashed potatoes out to the poor who stood in a line waiting for something to eat.

"You're Mary Mason," one of them said. "What are you doing here?"

"This is a bonanza," another reporter whispered to a colleague. "We never expected this... We came to do a story on the homeless..."

Someone flashed a camera and soon the television media appeared on the scene.

"I'm just trying to help the less fortunate," Mary explained.

"Will you hurry up!" a bum said impatiently as he thrust his empty plate at her. "We don't appreciate becoming part of a media circus just to eat."

"Do you know who this is?" a reporter asked a young woman in line. "Do you know who is serving you?"

"As far as I'm concerned," the woman said, "She's an angel of mercy."

A young child stood clinging to the skirt of the young woman.

"I'm hungry," the child said as she looked up at her mother with wide eyes.

"Why are you here?" the reporter asked.

"My husband skipped out of town and left me alone. No food...no money...nothing...took everything we had...." the young woman said.

"Can't you get assistance from the state?" the reporter asked.

"Sure," came the reply, "But I have to wait for that...they have to do an investigation on me first to make sure I'm not trying to commit fraud...laughable, isn't it?" the young woman asked. "I can't go to work because I can't pay for someone to care for my child, and I can't get public aid to pay for someone to care for my child so I can go to work...so here we are...letting this wonderful church help us..."

The reporter turned away. It wasn't the story he wanted.

The television media thrust microphones at Mary and asked questions that she didn't know how to answer.

"I can't tell you anything," she said. "Please let me help these people," she begged nervously. After all, she had promised Bob she would do volunteer work.

"Just tell us how you are feeling?" the reporter asked, "About all the publicity you are getting..."

Mary didn't know what to say so she said nothing.

"Come on Mary," one of the television reporters begged. "Give us a statement, please?"

Mary took a deep breath.

"People like us," she said, "Need help. "People need help so that they don't end up in situations over which they have no control. There are very few places one can go to get help when they are in a desperate situation, especially women," she said.

"But what about the druggies?" another reporter asked.

"They need help, too," came the reply. "I don't judge anyone here. I'm just here to pass out mashed potatoes and gravy and to give these people help," she said.

The crowd standing in line heard her and started to applaud.

"There ought to be more people like her!" someone shouted from the crowd.

The television cameras turned around to find the person. It was an old man with white hair.

"She did what she had to do," the old man told the reporters. "I don't care who her husband was, he was a jerk, plain and simple. There are too many of us out here on the street who wouldn't be here if they only could have gotten some help when they needed it...and we're slowly dying out here and no one gives a dam...except maybe her, and a few others like her, who know what it feels like to be in a hopeless situation with nowhere to turn..."

Mary looked down at the gravy. She felt like a hypocrite knowing she was at this place only because Bob had sent her, but she was starting to understand why she was sent; and more importantly, she was beginning to believe in what she was saying and she was beginning to believe in these people.

Doors

"They understand me," Mary thought. "Perhaps we aren't so different."

A man began to cough as he handed her his plate.

"I hope he doesn't have anything contagious," Mary thought. "Are you all right?" she asked.

"It's smokers cough," the man explained. "Had to quit a long time ago, but the cough is still there. Couldn't afford the cigarettes," he explained.

"Oh," Mary said simply as she handed him his plate.

The reporters were questioning the other servers in line now. Mary wondered what they were saying about her.

"I guess I'll have to watch the news tonight," she thought wondering if she would be able to keep her eyes open that long. It looked as though she had a long tough night ahead of her. Her feet were killing her already.

"Next time wear more sensible shoes, Mary," the priest said as he approached her from the kitchen behind her.

"Yes, father," Mary said as she fidgeted in her shoes shifting her weight from one foot to the other. "I guess high heeled pumps aren't exactly appropriate footwear for kitchen duty," she said.

The young priest smiled at her.

"You are one of a kind, Mary," he said.

"Is that bad?" Mary asked.

"No. That's good," the priest told her. "That's very good."

Mary smiled at the young priest.

"Too bad he's a priest," Mary said looking into the priest's dark eyes.

The priest turned away.

Doors

"Father Donovan," one of the workers said, "We're out of peas..."

"I'll bring out some more," came the reply as the priest disappeared back into the kitchen.

Mary had forgotten about the press now. Soon they began to leave and Mary was left with the unexciting mashed potatoes and gravy she was assigned to serve. Her feet were still killing her.

"I miss my little girl," she thought. "I miss Quinn. When I get home I'm going to tell Mom and Dad just how lucky I am to have them," she thought as she served a little boy and his parents. "Quinn and I could have easily ended up in this line if it weren't for them," she thought. She did not know that many of these homeless had families who had simply turned their backs on their less fortunate relatives out of shame.

Father Donovan returned.

"How are you doing on those mashed potatoes?" he asked her.

"Just fine, Father," came the reply.

"Let me know when you need more," he said.

"I will. Thank-you, Father."

"No. Thank-you, Mary," he said. "Thank-you."

Mary wondered again how a man as handsome as Father Donovan ended up being a priest.

The people in the line kept coming and more kept coming in the door. Finally, all the food was gone, but miraculously there had been enough for everyone to eat. Mary stayed to do the dishes in her bare feet.

"See you tomorrow," Father Donovan said as she walked out the mission

Doors

door. "Remember to wear sensible shoes," he said.

Mary laughed aloud. She held her high-heeled pumps in her hand. Her clothes were splattered with food. She never felt so good. She went home that night and held her child in her arms until they both fell asleep. Her mother tried to wake them as they slept in the big old chair by the roaring fire, but mother and daughter were too content to wake.

Mary missed the late evening news.

CHAPTER EIGHTEEN
ANOTHER MEETING WITH BOB

Mary was tired. Her head hurt and she ached all over.

"I wonder if I'm getting the flu," she thought as she approached Bob's office door and knocked,

"Come right in," Sandra said.

Mary walked through the door. She felt as though her face was as red as her hair.

"You don't look so good," Sandra said. "Aren't you feeling well?"

"It's either nerves or the flu," Mary told her.

"Don't give me the flu," Sandra said.

"Maybe I should re-schedule?"

"Nonsense," came the reply. "Mr. Grant is as healthy as a horse, and I know he wants to talk to you."

"Come In! Come in!" Bob Grant shouted from the other room as he got up from his chair, a southern sign of politeness when a lady enters the room.

"Please don't get up," Mary said.

"Nonsense," Bob replied. "Sit down," he directed.

Doors

They both sat down. She sat across from where he sat, facing his desk.

"I'm proud of you," he said. "You did a good job. The press is with you. That's good," he explained.

"Why is that good?" Mary asked.

"We need the press. We're going to show your husband for the kind of abusive jerk he was," Bob said.

"I don't understand."

"We are going to show everyone that you are a good and decent person and that you were merely an unwitting victim of all of this."

"I thought I was innocent until proven guilty?"

"In your dreams," Bob said laughing. "In an ideal world, maybe...not in this world of ours...not in a million years..."

"Then I did good?"

"You did good," Bob said. "Keep it up. Show everyone that the people of this town are behind you...Why...did you see this headline, 'HOMELESS WOMAN SAYS MARY MASON IS AN ANGEL OF MERCY'? We want more of that."

"I really didn't do much," Mary said. "All I did was pass out mashed potatoes and gravy..."

"Mary," Bob began, "Let me explain something to you. It's far easier to support a living saint than a dead son of a bitch, even though he was the chief of police..."

"Oh," Mary said quite simply.

"Now, what you have done so far has been the easy part. Now things are going to get more difficult. You are going to have to lay your soul bare," Bob explained, "And it won't be easy."

"It won't be pretty, either," Mary said.

"That's all right," Bob replied, "The uglier the better, especially when it comes to that husband of yours..."

"That's what I was talking about," Mary said.

"That's good. We understand each other," Bob said. "When did Mr. Mason first start beating you?"

"On our honeymoon night," came the reply. "Afterward, he made me kneel down by the bed and beg God for forgiveness for not being a perfect wife...It seems he thought I was flirting with the bus boy...I mean it was crazy...he hit me...he raped me...he impregnated me...all in one night....And then I was stuck. I had nowhere to turn...I had nowhere to go...and I thought it probably was my fault...I mean I was so young and so inexperienced, and my parents didn't tell me what to expect except that I was told to be obedient..."

Bob shook his head.

"Did he ever leave marks on you?"

"Not where anyone could see," Mary told him, "Except that he broke my ribs on a semi-regular basis...about every other month..."

"Did you see a doctor for that?"

"At first I did because it was hard to breathe, so I went to the emergency room the first few times, but after that Frank wouldn't let me go there anymore. He'd tape me up himself. Once, he punctured a lung, though, and I started coughing up blood and then he had to take me into the emergency room..."

"Did anyone suggest that he was abusing you?"

"Oh my God, no!" came the reply. "This was the chief of police we were talking about...No one ever reported it or anything..."

"How did he explain it to the doctors?"

"He told them I was clumsy..."

"They believed that?"

"Probably not. I figured that they just felt it was none of their business. After all, I was an adult. It wasn't like I was a child or anything, and there aren't any mandatory reporting laws on abused adults..."

"That's true," Bob said. "Did he ever hurt your child, Quinn?"

Mary looked away.

"Did he ever hurt your child, Quinn," Bob repeated.

"Yes," Mary said timidly. "Although I didn't find out about it until recently..."

"How recently?" Bob asked.

"A few days ago," came the reply. "Apparently, my daughter views me as some sort of a savior..." Mary said.

"What do you mean?" Bob asked her.

Mary began to cry. She took a tissue from her purse and dabbed at her eyes.

"I told you this wouldn't be easy," Bob said, "But you must tell me what he did to her.

Doors

"He raped her," Mary said.

"More than once?" Bob asked.

"Yes."

"Did you confirm it?"

"Yes. My mother took her to the doctor while I was still in jail and the doctor confirmed it."

"Did your husband beat your daughter?"

"No. He only raped her."

"Did he threaten her?"

"He threatened to kill me if she told anyone, even me..."

"You know that this will all have to come out in court," Bob said.

"Does it have to?" Mary asked.

"I'm afraid so..."

"...but this is such a small town..." Mary protested.

"You have to trust me, Mary," Bob told her. "You have to do what I say. I won't do anything that isn't in the best interests of you and Quinn, but you have to trust me. Quinn will have to testify in court..."

"Oh God!" said Mary wringing the tissue in her hands.

"Would you like some water?" Bob asked.

"I'd like a good stiff drink," came the reply.

Bob pulled a bottle out of his desk drawer.

"Bring me two glasses, Sandra," he said into the intercom.

"Coming, Boss!" came the reply.

Sandra brought in the two glasses.

Doors

"I know I'm not driving," Bob said. "How about you?"

"I took a cab," Mary said as Bob poured them each a drink.

"I only drink the best bourbon," Bob said.

"To your health," Mary said holding up the glass in a toast.

Bob held his glass high in the air.

"To your courage!" he said.

"To my courage!" Mary joined in, "May it forever wave!" she laughed.

Then they drank together and planned the strategy of the case.

CHAPTER NINETEEN

MOVING DAY

"The moving van will be here any minute," Nick said.

April stared out the window. Boxes lay all round her.

"I don't want to move," she said.

"It's a little late for that, isn't it?" came the reply. "We've already leased this place out, and we're all packed and ready to go."

"I'm not ready to go," April said.

"Look," Nick told her, "We've been over this time and time again, and we agreed didn't we?"

"I wasn't given much of a choice, Nick."

"What do you mean?"

"I mean first you buy the place without asking me, then you lease this place without asking me, then you move us out without asking me...Where did we come to an agreement, Nick?"

"I didn't want to bother you since you're pregnant and all..."

"That's stupid, Nick. I have a doctorate degree in law, Nick. Or did you forget that you married an intelligent woman and not some bimbo you met in a bar somewhere?"

"You're serious, aren't you?"

"Yes, Nick. I'm serious. What in the hell did you think you were doing?"

"I thought I was taking care of you," Nick replied.

"Bullshit, Nick. You thought you wouldn't involve me because I don't agree with the way you're doing things these days."

"But I love you, April..."

"Love and fifty cents won't get you any farther than a bus ride into town, Nick."

"Why do you keep saying my name like that?" Nick inquired.

"What am I supposed to call you? Jerk? Asshole? Shit head? Dork?"

"You really are mad, aren't you?"

"I'm angry, Nick. I'm very angry. Only dogs go mad."

"I thought I was helping us."

"You thought you would help yourself, and you gave up everything I thought you believed in..."

"You're disappointed in me. Aren't you?"

"I'm more than disappointed in you, Nick. I'm furious with you."

"Will you move with me?"

"I don't know, Nick. I'm pretty angry right now."

Tears filled Nick's eyes.

"I love you," he said.

"You're nothing but a big baby, Nick," said April, unmoved.

"But I really love you," Nick pleaded.

Doors

"You don't love me enough to respect what I feel or what I have to say about what we do with our lives, Nick. I'm not sure I can live that way."

"Are you moving with me?" Nick asked her.

"No, Nick," April said looking away from him and out the window again. "I told you. I'm staying here."

"But I leased the place..." Nick protested.

"You had no legal right to do that, Nick. Remember? My name is on the deed as well as yours and we happen to be tenants in common, not joint tenants."

"What are you saying?"

"I'm saying that I broke your lease?"

"You broke our lease?"

"I broke *your* lease Nick. God, you didn't even trust me enough to give me joint tenancy in this place after we were married. As a tenant in common I own 1/2 of this condo outright. You can't lease your half without leasing my half, Nick. Your mistake, Nick. If we were joint tenants you would have had legal rights to all of it as would I and I wouldn't have been able to break your lease with those people...but the lease was illegal, Nick. So I'm staying..."

"You're serious, aren't you?" Nick said more than asked April.

"I'm serious, Nick," said April. "...and, oh yes...you can expect a lawsuit from those people to whom you thought you leased this place. They were very angry when they found out the lease wasn't legal...very angry..."

"Come on, April," Nick said. "Don't do this to me. Please don't do this to me..."

"You did this to yourself, Nick, by not trusting me and respecting me."

"I trust you and respect you, April."

"No you don't, Nick."

"What about the house?"

"I don't give a damn about that house. It's a blood house, Nick. I don't give a damn about that house. I won't raise my child in a house like that..."

"But I love that house..."

"More than me and the baby, Nick?"

"I didn't say that."

"What are you saying, Nick?"

"I don't know, April. I'm in shock. It's as though this is coming out of nowhere. I thought that after we made love over there that everything was all right about the house..."

"Sorry to mislead you, Nick. You thought wrong. Blame it on hormones and pregnancy, if you like..."

"Why are you being so cold, April?"

"If you can't have what you want, then I'm being cold. Is that it? You are sick, Nick. You are sick."

"Will you stop saying my name over and over again like that?" Nick asked becoming agitated.

"Sorry, Nick," came the reply. "I just can't help it...comes with the territory of marrying an attorney, I guess. The prosecuting attorney should

Doors

never have married the defense, Nick..."

"We aren't in court now, April..."

"Aren't we, Nick? Aren't we in a court of sorts always judging each other, you playing your little manipulative games with me? I'm sick of it. I've had it. I can't stand it anymore. You are too used to winning, Nick. The cards are always stacked in your favor in the courtroom because you represent the political good guy...the state... and when the defense finds a loophole the press shouts loud and clear...Never mind that the state has a huge leg up to begin with...then if Nick is a good little boy and does as he is told, he'll get some privileges like a house for pennies on the dollar and then maybe a judgeship...When will that happen, Nick? Will you be on the take then, Nick?"

"If you stay here how will you support yourself?" Nick asked ignoring what April had just said.

"I'm suing you for spousal and child support, Nick. I promise you I'll make it messy...It won't be at all good for your image when the public finds out how you got that house..."

"You wouldn't dare..."

"Try me, Nick..."

"Don't you love me at all?"

"I do love you. That's why I'm doing this, Nick. It's better than finding you dead, Nick."

"You won't change your mind?"

"About finding you dead, Nick?"

Doors

"What makes you think something like that will happen?"

"Think about it, Nick. You bought the dream house of some drug lord and his wife...a drug lord you just happened to put away...the kind of guy I even I wouldn't defend...and I believe everyone is entitled to a defense..."

"I don't believe you," Nick said losing his temper.

"You're leaving, aren't you?" April asked.

"You can keep all the stuff, " Nick said as he walked out the door.

The next morning Nick was shot with a twenty-two caliber rifle.

CHAPTER TWENTY

THE HOSPITAL

April paced up and down the corridor of the hospital. Then she walked over to the nurses' station.

"How is he doing?" she asked.

"I don't know, Mrs. Wilcox," the nurse told her. "He's still in surgery, like I said..."

"I knew this would happen," April mumbled as she walked away and continued to pace up and down the corridor. "I told Nick this would happen, but he wouldn't listen to me..."

"Oh, Mrs. Wilcox..." the nurse interrupted. "Your husband is out of surgery now. He's up in recovery on the third floor if you want to go up there..."

"Thank-you," April said as she headed down to the elevator without looking back.

The elevator ride up one floor seemed as though it took an eternity.

"I think I'll kill him," April thought aloud.

Doors

A male nurse standing next to her looked at her inquisitively.

"My husband is so stupid," she said shaking her head.

The male nurse smiled at her.

"Do I know you?" he asked.

"I don't think so," came the reply as the two of them exited the elevator.

"Where did you go to high school?" he asked her.

"Hoover," came the reply.

"You're April Sanders..." he said. "You haven't changed a bit.

"It's been ten years," April said. "How can you remember me after ten years?"

"I'll never forget those eyes and that smile," he told her.

April blushed.

"Can you tell me where recovery is?" she asked.

"I'll take you there," the male nurse said.

They walked down the third floor corridor together.

"I'm Mike Rubin," the male nurse told her. "I had Biology with you..."

"I hated high school," April told him. "It was the most miserable time in my life..."

"Why was that?" he asked.

"Probably because I was fat," April told him.

"You were never fat," Mike said.

"Well...I thought I was..."

"Here it is," Mike said pointing to a door clearly marked recovery. "I'll get someone to come out and talk to you," he said as he disappeared inside.

A few moments later Mike appeared with an attractive female nurse.

"This is Janet," Mike said as he walked down the hall. "She'll help you," he said.

"Thanks, Mike..." April shouted after him as he walked away.

Mike waved back. April remembered she was in a hospital and was embarrassed she had thoughtlessly raised her voice.

"How is my husband, Nick Wilcox?" April asked Janet as she turned toward her.

"He'll be just fine."

April breathed a sigh of relief.

"Where was he shot?" April asked.

"Just below the left shoulder...a little lower and the bullet would have hit his heart..."

"Oh my God!" April said, her head reeling.

"Are you all right?" the Janet asked her.

"I'd like to sit down," April said.

"I can take you to the waiting lounge," Janet told her. "He won't wake up for at least an hour...'

"No, I'll wait here," April insisted.

"Then let me get you a chair,' Janet said as she disappeared thought the swinging doors into the recovery room.

April leaned against the wall.

Doors

A few moments later Janet appeared with a chair and placed it across the hall from the double doors.

"Sit here," she said. "I guarantee you won't miss a thing..."

"Thank-you," April replied. "Will you tell me when my husband wakes up?"

"Immediately," came the reply as Janet disappeared behind the swinging doors.

April sat in the chair and fell asleep. She hadn't slept all night thinking about Nick, and then the call in the morning came that he was shot as he walked out the front door to get into his car. Apparently, a neighbor saw the whole thing and called the police.

It seemed as though April had just closed her eyes when an orderly awakened her.

"You can come in and see your husband now," he said. "He's awake now..."

April followed him thought the doors and across the wide room to Nicks bed. The other beds in the room were empty.

"Not a big day for surgery," the orderly said as he pointed the way to Nick's bed.

April went to Nick's bedside.

"You son of a bitch," she said.

Nick smiled at her. She began to cry.

"How did you get so smart?" he asked her.

"I was born that way," she replied.

Doors

"How did you get so stupid?" she laughed between her tears.

"I was born that way, too..." he said and started to laugh. "Ouch...," he said. "It hurts when I laugh..."

"Don't laugh," April said. "It's not funny..."

"What are we going to do now?" Nick asked.

"You're going to come home with me," April told him, "As soon as you get out of here."

"You'll take me back?" he asked.

"I have to," April said. "I can't sleep a wink without you."

"I slept like a baby," Nick said lying.

"Oh Yeah?" April said. "Maybe I should get a gun myself and finish this job..."

"I don't think they wanted to kill me," Nick said.

"What do you mean?" April asked him.

"Well," Nick explained, "I think they were only trying to scare me...or I would be dead...Guys like that don't hire guys that miss..."

"You were lucky, Nick..."

"Maybe...Maybe..." Nick said as he started to fall asleep. "I love you..." he said as April sat on a chair next to his bed and waited for the doctor.

"You stupid fool," April told him as he drifted off into sleep. "From now on you better listen to me..." she whispered. "I wasn't born yesterday, you know..."

Not long after that the doctor appeared.

"Your husband had a close call," he said.

Doors

"Tell me about it," April told him.

"How is it he came to be shot?" the doctor asked.

"He was in the wrong place at the wrong time," April explained.

"That goes without saying," the doctor said.

"It's really a long story..." April began.

"You don't have to tell me," the doctor replied.

"I don't know if I can, Doctor..."

"That's all right. I understand. It's none of my business, Mrs. Wilcox...Your husband will be in here for a few days...Do you want to see the bullet?" he asked.

"No, Doctor. But you better save it for the police," April told him, "For identification purposes..."

"Of course, Mrs. Wilcox," he said. "Of course."

"I'm an attorney," April explained.

"I thought you might be," the doctor said. "Anyway," he continued. "He'll have to stay in here a few days to make sure infection doesn't develop. Bullets aren't known for being sterile and germ free, you know..." the doctor said attempting humor.

April yawned.

"Can I get you anything?" the doctor asked.

"I'm all right," April said as she placed her hands on her stomach as if she could feel her unborn child. "I'm just tired," she said as she reached for her husband's hand. "I love this guy," she told the doctor. "I just don't want to lose him..."

Doors

"He'll be fine," the doctor explained. "It will just take some time...That's all...it will just take some time..."

CHAPTER TWENTY-ONE

MORE FOR THE DEFENSE

"You got a call from a woman at the police department today," Sandra told Bob as she poured his morning coffee.

Bob lit his cigarette and took a puff.

"Tell me <u>after</u> I've had my morning coffee," he said.

"It's important," Sandra told him.

"This better be good," Bob said as he took a sip of his coffee.

"Trust me," Sandra told him.

"All right. Shoot!" Bob said.

"Well..." Sandra began, "It seems that several of the women officers at the police department have been sexually harassed..."

"So?" Bob asked.

"...So they have been sexually harassed by none other than our great illustrious police chief," Sandra explained.

"You're kidding me. Right?"

"No, Bob. I'm not kidding you. I couldn't be more serious."

"Why are they coming forward now?"

Doors

"Why not?" Sandra laughed sarcastically. "He's dead...I'd come forward too!"

"But you'd come forward anyway," Bob said.

"True," Sandra replied, "But that's me...Anyway I figured that this would help Mary Mason's case..."

"It will put the lid on it," Bob said smiling.

"That guy was a major jerk," Sandra added unasked for an opinion.

"Jerk is too nice a word for a guy like that...He reminds me of my father," Bob said. "My father was so stupid. I can't believe how stupid he was. For the life of me, I don't know what my mother saw in him. I mean, she was a smart woman, a real smart woman...And he was so abusive to us kids. I don't think he ever said more than two words to me at any one time when I was growing up. He called me 'that blind son of a bitch,' and I don't think he ever even called me by my name. He beat me daily. Sometimes I'd hide all day in the corncrib until he drank himself to sleep...just to avoid the beating. He considered me inferior because I was blind..."

"Now look at you," Sandra said.

"Yeah," Bob replied, "I'm still blind..."

"...But you're the most successful one in your family," Sandra protested. "You're an attorney..."

"Well, I am happy that I can help people," Bob said, "But I'll probably never stop thinking of myself as 'that little blind son of a bitch'," Bob laughed.

Doors

"You have spirit," Sandra told him.

"I'd rather have eyes," Bob said. "Did I ever tell you that I could see until I was about two? I got a fever and it blinded me...My father was too stupid to take me to a doctor. There were eleven of us, you know. We were a big, poor family."

"There were ten in my family," Sandra said.

"All the same Mom and Dad?" Bob asked.

"No."

"Well, you see...That's the difference. We all had the exact same Mom and Dad. How my Mom put up with it I'll never know..."

"She must have seen something in him..."

"She must have. They had eleven kids together. She was still having kids until she was forty-five!"

"What happened to your mother?"

"She died."

"How?"

"Heart attack."

"That's sad."

"Not really."

"How do you figure?"

"When it's your time to go, that's it," Bob said.

"Well, she's in a better place."

"You know I don't believe in that stuff," Bob told her.

"Why not?" Sandra asked him.

Doors

"Because there is more harm caused by so called 'organized religion' in this world than caused by any other cause...that's why...Look at the utter stupidity of the holy wars," Bob said. "Look at all the people who have killed and been killed in the name of God. If there is a God," Bob went on, "You can't tell me he would let people go out and commit such atrocities in his name."

"Sure there's a God," Sandra told him.

"You won't convince me," came the reply.

"But you're such a good person, Bob. I can't believe you don't believe in God..."

Bob took another sip of his coffee.

"Want to heat his up for me?" he asked changing the subject and handing the cup to Sandra.

"Sure, Boss," came the reply, and Sandra took the cup and turned to leave the room.

"By the way," Bob told her, "You make terrible coffee!"

Sandra laughed.

"Make a fresh pot," Bob told her, "Like I showed you..."

"You mean you want me to spill half the grounds on the floor?" Sandra asked.

"I told you I was a 'blind son of a bitch'," Bob said laughing.

"I'll remember that," Sandra said laughing back at him as she left the room.

"Make an appointment with those women to come in here and talk with me!" Bob called after her.

"It's already done," Sandra said. "They'll be here at noon."

"Good girl," Bob said.

"Don't call me 'girl'," Sandra told him. "It's demeaning."

"Sorry!" he called after her. "I told you I was a blind 'son of a bitch'..."

Sandra laughed.

"You need a sense of humor to make it in this business," she thought as she walked toward the coffee maker to make the coffee.

Bob continued to smoke his cigarette as he sat at his office desk. He felt good. His case was coming together just fine...just fine...

Later, when Sandra returned with the coffee she asked Bob, "Did you know that the other attorneys in this building presented me with a plaque after I was here for a month?"

"Really?" Bob asked. "What for?"

"Well," Sandra told him, "It seems that no other secretary has lasted with you in this office for over a week...so they have me a congratulatory plaque for being secretary of the month. . . or rather for a month. . ."

Bob laughed.

"Is that true?" Sandra asked.

"Practically," Bob said.

"Well, how am I doing?" Sandra asked him.

"You're the best secretary I ever had," he said laughing again.

"Well, I've been here six years now," Sandra told him. "I guess I must be doing all right," she said laughing with him. "I told them way back then that you weren't <u>really</u> a 'blind son of a bitch'."

"Did they believe you?" Bob asked.

"No," came the reply...

They both laughed.

"Well," Sandra said as she turned to leave the room again, "I've got work to do."

"That's what I pay you for," Bob told her as she left his office.

"I almost have that research you asked for completed," she said looking back at him.

"Can we start to go over it this afternoon?" he asked.

"Sure," came the reply.

"Good!" Bob told her. "Good job..."

CHAPTER TWENTY-TWO

NICK'S RECOVERY

"You can go home today," the nurse said as she entered Nick's room.

"Finally," came the reply.

April looked at Nick from the chair where she sat.

"You can leave as soon as the doctor comes in and signs the papers," the nurse said. "...Just one more examination and you can go home."

"When will he be here?" Nick asked.

"Any minute," came the reply. "I just saw him in a room down the hall.

Nick smiled.

"You won't get yourself shot again, will you?" the nurse asked.

"It's not exactly my favorite thing to do," Nick said.

"He's coming home with me," April added. "I've got a gun..."

"You've got a what?" Nick asked her.

"I've got a gun. I couldn't get police protection for you, so I bought a gun..."

"You don't know how to shoot," Nick protested.

"Wrong." April replied. "My Dad taught me years ago. It's like riding a bicycle. You never quite forget how it is done."

"Where is this gun?" Nick asked.

"It's in my purse."

"Do you have a permit for it?"

"Yes, counselor," came the reply, "I have a permit for it. I got an emergency permit. The judge walked it through for me..."

"I thought you didn't believe in calling in favors, April."

"This is different, Nick."

"You mean *you* are *compromising* yourself?"

"I mean it's a matter of life and death, Nick. You almost got yourself killed because you didn't listen to me, so shut up and listen. We are having a baby now, and I'm not taking *any* chances!"

"All right...All right...You win...." said Nick resolutely.

"Can I see the gun?" he asked.

April pulled a small ladies' gun out of the handbag on her lap.

"I opted against the diamond studded handle," she said as she displayed the gun for Nick.

Just then the doctor came into the room.

"You aren't going to shoot him again? Are you?" the doctor asked April with a grin on his face.

"This is just for protection," April said.

"Just don't point that thing at me," the doctor warned her, "Or I'll have to attack you with a scalpel and that won't be pretty."

April and Nick laughed.

"Let me have a look at that bullet hole," the doctor said as he moved Nick's hospital gown down from Nick's shoulders.

"How am I Doc?" Nick asked.

"You're doing fine," the doctor said. "No sign of infection. You can go home today. I just want to give you a prescription for antibiotics and something for pain...just a little Tylenol with codeine, just to take the edge off the pain. You'll be sore for awhile."

"Can I have sex?" Nick asked.

"That's not what was shot," the doctor said sarcastically. "You can do anything you feel up to doing, if you know what I mean," he said.

April blushed.

"How soon can I go back to work?" Nick asked.

"Is Monday too soon for you?" the doctor asked him. "I want you to take it easy this weekend," he said.

"Monday's great," Nick replied. "I have a preliminary hearing on the Mason Case next week," he explained, "And I don't want to send in another trainee. Last time the guy messed things up a bit and all it was an arraignment and bail hearing."

"I don't understand a thing you are saying," the doctor said.

"That's all right," Nick told him. "I don't know much about medicine either.

"You only know how to get shot, right?" the doctor asked.

"Maybe I will shoot him," April teased. "I'm a better shot than the guy they sent after him..."

Let me sign the release papers," the doctor said as he filled out the prescription forms and handed them to April. "Take care of this guy," he told her as he continued to fill out papers. "I want him in my office in a week. No showers. Bath only. I'll change the dressing when I see him..." he said. "Can you remember all that?" the doctor asked.

"I think so," April said tossing her long blond hair. "I _am_ a lawyer, after all..."

"I didn't mean anything..." the doctor protested.

"It's all right, Doctor. Don't worry about it. I'm used to it," April said shaking her head.

"All right, then," the doctor said as he handed the release papers to a nurse who was just walking in the door. "Get dressed and I'll see you in my office in a week," he said leaving the room.

The nurse took the papers, handed April the standard patient care instruction sheet and left.

"Did you keep the bullet?" April asked. "It's evidence."

"Turned it over to the police," came the reply.

"Good," August said. "Maybe they can trace the gun."

"The sooner the better," Nick said. "Then we can put that guy away."

"Oh yes," April interjected. "I forgot to tell you...The house you bought is no more..."

"What are you talking about, April?" Nick asked.

"They burned it, Nick. It was Arson. It's gone. Adios. Good-by, No more..."

"Are you serious?"

"Didn't you read the morning paper, Nick?"

"No. I was sleeping all morning. I haven't had a chance to read anything..."

"Well, it's gone, Nick. Your little investment for pennies on the dollar is now a heap of ashes."

"I can rebuild," Nick said. "I have insurance..."

"No," April protested. "You will *not* rebuild. You can sell that lot and take that money and get a house somewhere else...somewhere far away from that place."

"You mean something small with a white picket fence? Nick asked her.

"Precisely."

"I'll have to pay off the loan first."

"Did you insure it for more than the loan, Nick?"

"Of course, I insured it for full value."

"Then we can use the extra money for a down payment on my little house with the white picket fence."

"Isn't that compromising your values, April?"

"It's the cost of the bullet, Nick. It's not a compromise. It's the cost of that bullet."

"You're very strange, April..."

"I want that little house with the white picket fence, Nick and I want you and me and the baby safely in it. I need to make a nest, Nick. I'm having a baby, remember?"

Nick reached out to April and drew her close to his bed. He put his head on her stomach.

"I love you, little baby," he said. "Daddy loves you..."

"Get up and get dressed," April told him. "We'll go out to lunch and then I'll drive us back to the condo. Tomorrow we'll put the lot up for sale and go house hunting."

"You have your mind made up, don't you?"

"This time you don't have a choice, Nick. This time you're going to listen to me..."

"Are you sure *you* didn't shoot me?" Nick asked her laughing as he got up from his bed and took his clothes from a bag in the closet.

"You can't wear those," April said. "They're covered with blood."

Nick reeled and sat on the chair next to his bed.

"I guess I forgot," he said feeling rather queasy.

"Are you all right?" April asked him.

"I'm all right," came the reply, "But what am I going to wear?"

"Look in the closet again," April directed him.

"I'm not sure I can. I feel kind of sick," came the reply as Nick ran to the bathroom toilet to throw up.

April took a clean set of clothes out of a bag she had brought with her and stuffed under her chair when she came in to see Nick and laid them out on the bed. She wrapped up the bloody clothes so that Nick could not see the blood.

Doors

"Get dressed," April said coolly. "I'll take the clothes you were shot in to the police department for identification. They may need them for evidence."

"They're all cut up," Nick said. "They cut those things off of me..."

"Nick," April told him, "You've seen this stuff before. Why is it bothering you now?"

"It's never been my own clothes cut up, or my own blood," Nick explained.

"Will you listen to me now?" April asked him?

"I'll listen to you," he said.

"Then get dressed and let's get out of here," April said taking charge.

Nick got dressed. They went to lunch. Then they went back to the condo. The next day they put the lot up for sale and went house hunting. They found a cute little house with white siding, surrounded by a picket fence. There was a flower garden filled with roses, marigolds, tulips and daffodils, and a big tree out back with a swing in it. It was April's dream come true. They bought the house, and April began building her nest.

CHAPTER TWENTY-THREE

THE PRELIMINARY HEARING

"Mary, we're about to go in for the preliminary hearing," Bob said.

"What does that mean?" Mary asked.

Sandra smiled at her and Bob bent over and patted Duke on the head. Duke sat at Bob's feet.

"The preliminary hearing is the hearing where the court determines whether or not there is enough evidence to hold a trial," Bob explained. "For us it will give us an advance peek at the case for the defense. Just because the court says there's enough evidence to go to trial, it doesn't mean we are going to lose at trial," Bob said. "The preliminary hearing has a different standard. The prosecution doesn't have to prove guilt beyond a reasonable doubt at this stage of the proceedings..."

"I'm scared," Mary said. "Will you present my defense?"

"No, Mary. I probably won't even object to holding you over for trial," Bob said. "There's really no point in that. It will cost too much money to fight at this stage of the game and we'll probably lose of we do."

Doors

"I don't understand. This was self-defense..." Mary protested.

"Sure it was, Mary. I know that, but that's not the point. The point is you killed your husband, and you aren't denying it. Your defense is that you were justified in killing him because it was self-defense...he was trying to harm you...But that's for the jury to decide, whether it's self defense...they have to decide whether you were justified or excused in committing murder, in essence..."

"I don't understand," Mary said.

"Do you trust me, Mary?" Bob asked.

"Yes."

"Then trust me now, Mary...Everything will be all right. I promise you that."

As the three of them and Duke entered the courtroom, flashbulbs flashed at them. Mary did not hide her face. She saw no point in it. Everyone knew who she was anyway.

When the judge entered the room, he admonished the press for taking pictures and told them there would be no photography while he presided before the court.

"Are you ready to begin?" Judge Goldstein asked.

"Prosecution is ready, your honor..."

"Defense is ready, your honor..."

"Please state your appearances for the record," the judge said as his court reporter carefully took her notes.

"Nick Wilcox appearing on behalf of the State of California," Nick said

Doors

standing.

Bob and his dog stood next.

"Robert Donald Grant appearing on behalf of the defendant, Mary Mason," Bob stated clearly and then sat down.

"Thank-you," said the judge. "You may begin Mr. Wilcox."

"Mary Mason killed her husband in cold blood," Nick began. "The prosecution has a witness, her three year old daughter, Quinn, who was at the home and heard her parents arguing just prior to the death of Mr. Mason."

"Is that all you have?" the judge asked.

"The prosecution has the murder weapon with Mrs. Mason's fingerprints on it which we have labeled as Exhibit A. and a statement from Mrs. Mason made to the arresting officer that she killed her husband labeled Exhibit B."

"Objection," Bob said standing. "Hearsay."

"Admission exception," came the reply.

"Admission allegedly made prior to reading of rights," Bob said emphatically..."according to the record of the prosecution..."

"I'll decide matters of admission of evidence at time of trial," the judge said.

"With utmost respect, your honor," Bob protested. "If you are deciding whether to hold this matter over for trial, shouldn't you only be considering *admissible* evidence?"

"I'm going to consider all of the evidence," the judge responded.

Mary looked worried. Bob squeezed her hand to reassure her.

"It's as though he can see my face," Mary thought.

"Do you have anything else?" the judge said.

"Your honor, we have evidence in the form of a statement of neighbor Gloria Brown that no one came into or left the house during the period of time in which the death occurred; and we have a transcript of the call the child of the Mason's made to 911, as well as the original recording in which the child states that 'Mommy killed Daddy.' which we have labeled Exhibits C, D, and F."

"Objection to tape and transcript evidence," Bob said rising again, "Best evidence rule. Prosecution is attempting to characterize the statements on the tape and transcript and is not quoting full context."

"I told you counselor, I am not judging on admissibility of the evidence at this time..." the judge said rather annoyed at Bob.

"Just making the record, your honor," Bob said knowing he would later challenge this judge and not allow him to try the case anyway based on these rulings. Besides Goldstein was a hanging judge...strictly for the prosecution. Mary would never get a fair trial out of him. Goldstein was one of the good old boys and he had to protect his political interests; and Bob Knew it.

"Keep it up and I'll find you in contempt of court," the judge told him hitting his gavel against the judge's podium where he sat above the court..."

Bob sat down.

Doors

"We also have the forensic pathology report of Dr. Jack Bugelman that states the death was caused by repeated stabbing which was continued after the victim was incapacitated and could no longer threaten Ms. Mason or defend himself. This report is labeled Exhibit G," Nick said.

Bob smiled. Nick had given him a piece of information he didn't have before this. While Bob knew about the pathologist's report, he didn't know the prosecution was going to use it this way. Now Bob knew how to counter it. Bob also knew something about Dr. Bugelman that wasn't common knowledge. He knew that Dr. Bugelman was either incompetent or on the take, and he could prove it.

"I want to review this evidence at this time without judging it for admissibility," the judge said. "I'll take an hour recess to review the evidence before the court," he said. "Anything else?"

"Not at this time, your honor," the prosecution said.

Bob stood up. Duke was beside him.

"No need to review the evidence at this time, you honor," Bob told the judge. "Defense is going to stipulate to holding this matter over for trial in light of the fact that your honor will not omit any of the evidence offered for lack of admissibility. Defense also hereby waives its right to a speedy trial. Defense further requests trial by a jury of her peers."

Nick looked surprised. He gathered the evidence together.

"Any objections, counselor?" the judge asked Nick.

"I wonder what he's up to?" thought Nick. "No objections," he told the judge, having no other choice.

Doors

April was watching it all and she thought it was funny.

"This is going to be good," thought April. "He's going to give Nick a run for his money. It'll do Nick some good. He's too used to winning. It'll cut him down another peg or two."

"All right, then," the judge said. "I'll see you back here for trial setting dates in two weeks from today...Check your calendars, counselors. Is that agreeable?"

"Agreeable," Nick replied stoically.

"It's fine with me," Bob added, smiling.

"Thank-you counselors," the judge said, "For making my job an easy one today."

Mary sighed with relief. She wasn't sure she understood what was happening, but she trusted Bob; and she was glad this hearing was finished.

"We have a lot of work to do," Bob said as they exited the courtroom to the flashing of cameras.

"Do you have a statement for the press?" a television reporter asked as a microphone was thrust in Bob's face.

"My client is innocent of all charges," Bob said. "This was self defense, pure and simple; and we have ample evidence to prove it."

"How can you be so sure you'll win this one?" the reporter asked Bob.

"In twenty-two years I've never had such a clean cut case of self-defense," Bob said. "The evidence in favor of my client is overwhelming..."

Doors

The next day the newspaper headlines read 'EVIDENCE OVERWHELMING...MARY MASON KILLED HUSBAND IN SELF DEFENSE'.

"God Damn it!," Nick told April over breakfast as he read the newspaper headlines. "How can a fair trial go on with headlines like this?"

"This may be the only way Mary <u>can</u> get a fair trial," she said.

"Whose side are you on, anyway?" Nick retorted.

"Why, I'm on the side of truth, justice and the American way," April told him, "Just like Superman?"

"Are you saying Bob Grant is Superman?" Nick asked sarcastically.

"I might be," said April. "I just might be..."

"Well, he doesn't leap tall buildings in a single bound!"

"How do you know he doesn't?" asked April.

"Because he can't see," replied Nick.

"I wouldn't be too certain about that," April smiled. "There is more than one way for a person to see."

CHAPTER TWENTY-FOUR

A NEW LOOK FOR MARY

"I like your hair short like that," Mary's mother told her as Mary got ready to leave for the mission.

"Thanks," Mary said. "Bob told me to get a new look, so I had a makeover."

"That's right," her mother said. "You aren't wearing as much make-up are you?"

"That's part of the change. I'm supposed to have that wholesome look."

"Wow!" her mother said. "Even your clothes look different."

"I'm going for that conservative look," Mary told her. "It's all part of it."

"All part of what?"

"Well, I'm supposed to look wholesome and conservative...not like someone who would do anything irrational..."

"You mean like killing your husband?"

"Precisely. I'm supposed to project an image of innocence."

"But you *are* innocent, Mary."

"I know that and you know that, but you must remember, Mom, I killed this town's chief of police...Mr. perfect...Mr. Rid the Streets of Crime..."

Doors

"Is that why you're doing all this volunteer work?" her mother asked. "To be a 'do gooder'?"

"Well," Mary told her, "It started out that way, but it's changed. I've changed, Mom. I like helping people now. I like being around other people, and I feel good when I'm being useful. I really do. Besides, Quinn goes to bed early, and you're here to watch her while I go to the mission..."

"Is that all?" her mother asked.

"It keeps my mind off things," Mary confessed.

"Off what things?"

"It keeps my mind off what I did," Mary said.

"But you didn't do anything wrong, Mary. You only defended yourself."

"I know that, Mom. They keep telling me that in group therapy, but just because everyone thinks I didn't do anything wrong, it doesn't make it any better?"

"Make what any better, Mary?"

"The nightmares, Mom, and all the terrible thoughts. I killed Quinn's Daddy, Mom. He was a terrible Dad. He was sick and needed help, but I keep thinking maybe there could have been another way..."

"You can't think about that," her mother told her. "What is done is done, and that's all there is to it. You can't look back and you can't undo anything, so you have to learn to live with it..."

"I don't know if I can..."

"You have to, for Quinn's sake. You just have to be brave and go on with your life. You can lean on me, Mary. I'll help you. You're my baby. I love you. Don't you know that?"

"It's not fair to you," Mary said.

"It's something I want to do, Mary. Life isn't always fair, you know. God knows life isn't always fair..."

"Did you know that I couldn't collect on the life insurance?" Mary asked, changing the subject for a moment.

"Why not? It was in Quinn's name?"

"Because they figure that because I killed him, that I would make an illegal profit as long as I had custody of Quinn," Mary explained. "But Bob said he'll take care of that. He said He's going to get a court order to put everything in trust for Quinn...the house, insurance, the car...everything...at least until after the trial. Then after the trial everything that should come to me will come to me...providing I'm found innocent, of course. Otherwise, everything will remain in trust for Quinn until she's eighteen."

"It'll be rough on you if that happens," her mother said.

"I know, but I can't think about that right now. I just want to get through this thing one day at a time...just one day at a time, Mom...That's all I can handle right now..."

"Are you going to go back to school?"

"I'll have to, Mom. I'm not qualified to do anything except be a mother. I can't even collect on my dead husband's social security right now because of this trial and Quinn's will go into the trust."

"When are you going to start?"

Doors

"Spring semester starts in a few weeks," Mary said. "I'm going to enroll at Central City College tomorrow and pick out my classes and all... If I can't start then, I'll start later."

"Do you need some money?"

"I have some I set aside," Mary said. "Some the court doesn't know about. That should cover things."

"Are you sure?"

"I'm sure. You've already done too much, Mom."

"It makes your father and me happy to help you, Mary."

"I know that, Mom; but I also know that this is going to set back Dad's retirement a bit..."

"We're not worried about that, Mary."

"I know, Mom; but it's not fair. It's just not fair."

"I told you, Mary, life isn't fair."

Suddenly, Mary looked down at her watch.

"Oh my God!" she said. "If I don't leave right now, I'm going to be late!"

"You always were a punctual child," her mother said.

"I love you, Mom," Mary said as she walked out the door.

"I love you, too," her mother replied as the door drew shut.

When she was alone, Mary's mother sat and had a good, long cry.

"Why <u>does</u> life have to be so dammed unfair?" she said over and over again through her tears.

No answer was forthcoming.

No answer was forthcoming because that was just how things were. Sometimes life just didn't have any answers. If Mary had just been able to get that retraining order enforced, then none of this would have happened. Mary wondered how many other women lived in fear like she had lived in fear for so long. Mary wondered if anyone would ever do anything to help other women like her so this would never happen again. Mary knew there must be help out there somewhere for women like her. She just never knew how to find it, and now it was too late.

CHAPTER TWENTY-FIVE

THE PROBLEM WITH THE PRIESTHOOD

Father Donovan had a problem. He found he was strangely attracted to Mary and he didn't know why. This kind of thing wasn't supposed to happen to priests. After all, he had sworn himself to a life of celibacy. At first he thought it was priestly concern he felt. Mary was so small and fragile. She couldn't weigh more than a hundred pounds, all five feet one inch of her. He noticed that her hands were small and delicate as she carried the trays to the steam table each night. Priests weren't supposed to notice things like that. He found Mary's eyes to be somewhat hypnotic, and he was afraid to look at her too long for fear he would get lost in the blue of her eyes. He was also afraid his secret would be found out. He didn't want anyone to know he was human, after all...

Mary felt something between them. She wondered why father Donovan was so helpful.

"This isn't a sin I want on my head," Mary thought. "God will surely crucify me if I tempt a priest."

That night as Mary fed the hungry who came to mission for food, she thanked the Lord that she had a roof over her head and loving parents who were willing to take care of her and Quinn, especially during these difficult times. Mary wondered why it was that these many homeless had no one to help them through their times of sorrow.

"Thank-you," a woman Mary had come to know as Leanne said as Mary handed out food to her and her daughter. "I'll try to repay the mission someday," she told Mary.

Father Donovan heard the woman's words.

"No need to repay us," Father Donovan told the woman. "We are here to dispense love. We only want you to pass it on," he said.

Mary smiled at Leanne.

"God bless you both," Leanne said.

"God bless you," Father Donovan told her. "God bless you and your daughter all the days of your life."

Mary mused at how simple it all was. You get love, then you give it. Pretty soon, if enough people get and enough people give, the world would be free of all its problems...Too bad it really didn't work that way.

"I like it here," Mary thought. "I wish I was a nun so I'd never have to leave," she thought momentarily. Then she changed her mind when she remembered Quinn. "...The only problem is...if I had become a nun I wouldn't have Quinn..." she thought.

Father Donovan couldn't help admiring Mary as she stood there at the steam table. Even in sensible shoes he found the turn of her ankle attractive.

"Is there anything I can do to help you?" he asked Mary.

Doors

"No, Father," came the reply.

"Are you sure?" he asked. "You've been standing here working for over two hours now without a break...At least take a break, Mary, before you pass out from exhaustion..."

"Maybe I will take a short break," Mary said. "I am rather tired," she said. "I haven't been sleeping much lately," she told father Donovan.

"You have to take care of yourself, Mary, or you won't be any good to anyone," he said, "Least of all to yourself."

"You sound like my mother," Mary told him as she wiped her hands on her apron and put down the spoon she was holding.

"Can I take over for you?" he asked.

"I'll do that," one of the nuns said overhearing the conversation. "You go ahead and take a break with Mary," she said. "Mary looks like she could use some company."

Mary couldn't help blushing as she and Father Donovan went into the kitchen to take a break.

Father Donovan got some water from the sink.

"I'd offer you wine," he said, "But this is a poor parish..."

"Wine would put me to sleep," Mary said.

"I thought you said you needed sleep, Mary?"

"Well, that's true," Mary replied, "But not right now...I have work to do here..."

"You need to take care of yourself, Mary."

"I will. I promise," came the reply.

Doors

"By the way," Father Donovan asked, "How is your case coming?"

"Well...I'm going to trial on the charges, Father, but my attorney seems optimistic..."

"Only God can really judge you," Father Donovan said.

"Do you think I'm guilty, father?"

"Of course not, Mary. How could anyone blame a little thing like you for what happened?"

"Well, apparently the district attorney's office can, Father."

"What do they know, anyway?" Father Donovan told her. "What do they see of life the way it *really* is? Who are they to judge? The bible says judge not lest ye be judged, Mary," Father Donovan said trying to sound religious. He didn't want his true feelings for this woman to accidentally come pouring forth.

Mary looked away from him.

"Is something wrong, Mary?" he asked.

"Sort of," came the timid reply.

"Tell me what's bothering you?" Father Donovan implored of her.

"I don't dare, Father..."

"Mary," he said lovingly, "You can tell me anything...anything at all...I am a priest, after all..."

"I don't think I can tell you this, Father."

"Is it about the trial, Mary?"

"No, Father."

"Is it about what you did to your husband, Mary?"

Doors

"No."

"Nothing can be that bad, Mary."

"I don't know, Father."

"Please tell me what it is..."

"Maybe I should go to confession," Mary said.

"Well, that's up to you, Mary, but if you want to talk, I'm here for you."

"I think I'll go to confession," Mary resolved not willing to tell him her deep dark secret.

Mary could never let him know that she was in love with him. After all, he <u>was</u> a priest.

"You're very special, Mary," Father Donovan told her as she rose to return to work.

"Why is that?" she asked.

"It takes a lot of courage to have gone through what you have gone through and are going through now and to still be able to get up and face the world each day," he told her.

"It's not courage," Mary replied. "It's just something I have to do, that's all. Some things in life give you no choices."

"That's where you are wrong, Mary," Father Donovan told her. "God gives us all choices, everyday. It's up to us what we do about them," he said knowing in his heart that very soon he might be facing a choice about Mary that he would rather not face.

"I guess you're right," she said. "I just hope I've made the right choices, that's all..."

Doors

"Only God knows that," Father Donovan told her. "Only God knows that..."

Mary returned to the steam table and dished out food until all the hungry were fed. She was grateful there was enough food for all the people who came into the mission. It seemed as though everyday the crowds of the hungry kept getting bigger. Mary wondered how that could be and whether one day they would not have enough food and have to turn some of them away from the mission and into the darkness of night without a morsel of food in their stomachs.

"I only know this," Mary thought, "Father Donovan has been called by God to this mission to do something special, and I will not be the one to interfere with that...even if it means that I will never know love...even if it means that..."

Mary went home that night feeling both tired and secure in her convictions that she would not come between this great man and his church.

CHAPTER TWENTY-SIX

MORNING SICKNESS FOR APRIL

"Are you all right?" Nick asked April as he stood outside the bathroom door listening as April threw up the contents of her stomach.

"Of course, I'm all right," April said between heaves. "It's only morning sickness."

"Can I get you anything?"

"Leave me alone, Nick. Just leave me alone."

"I think I'm going to be sick, too!" Nick said as he ran to the other bathroom and threw up in the toilet.

"He's so stupid," April thought as she finished being sick, "But he <u>is</u> sweet. Imagine! Sympathetic morning sickness..."

April returned to the kitchen and sat down at the table in front of her cup of herb tea. It was a special blend that was supposed to soothe her stomach and help with morning sickness...peppermint and almond...

"I wonder if I should drink this," she thought aloud as Nick entered the room.

"I think I have the flu," Nick said as he sat down.

April smiled at him knowingly.

"You're sweet," she said, "And I love you," she told him as she reached over and fondly touched her hand against his unshaven cheek. "You need a shave," she told him.

Nick opened up the Sunday paper and looked through it for the comic section.

"I love Sunday's," he said. "Lots of comics to read..."

"You're funny," April told him deciding to gingerly sip her tea. "Would you like a cup of herb tea to soothe your stomach?" she asked.

"I'll stick to my black coffee," he said. "It's a man's drink."

"I thought you said whiskey was a 'man's drink?'"

"Not in the morning, April...Not in the morning...at least not before noon," he teased.

"Well," April told him, "I won't be having any coffee, colas *or* spirits until after the baby...It's not good for her..."

"What do you mean, her?"

"Didn't I tell you it's a girl?" April asked him.

"How could you know that?" Nick asked reaching over and placing his hand on her stomach.

"Well...they think it's a girl from the ultrasound...I have pictures, Nick...Do you want to see them?"

"Sure."

April went to the living room and came back a few moment's later.

"There's your baby," she said pointing to a series of photocopies the doctor had given her from the ultrasound machine.

"Oh my God!" Nick said excitedly. "Look at that! Look! It's a baby! A real baby!"

"Of course, it's a real baby, Nick. What did you think it would be?"

"I don't know," he said. "I mean, now it all seems so real...We're actually having a baby!"

"I told you that, Nick. Why do you think I'm getting fat?"

"I don't know. I didn't think about it, that's all," he said as he started to walk around the room. "I can't contain myself. Let's go buy a crib or something..."

"All right, Nick. We'll go buy a baby buggy today and you can fill it with stuffed animals...all right?" April said laughing as she rose and put her arms around Nick to hug him.

"I love you," he said kissing her.

"Show me," she said reaching down and unzipping his pants.

Nick's pants fell to the floor.

"Is it safe for the baby?" he asked.

"Of course," April said dropping her nightgown to the ground and pulling off Nick's underwear.

Nick pressed against her.

"I can't stand it," April said. "Make love to me and make love to me now."

Nick kissed her all over as she stood naked and pregnant before him. He found the swelling of her belly exciting.

April pulled off his white tee shirt.   Nick was naked against her body now and it felt good. She caressed him lovingly.

"God! I love you!" she said. "You can't imagine how much I love you! You just can't imagine!"

Nick took her into the living room and threw the sofa pillows on the floor. They lay down on the pillows and they made sweet love. It felt good. It felt very, very good.

Nick kissed her, and April swooned for him.

"I love you, Nick," she kept saying between kisses that continued and did not stop.

"I love you too," he said as he continued to hold her tight, not wanting to ever let her go. "You're so wonderful," he told her kissing her again. "You're so wonderful..."

Later that afternoon they went shopping and picked out a buggy fit for their little princess. It was an Italian import. It was the best and the most expensive they could find. After all, this buggy had to last. Nick figured they'd have at least a half dozen kids. April planned on two.

They went to a toy store and Nick could hardly be controlled. April insisted that the baby should be well-rounded, and they should buy toys suitable for both sexes. After all, they didn't want to be sexist stereotypical, did they?

"This will be the most loved baby ever to have been born," Nick told April as they made love again that night.

April smiled. She was happy. She was happier than she had ever been

Doors

in her entire life.

"This is what it's all about, Nick," she said. "It's not about money, or big cars or a fancy house. It's about love and being together and raising a family. That's why we were put on this earth."

"Are you getting sentimental on me, counselor?" Nick asked as he kissed her tenderly.

"I suppose so," she told him between kisses, "But I mean every word of it. I really do."

"You and this little white house with the picket fence and the swing in the tree out back are really getting to me," he said. "I guess I'll have to rethink my priorities..."

"What do you mean?"

"I mean I used to think that things were what life was about...having things...making money...making money to have things," he said. "Now I realize that we don't need things. We only need each other."

"It's inconvenient being rich, didn't you know that, Nick?"

"What do you mean?" Nick asked.

"A rich man has to rent a big truck to move his possessions when he is required to leave one place to live in another," April said. "A poor man can move with only a few bags... and he can carry his bags with his own two arms."

Nick sat and thought about what April had just said.

"How did you think up that?" Nick asked her.

"One of my clients told me," April said, "...One of my clients from legal aid...It seems that when I expressed my sorrow at how little this particular individual had, he was surprised. He said that he was happy and didn't need much. He said that he was free and could go where he wished. He worked here and there and lived here and there, but he was free of all cares. He wasn't a blight on society or anything like that...He was simply satisfied with what he had. It was that simple. This guy lived for the moment. He lived for the day. He did what he thought was right. He helped the poor. He was kind to everyone."

"He sounds like Jesus Christ..."Nick said.

"He said he was walking in His footsteps," April told him.

"It kind of makes you think, doesn't it?" Nick asked her.

"Yes, it does, Nick."

Then they lay for a while thinking and staring up at the ceiling. Nick's hand moved over to touch April's swelling stomach. April rolled over on top of Nick and kissed him over and over again.

"I love you," she said, as he rolled her off of him and made love to her again.

"Life is so wonderful," Nick said. "It's so wonderful..."

CHAPTER TWENTY-SEVEN
THE TRIAL IS SET

"Bob Grant is on the telephone," Mary's mother called out to her.

"Coming..." came the reply.

"She'll be right here," Mary's mother told Bob. "She's just getting out of the shower..."

"I can call back," Bob said.

"Nonsense," came the reply. "She's here right now," Mary's mother told Bob as Mary appeared in the kitchen door in her robe, drying her short red hair with terry cloth towel.

Mary took the telephone receiver from her mother's hand and leaned against the kitchen wall.

"Hello," she said.

"Better sit down," Bob told her as if he could see she was standing up.

Mary pulled out a kitchen table chair and sat down.

"I'm sitting down," she said.

"Good," came the reply. "I have something to tell you. The date for the trial has been set and it's sooner than we thought," Bob explained.

"Is that good or bad," Mary asked him.

"It's good and bad," Bob explained. "It's good because it means that the district attorney's office is worried about all the favorable publicity you're getting..."

"I don't understand..."

"Well, it's bad because this gives us less time to prepare and less time to get even more favorable publicity," Bob explained. "The simple truth is that we're getting to them. You're doing good, Mary."

"I haven't done anything," Mary said.

"Look out the kitchen window," Bob told her.

Mary stretched her neck and looked out the window through her mother's organdy white pricilla curtains.

"Do you see anything?"

"Reporters..." Mary replied. "Lots of reporters."

"They want to know how you feel about the trial date."

"What should I tell them?" Mary asked.

"Tell them the truth," Bob told her.

"What's the truth, Bob?"

"The truth is that you acted in self defense. Tell them that, Mary; and tell them that you feel confident that a jury of your peers will agree with you and your attorney."

"Should I say anything else?"

"If they ask you if you're going to plea bargain, tell them you're not doing anything of the sort."

Doors

"What does that mean?"

"That means that we are not going to plead guilty to anything, Mary. You're simply not guilty, and you're not going to go to jail or have a record of any kind if I can help it."

"I thought it was good to plea bargain."

"Sometimes it is, and sometimes it's not," Bob said. "In this case it's not."

"How soon are we going to trial? Mary asked.

"Next month," Bob told her.

"That soon?"

"That soon. Are you scared, Mary?"

"I'm scared as hell, Bob."

"Do you trust me, Mary?"

"Yes."

"Then don't worry. Right now I'm going to tell you to do something...all right?"

"All right."

"I want you to go down to the mission chapel and pray," Bob said.

"I thought you didn't believe in God, Bob."

"I don't, Mary, but it makes good copy. Don't you get it? The reporters will follow you and make a photo opportunity out of it..."

"But I really think I need to pray..."

"That even makes it better, Mary, because you'll look sincere."

"But I am sincere. I'm scared, Bob. I'm really scared."

"Then talk to the priest while you're down there and make sure the press sees you."

"I don't know," Mary said. "I'm not sure it's right to use the church that way."

"What would you do under normal circumstances?" Bob asked.

"I'd be scared as hell, like I am; and I'd want to talk to a priest," Mary told him.

"Well, then...how could you be using the church? The reporters are going to follow you anyway. Just let them take some pictures. Trust me, Mary. You said you trusted me."

"All right, Bob. I trust you. I'll do it."

"Wear something conservative. Something black or navy with a hat and gloves...white gloves if you have them...It will add a nice touch...but don't put a veil or anything over your face...all right?"

"For someone who can't see, you certainly are concerned about appearances, Bob..."

"Will you do it, Mary?"

"I'll do it."

"Good girl. I'm going to hang up now, but if you have any questions, call me..."

"Good-bye, Bob."

"Good-bye, Mary."

"What did Mr. Grant want?" Mary's mother asked as she entered the room.

Doors

"The trial date has been set," Mary told her mother as she explained what Bob had just told her. "It looks like I'll have to put off going back to school for awhile..."

"I can't believe they've set the trial so soon," her mother said.

"Apparently, the man I killed was no ordinary man," Mary told her.

"Well, you're no ordinary woman," her mother replied.

Mary's thoughts turned to Quinn.

"Where's Quinn?" she asked.

"Don't you worry about Quinn. She's upstairs playing. I'll watch her today. We'll stay inside and bake cookies. I'll pull down the window shades. Nobody will bother her, I promise. You go down to the mission and you do what you have to do. Have a nice long talk with Father Donovan...He's a wonderful priest. He'll take care of you."

Mary looked away afraid that her mother would guess her secret that she had fallen in love with the handsome priest. It was ironic. Mary had looked all her life for love and when she finally found someone she could love, it was forbidden by God and the church. Mary loved the church, but she didn't understand this at all...It didn't seem fair...

"Thanks, Mom," she said as she left the room carrying her towel with her. "I'll go up and get dressed now and kiss Quinn good-bye."

"You do that," her mother told her, "And don't you worry about a thing...not one little thing."

"I love you, Mom," Mary said as she started up the stairs to her room.

Mary's mother watched as her daughter climbed the stairs. She wondered how this ever could have happened to someone as sweet and loving as Mary.

"I love you, too," her mother shouted after her.

Mary dressed in a little black short-sleeved sheath dress with a strand of fake white pearls around her neck. She put on a little black pillbox hat and wore wrist length white gloves. The press had a field day with her. Mary did exactly as she was told. The next day the headlines in the papers read, 'ACCUSED MURDEROUS SAYS SHE ACTED IN SELF DEFENSE...SPENDS DAY IN PRAYER..."

"Oh shit!" Nick Wilcox gasped as he opened his morning paper and showed it to April as she sat across the table from him.

April laughed.

"It's not funny," he said.

"Better get used to it," April told him. "You're going to lose this one...

"That's not funny, April. It's not funny at all," Nick told her.

"It wasn't meant to be funny, Nick," came the reply. "It was meant to be the truth."

Nick shook his head. He knew April was probably right. This was one he was probably going to lose...and he probably should...but he simply did not like losing. He didn't like it at all.

"Nobody says you have to like losing," April said as if reading his mind.

"I haven't lost yet," he said.

CHAPTER TWENTY-EIGHT

OUT TO LUNCH AGAIN

April sat alone in the restaurant booth waiting for Nick. She had purposely picked a far corner booth in a place that was both dark and romantic. So what if it was lunchtime, anyway? She was in the mood for a little romance.

Suddenly, Nick appeared.

"You're on time for a change," she said. "I've ordered us drinks. They're coming."

"Thanks," Nick said as he sat down next to her and gave her a quick little kiss.

"How did it go this morning?" April asked.

"Picked the jury," he said.

"That was quick," April told him.

"Not quick enough," came the reply. "First Grant challenges Judge Goldstein and gets him off the case on the basis that he was unwilling to consider admissibility of evidence at the preliminary hearing, then he serves the prosecution with a motion to suppress evidence, then Judge

Doors

Ramsey takes the bench to take over the trial."

"Judge Ramsey's a fair judge," April told him. "He's one of the best."

"For civil plaintiffs and criminal defendants, maybe...the guy is way too liberal for me..."

"You've got to be kidding," April said. "The only trouble with Judge Ramsey is that he doesn't have any political interest in any of his cases. He's close to retirement. He's an ex-state senator. He can't be bought simply because he comes from old money; and quite frankly, Ramsey is the best judge on the bench as far as I'm concerned...Unless...you don't want a fair trial, that is."

"Of course I want a fair trial."

"You could challenge him."

"You know better than that. If I did that I'd never be able to face him on the bench again."

"Bob Grant does it all the time. He challenges judges if he feels he has to..."

"He's also blind," Nick said sarcastically. "He doesn't have to look them in the eyes when he does it..."

"That's not nice," April said.

"I know. I'm sorry came the reply. It's just that I'm so frustrated. I don't like to lose."

"Look at it as being against a worthy opponent," April told him. "Let the best man win, as it were..."

"You're right. You're right. I should only be concerned about justice

Doors

having its day."

"That's right," April told him as she slid his hand under her skirt.

"You aren't wearing any panties," he whispered and then he smiled. "Did you have something in mind other than lunch?"

April's napkin slid off her lap and she reached over to pick it up. She could feel Nick's hand against her. Then she reached under Nick's napkin and unzipped his pants.

"You aren't wearing any underwear either," she said surprised as she touched him.

"I guess we had the same thing in mind," he said as they looked into each others eyes and smiled.

Their drinks came and they were forced to stop. April sipped her sparkling water and Nick drank his beer.

"I don't know why they call this sparkling water," April said. "Even with the slice of lime, it still tastes like club soda to me..."

"That's because it is," Nick told her. "Even if it comes out of the ground that way, it's still nothing more than club soda."

April looked at him and smiled.

"I ordered lunch already," she said. "We're having raw oysters on the half shell," she told him as she pulled back her suit jacket to reveal that she wore no bra underneath her see through blouse.

Nick found April to be more than exciting.

"Are you trying to turn me on?" he asked her.

"What do you think, counselor?"

"Guilty as charged," came the reply.

"Am I succeeding, Nick?"

Nick put her hand back underneath the napkin.

April smiled.

"What do you think?" he asked.

"I think I want you," came the reply.

The oysters came and they fed one another. Then they paid the bill, left the tip and went outside to Nick's car and inside and kissed each other over and over again like a couple of necking teen-agers. They ran their hands over each other's bodies as though they couldn't get enough of one another.

"Leave your car here," Nick said. "We'll get it later."

"It'll be towed," April told him between kisses.

"I don't care," came the reply. "I'll pay the charges."

"I took the afternoon off," April said, "I was hoping we could spend the day together."

Nick reached up and turned on the motor. Then he picked up his car phone and dialed.

"I won't be in this afternoon," he said as they drove away. "I have a headache."

April smiled at him.

The person on the other end of the telephone line agreed he had had a big morning; and that Nick should take the afternoon off. Nick and April drove home, jumped out of the car, raced into the house and removed

Doors

what was left of their clothing, letting all theirlclothes lay strewn and rumpled on the living room floor. Then Nick carried her to the bedroom and they made love there in their bed, over and over again. Nick marveled at the beauty of April's swelling body, and April marveled at her love for Nick, the man who had given her the gift of the child within her womb.

"I love you more than you'll ever know," she told him.

"That's good," he said, "Because I love you too."

April's car was towed away later that afternoon. Nick paid the price to recover it without as much as a grumble.

CHAPTER TWENTY-NINE

ROMANCE BLOOMS AGAIN, UNEXPECTEDLY

"Did you read the paper this morning?" Bob asked Sandra as he entered the door.

"No, Boss. Did you?" Sandra giggled.

"As a matter of fact, I did," Bob told her.

"How?" she asked.

"Never mind that. I just did that's all. All right, I had it read to me. Are you happy now."

"It makes more sense," Sandra told him.

"Anyway, it seems some guy took a break from a deposition in San Francisco, went out to his car and got a couple of Uzis and a bag of ammunition, went back up to the deposition and blew everyone away."

"You're kidding!?!"

"Nope. Wish I were kidding. Eight dead. Six wounded. The Police minister said it was the most terrible thing he'd ever seen."

"Why did the guy do it?"

"Apparently the lawsuit wasn't going his way and he thought the

Doors

insurance company should give him three hundred thousand dollars and they wouldn't give him a penny."

"Was he desperate?"

"I don't know, but they think the shooting was planned. He definitely knew who he wanted to shoot and why."

"What is this world coming to?"

"I'll tell you this, Sandra, if the law doesn't start working, a lot more of this kind of thing is going to happen."

"What do you mean?"

"The law is supposed to abide by certain standards. It's supposed to protect everyone blindly, evenly, the same; but you and I know for a fact it doesn't work that way. The little guy can't afford to litigate. He thinks he can, but he can't. The big guy will win simply because the little guy doesn't have the money to fight, never mind the time and the energy. Criminal lawsuits work the same way. A guy can steal millions in working white-collar securities fraud and get off with a few months in a country club prison, complete with pools and tennis courts. Another guy can steal a few hundred from a convenience store and end up spending years behind bars, the girlfriend of some sadistic bully with the aids virus. He ends up dead. The first guy gets little more than a forced vacation and time to meditate."

"Is it that bad?"

"It's worse. There's a lawsuit pending right now against the city because a guy who was doing thirty days in county jail got raped by his cellmate."

"What's the basis of the lawsuit?"

"Inadequate protection from the guards?"

"Do the guards have a duty to protect him?"

"That's for the trier of fact to decide. I suppose that if there's a jury, though, it will decide there was no duty because the guy is suing for three million, and if he wins they will be afraid that their taxes will go up to pay for it."

"Won't they want to preserve their own rights? What if happened to them?"

"People these days don't look at anything from a long term standpoint. It's only the short term that counts," Bob told her.

Suddenly, the phone rang and interrupted their conversation.

"Bob Grant's law office," Sandra said as she picked up the receiver.

"May I speak to Mr. Grant," a female voice on the other end asked.

"May I say who is calling?"

"Tell him it's Donna Fairmont Baxter," came the reply. "I'm an old friend."

"It's Donna Fairmont Baxter," Sandra said, putting her hand over the receiver in order that the caller wouldn't hear her.

Bob beamed.

"I'll take it in my office," he said as he and Duke went into the other room that comprised his office.

"Donna Fairmont!" Bob said as he answered the phone. "How is the prettiest girl that ever graced the state of Alabama?" he asked.

Doors

"I'm divorced and missing you," came the reply. "And how are you?"

"I'd like to see you," Bob said. "How did you find me?" he asked.

"I had a terrible time finding you," came the reply, "Because I always knew you as Don. You always went by the name of Donald at home. But when I couldn't find you under that name, I called the state bar and they told me they had a listing for Robert Donald Grant, so I took my chances and made the call. Do you know it took me five years to track you down?"

"So where are you now?" Bob asked.

"I'm in Los Angeles. I'm working out here for an insurance company. I transferred out here from Alabama. I'm coming up to Central City this weekend," she said.

"Can we have dinner?" Bob asked.

"I should hope so," she said.

"I'm looking forward to it then," Bob told her.

"Are you married?" Donna asked.

"Not at the moment. Three times divorced, but nor married at the moment," came the reply.

"Are you still a ladies' man?"

"Not quite."

"Why not?"

"Nobody wants a blind old guy like me..."

"I'll bet you're as handsome as ever..."

"My hair is white now..."

"I don't believe you."

"You'll see."

"It's a date then?" Donna asked him.

"It's a date," he said.

"I'll call you when I get into town," she said.

"I'll be waiting," Bob said.

"Good. I've spent the last five years looking for you," she said again as a matter of fact.

"You're kidding?"

"I don't kid about things like that," she said.

"Why did you do that?" he asked her.

"I wanted to find you again," she said quite simply.

They said their good-byes and Bob hung up the receiver. He wondered if it could really be true. Could it be possible that Donna Fairmont had been looking for him for five years?

"She's probably just joking," Bob thought.

Sandra entered the room.

"An old friend?" she asked.

"I was secretly in love with her, but she was only seventeen and I was twenty seven, so I didn't think it was proper to pursue her. Instead, I introduced her to my best friend. Now three grown kids and thirty years later he left her for another woman."

"Did she tell you that?"

"Not exactly. She told me she was divorced. The rest I heard from my sister. We come from a small town, you know...you know how it is...Everybody knows everybody else's business..."

"What made you keep tabs on her?"

"I told you. I was secretly in love with her," he said. "She was so beautiful."

"How would you know that?"

"I just know. She had a good figure too! Everthing in the right places."

"People change," Sandra told him.

"Beauty is more than how you look," Bob said, "Especially to a blind man.

Sandra smiled and returned to her work. Bob spent the afternoon trying to work, but mostly reminiscing about the past and about Donna.

CHAPTER THIRTY

DONNA COMES TO TOWN

It was Friday. The office telephone rang. Sandra was out at lunch, so Bob picked it up.

"Law Office," he said.

"This is Donna," said the voice on the other end of the line. "I'm in town. I just arrived. Just drove into town minutes ago."

"Where are you?"

"I'm downstairs in your office building lobby."

"Why didn't you just come up?"

"I said I'd call, remember?"

Bob laughed.

"Do you still want to see me?" Donna asked.

"Does a fish want to be in water?" Bob replied.

"I'm on my way up now," Donna told him, hanging up the phone.

"Can't wait to see you," Bob said.

Doors

A few minutes later Donna entered the outer office where Bob stood with Duke waiting for her. They hugged.

"I hardly recognized you," she said. "Your hair is so white."

"I told you," Bob laughed, "But you wouldn't believe me."

"You're as handsome and dashing as ever," Donna told him, "White hair and all..."

"You still have a great little figure," he said.

"You can't see me, Don," she protested.

"No one has called me Don for a long time," he said, "And I know you still have a great little figure because I could feel it when I hugged you," Bob told her.

"No, I don't," Donna protested.

"Yes, you do," Bob told her, "It's all there. It's just moved down and around a little bit...that's all."

Donna laughed.

"Have you had lunch?" Bob asked her.

"Do you eat lunch now?" Donna asked. "You never used to eat lunch."

"I do on special occasions," Bob told her.

"Then let's have lunch," Donna said. "I'm famished."

"Let's go," came the reply as Bob, Duke and Donna exited the office door.

"Shall I drive?" Bob asked. "Or would you rather walk?"

"Let's walk," Donna said. "It's much safer."

"There's an excellent restaurant in the hotel across the street. It's

Doors

called the grill. The chef there serves a marvelous rack of lamb braised and then baked with honey mustard and ground pistachios."

"Your tastes have gotten quite sophisticated," Donna told him. "I guess you've come a long way from hamburgers and grilled onions."

"Let's stay away from the onions until later," Bob said. "I might want to make love to you, or something."

"I hope so," Donna said. "I've been waiting for you for over thirty years and we don't have all that much time left."

Bob said nothing as they entered the restaurant called the grill.

"Can we have a nice dark romantic booth?" he asked the maiter'd as they entered to be seated.

They were seated.

"Is it dark and romantic?" Bob asked her.

Donna laughed.

"You have to tell me," he said.

"Anyplace is romantic if I'm with you," Donna told him. "I have a confession to make," she said. "I have been secretly in love with you since the day I met you."

"You're kidding?" Bob said more than asking.

"No. I'm not," came the reply.

"Then why did you marry my best friend?"

"I didn't think *you* were interested," came the reply.

"Well, I was," Bob told her.

"Then why did you introduce me to your best friend, Don?"

Doors

Bob smiled. It felt good to be called Don again. The years melted away.

"I guess I was afraid," he told her. "I was ten years older than you at the time and I guess I just didn't think it was the proper thing to do."

"Does it make any difference now?" Donna asked him.

"Hell, no!"

"Thank God," she said. "Maybe we can give the home town something to talk about."

"I hope so," Bob laughed. "What made you come looking for me?" he asked.

"Jack ran off with another woman after twenty-five years of marriage...a younger woman. I stewed about it for a few days. The kids were all grown, so I got myself transferred to California and decided to go looking for you. I'd never gotten over you, Don...I just couldn't stop thinking about you and dreaming about you all those years..."

"You know something?" Bob asked her. "I think I must be the luckiest man on this planet right now. I've been married three times to three very wonderful women, but somehow something was always missing. I could never really love them the way I wanted to...the way they deserved to be loved...completely...because something was always missing...I think that something was you," he confessed.

"Do you have any court appearances or anything this afternoon?" Donna asked.

"Why?" Bob asked her.

Doors

"I have a lovely hotel room," she said.

"Where?" Bob asked.

"Why, right here in this hotel..." Donna told him smiling.

Bob patted Duke.

"Can the dog come too?" he asked.

"As long as he doesn't interfere," Donna told him.

"With what?" Bob asked.

"With my seduction of you," came the reply.

Bob laughed heartily and kissed Donna on the cheek.

The food was served, and they ate, paid the bill and got a room at the hotel. Bob called Sandra and canceled all his appointments for the rest of the day.

This was the beginning of something old. Bob had never been happier. By the end of the weekend they had decided to get married.

CHAPTER THIRTY-ONE

APRIL AND NICK AND BABY MAKES THREE

Nick came through the door with his face askew.

"What a way to spend a Saturday morning!" he said.

"How was the funeral?" April asked him as she looked up from the television set.

"It was weird," Nick said.

"What do you mean?" April asked him.

"Well," Nick said. "There was Judge Bloom and his wife all upset about their son driving over a cliff in a drunken stupor and killing himself at the tender age of nineteen, and there were all his friends glorifying the thing..."

"What are you talking about?" April asked him.

"It was weird. That's all. It was weird. His friends got up one by one and did a eulogy on how much Jeff Bloom enjoyed life...about what a great guy he was and how much he loved to party and all..."

"So?"

"So...In the casket with him was a bottle of tequila...I mean it was macabre...it was strange, to say the least. The stuff actually killed the kid, and they were glorifying it, like it was their god or something...Everyone passed by the casket and said how peaceful Jeff looked...and how handsome he was...The kid was an alcoholic, pure and simple and the stuff killed him...and they celebrated it."

"Did you give my apologies for my not attending?" April asked him.

"Yes," came the reply. "The Blooms said they understood."

April got up, turned off the television set and then returned to her overstuffed chair to talk to Nick.

"I hope this morning sickness doesn't last much longer," she said as Nick sat on the sofa across from her stretching out his long legs. "I'd like to get on with things. Hanging over a toilet each morning isn't exactly my idea of a fulfilling accomplishment!"

"You'll get over it," Nick said. "They say everyone gets over it after awhile."

"Who says that?" April asked.

"I don't know," Nick said. "Everybody says that..."

"I hope they're right..."

"So do I. I don't like seeing you sick."

"It'll be worth it, Nick."

"I know," Nick said smiling at her. "I know it'll be worth it. I'm just sorry it's so hard on you."

"Come on, Nick," April teased. "I hear you throwing up first thing in the morning."

Nick blushed.

"I can't help it," he said. "I love you so much. When you get sick. I get sick too! I know it doesn't make sense...but I just do, that's all...I just do..."

"Did you hear about the rock quarry going in just outside of town?" April asked him.

"The Bailey Rock, Sand and Asphalt Quarry?" Nick asked.

"Yeah...that's the one...How can that possibly get approved, Nick? It's going to destroy natural wetland areas and harm wildlife, and its going to cause havoc on the rural community they want to build it in due to the excess traffic, sulfur dioxide emissions and all..."

"The Bailey's are a powerful family in this town," Nick told her.

"I know that, but it's not fair."

"The Bailey's are calling in their 'pay backs'," Nick told her.

"What do you mean?"

"Well, the old man Bailey, before he died, did a lot for the community, especially that rural community...the old timers that are there trust the family and don't really believe anyone in that family would do anything to harm them..."

"Are they nuts or what?"

"It seems," Nick went on, "That in the old days the Baileys provided transportation for field trips for the local school in the area and furnished hay for the horses that the kids rode to school and stuff like that. They also provided the refreshments for school parties, graduations, sent watermelons to community picnics, loaned out their tractors, tilled fields if a farmer was sick...stuff like that..."

"Doesn't sound like much," April told him.

"No it doesn't," came the reply, "But the Baileys did this during the time of the Great Depression and the memories stick...Everyone forgets that they aren't so generous now, except when they want something..."

"Like what?"

"Like building a football stadium at the high school so the Bailey boy can play on the football team..."

"I see..."

"Yeah..." Nick told her, "And when they wanted one of the sons to get into law school, they donated a wing on the building...that kind of stuff...The old man may have been a saint, but the new Baileys are opportunists," Nick told her. "It's just that the general public hasn't caught on..."

"Is that how they got their subdivision approved when there was a building moratorium and nobody else could build?" April asked.

"Precisely," Nick said. "A few well placed donations, memories of watermelons and hay given to school kids long grown, and they can write their own ticket...Everyone forgets they got their property by foreclosing on a loan and putting a farmer out on the dusty streets, so to speak...Everyone forgets that..."

"So now they can destroy wildlife and pollute the watershed and the air...And nobody gives a damn?"

Doors

"Cross a few palms with the color of green," Nick told her, "And you can pretty much buy whatever you want..."

"It's disgusting," April said.

"I agree," Nick told her, "But people like us can't do anything about it. We don't have the time, the energy, the funds, the means <u>or</u> the correct political support."

"Don't people understand what is happening to their environment, Nick?"

"Buy them a community center and promise them jobs and they don't care. I suppose they think it's survival of the fittest, but what they don't understand is that the environment they are killing is their own. Once they accomplish that, man will be as extinct as the dinosaur..."

"Aren't you being a little melodramatic, Nick?"

"Perhaps...But I don't think so...We have to preserve what we have for our little ones...I want our baby to have fresh air to breathe...I want her to see a deer crossing a country road...to hear the hoot of an owl...to see butterflies..."

"I don't see many butterflies anymore, Nick..."

"They're disappearing," Nick said. "That's what I mean. First the butterflies go and then the bees and then the birds...and then..."

"I get the picture, Nick, but what can we do?"

"Not much," came the reply, "But if everybody does just a little something, that little something will combine with everybody else's little something and become a lot. One grain of sand is nothing, but put a lot of

Doors

grains together and pretty soon you have a shovel full of sand, then a pile of sand, then a mountain..."

"I guess so," April told him, "But do we have to think about that now? I just want to think about this wonderful little baby inside of me..."

"That's what I am thinking about," Nick told her, "About that baby and that baby's baby and so on and so forth...what will be here for them? I want them to play in meadows of butterflies like I did when I was a kid."

"It sounds like fun," April said.

"It was," came the reply.

"What can we do, Nick?"

"I don't know," Nick told her, "But we've got to do something before it's too late..."

"There must be others of us who feel this way, Nick."

"I hope so, April. Otherwise we'll never build a mountain..."

CHAPTER THIRTY-TWO

THE MOTION TO SUPPRESS

The attorneys were all in the courtroom waiting rulings on their motions.

"The first case will be The State of California verses Mary Mason, Motion to Suppress," Judge Ramsey said.

The attorneys stood.

"Nick Wilcox appearing on behalf of the State of California," Nick said.

"Robert Donald Grant appearing on behalf of the defendant, Mary Mason, who is the moving party," Bob said as he and Duke stood before the court.

My tentative ruling is to grant in part and to deny in part," the judge said. "I'm going to grant suppression of evidence as to the statements made by Ms. Mason prior to her arrest and being read her rights. I'm going to deny suppression of all evidence having to do with the pathology report, and statements of the young child, Quinn, because I feel at this time that these are matters that should be properly heard before a jury. I'll take argument on the matters before this court if the parties so desire."

"I'll stipulate to the rulings," Bob said.

"We so stipulate," said Nick Wilcox.

"Mr. Grant, this was your motion, and you did partially prevail; therefore, I will have your office prepare the order for the court and at this time I will request that the minute order be recorded in the record," the judge said slamming down his gavel.

Bob and Nick left the courtroom. Outside they shook hands.

"Congratulations," Nick said.

"That's very sporting of you," came the reply. "I thought you didn't like to lose."

"Who told you that?"

"Nobody, but since you don't lose much, I figured that was the reason," Bob laughed as he reached down to pet Duke.

"You're a good adversary," Nick told him. "All I want out of this one is justice. I don't really know who is right here, so I've decided the court should decide..."

"...A change of position?"

"Not really. I intend to fight you dammed hard, Mr. Grant, dammed hard..."

"That's good," Bob told him. "It'll be more fun winning that way!"

"How can you be so sure you're going to win?" Nick asked him as they started walking down the hall.

"I'm sure I'm going to win because I *know* I'm right," Bob replied.

Doors

Nick became uneasy.

"Nice talking to you," he said as he darted down a side hall. "See you in court..."

Bob went back to his office.

"Donna and I are going to get married right after the Mason trial," Bob told Sandra as he sipped coffee later that day. "We're going to go to Las Vegas. Nothing fancy. We're too old for that."

"Do you want something frivolous or practical for a wedding gift?" Sandra asked Bob.

"We both already have all our household stuff, so we're going to be pretty much doubled up on that when Donna moves up here to Central City, so I say frivolous...something frivolous would be very nice...very nice indeed..."

"I know just what I'll get you," Sandra said thinking about the silver goblets and the special bottle of Champagne she would buy them. Sandra knew Bob loved champagne!

"Will it be expensive?" Bob asked her.

"Will you give me a raise?" Sandra retorted laughing.

"You drive me crazy," Bob said. "Aren't you ever serious?"

"Who said I'm not serious?" Sandra asked him.

Just then the telephone rang. It was Mary Mason.

"You told me to call," she said as Sandra handed Bob the phone.

"Well," Bob told her, "We wiped out your pre-arrest confession," Bob said.

Doors

"Is that good?" Mary asked.

"Well, in some ways it is," Bob explained, "Because they won't be able to show that you knew what you were doing when you killed your husband. I mean that's how that statement sounded, even if you *didn't know* what you were saying at the time...So that's good. That means the jury will be started from scratch...our scratch...and we can get all the abuse evidence before the court before we get to the part where you killed him."

"I'm scared," Mary said.

"You have to stop thinking that way, Mary. We can't have any negative thoughts now. If we're going to do that, we may as well accept the plea bargain the District Attorney offered and call it a day."

"You mean the manslaughter offer?"

"Yup, and that means fifteen years. If you do half of the time with time off for good behavior, you're still doing seven and a half! Quinn will be almost eleven years old when you get out. Do you want to miss her growing up, Mary?"

"You know I don't."

"Then you have to trust me."

"Why do you keep telling me that?"

"I'm telling you that because it's true, Mary. You *have* to trust me...That's all...You have to trust me...."

"I trust you Bob, I do..."

"Then you can't be scared, and even if you are scared, you can't act that way because acting scared is too close to acting guilty...You know what I mean?"

"I think so..."

"I mean people think that if you're not guilty then you have nothing to be afraid of...People actually believe that if you're not guilty you won't go to jail...And it doesn't always work that way...A jury is quite subjective...and we're going to have to fight hard to present all our evidence. That's the way it is. We have a good judge, though, one who doesn't play political games; and that's good..."

"What do you want me to do now, Bob?"

"Just keep up what you have been doing. Keep up your volunteer work at the mission, spend time with Quinn, go grocery shopping, visit with friends, don't act scared..."

"All right," came the reply as the two of them said their good-byes and hung up their telephone receivers.

"I'm worried about that one," Bob told Sandra as he hung up the telephone.

"Why? You have a good case."

"I just hope she can hold it all together," Bob said. "She's walking a thin line between sanity and insanity right now..."

"She'll be fine," Sandra told him.

"And how can you be so sure?"

"She was strong enough to blow the guy away before he did her in," Sandra said, "She's strong enough to keep standing up for herself."

"I hope you're right!"

"I *know* I'm right!" Sandra told him, "Besides, you said you have a fair judge on this one."

"That's true. That's true," came the reply.

"So don't worry or *you'll* look like you think you have a guilty client," Sandra said.

"Where did you learn that?" Bob asked.

"From you...Just now...Isn't that what you told Mary Mason just now?"

"Sort of..."

"Physician, heal thyself..." Sandra said laughing as she left the room with a stack full of papers to copy at the copy machine.

"Where are you going?" Bob called after her.

"Out to copy papers, boss!" she yelled back at him. "I'll be right back..."

CHAPTER THIRTY-THREE

MARY AND FATHER DONOVAN, THE PRIEST

"I have a confession to make," Mary told Father Donovan after her volunteer time was over for the night, and they sat alone at the kitchen table with cups of coffee. Mary needed to talk to someone who cared, someone who *really* cared. Mary needed a friend. She needed someone who could give her strength.

"What ever could you have to confess?" he asked her.

"I'm a little bit embarrassed," she said.

"Maybe I can help you," he said as he leaned over the table almost involuntarily and kissed her.

"Oh my God!" Mary said, breathless and surprised from the kiss.

"We may as well face facts," Father Donovan told her.

Mary turned away from him.

"This is not exactly good for my image," she said.

"What are you talking about?" he asked.

"I'm supposed to be pure and innocent," Mary said. "I can't go around seducing priests...that doesn't fulfill the image my lawyer wants me to portray."

"You haven't exactly seduced me..."

"I may as well have..."

"But you haven't. Besides, this is my choice, Mary. I love you and I won't be complete without you. I've been fighting it for a long time, but I just can't fight it any longer...I want to marry you, Mary..."

"You're already married," Mary told him, "To the church..."

"I know that being a priest was supposed to be a forever kind of thing, Mary, but it just hasn't turned out that way. Whether you marry me or not I'm going to resign from the priesthood. Celibacy is not something I can live with anymore. I just don't think it's right. I don't believe in it anymore."

"I don't know what to say," Mary said.

"Are you afraid I can't take care of you?" Father Donovan asked her. "I can, you know. I have a doctorate in psychology, you know. I can teach or become a clinical psychologist. I *can* take care of you and your daughter, Quinn."

"Quinn loves you," Mary told him.

"And her mother?"

Mary turned away.

"You're asking me at a bad time," she said.

"I was never much good at timing. That's probably how I ended up being a priest..."

Doors

"What I mean is with the trial and all...I might be going to prison..."

"You won't go to prison, Mary. I promise you, you won't. You're too good and too wonderful for that."

"Being good and being right doesn't always mean you win in this world."

"Who told you that?"

"My lawyer..."

"Doesn't he believe in God?"

"As a matter of fact he doesn't, but he's so good it's hard to believe he doesn't believe in God or anything," Mary said. "In fact, he's the best Christian I know...if you want to talk about leading a God-like life..."

"You're changing the subject, Mary."

"How can you do this to me right now," Mary asked him. "I wasn't going to confess I was in love with you. I was going to confess that I was scared and that I needed help and prayer. Now you've put something else in my path to consider."

"Do you love me, Mary?"

"Yes."

"What's so wrong with that?"

"You're a priest for God's sake!"

"I told you not for long. I'm resigning the priesthood."

"Will you promise me one thing?"

"Anything."

"Don't do anything until *after* the trial...please?"

"All right."

"Do you promise?"

"I promise...But will you consider my proposal of marriage then?"

"I'll consider it," Mary said, her head spinning. "I just hope God doesn't strike me down..."

"Our God is a just and wonderful God," Father Donovan told her. "He won't heap on our shoulders any greater burden than we are able to bear."

"I hope you're right."

"I know I'm right."

"Will you promise not to talk of this until after the trial?"

"I promise...reluctantly, I promise."

"Do you understand why?"

"I understand."

"All right," Mary said. "It's settled then...No more of this kind of talk until after the trial; and don't talk about this to a soul...It might hurt my case...I might go to prison for sure...besides it would ruin you as a character witness for me; and I know my lawyer is going to call you as a character witness...He told me so...."

"The cross-examination would be hell, wouldn't it?"

"Yes."

"Don't worry. This is just between the two of us. I just wanted you to know that I'm waiting for you no matter what happens at the trial," Father Donovan said.

"I don't know what to say."

"Don't say anything," Father Donovan said as a nun entered the room.

Doors

"Is there anything I can do to help you, Father?" the nun asked him.

"Nothing," came the reply.

"I must be going home now," Mary said as she rose from the chair in which she was sitting and headed for the door. "Thank-you for your kind words, Father," she said in front of the nun, feeling somewhat hypocritical.

"Drive safely," the nun said.

"Thank-you," Mary told the nun.

"God be with you," said Father Donovan as she left.

Mary didn't sleep that night. It seemed as though her world was getting more and more complex by the moment, and she didn't know what to do about it. It was the early hours of the morning when she finally fell asleep. She needed her rest. She was going to spend the day with Quinn at the zoo.

CHAPTER THIRTY-FOUR

GETTING READY FOR THE TRIAL

"Did you listen to the morning news?" Bob asked Sandra as he entered the office for the day.

"No."

"Well, it was a great day for news! A twenty-four year old woman in Virginia cut off her husband's penis while he slept. She said she took a knife from the kitchen and did it in one sweep."

"How gross!"

"That's not all. She said she did it because he kept raping her, and she was so scared after she did it that she ran out of the house taking the penis with her. Then she threw it out the car window as she drove away from the house."

Sandra started to laugh. Bob smiled.

"I told you it was a good day for news!~

"What happened when the guy woke up?"

"Well, he noticed his penis was missing and ran to the neighbor's house for help. The neighbor drove him to the hospital, notified the police; and the police found the severed penis lying on a road not far from the scene of the crime. They packed it in ice and took it to the hospital where a team of specialists in urology re-attached it."

"Can they do that?"

"It's not a common procedure, only about a hundred documented cases so it's largely an uncharted area of medicine...I mean it's not something that tends to happen on a daily basis or anything."

Sandra shook her head.

"Mary should have done that," she said, "And thrown it down the garbage disposal. The bastard could have suffered a little. He would have had to wait for a donor penis."

"Now who's being gross?"

"I guess it comes from working in this business," Sandra said. "What charges were brought against her?"

"Aggravated assault."

"Doesn't sound too bad."

"She hasn't brought charges against him for rape yet, though, so her defense will be difficult..."

"You aren't going to fly out and defend her, are you?"

"Might be fun."

"You are gross."

"Want to hear what else was in the news?"

"I don't know. Do I?"

"Sure you do."

"All right. What else was in the news?"

"A kid in Washington State found a frog cooked in a pretzel, and the defense is that the pretzels were made in New Jersey, and they don't have those kinds of frogs in New Jersey."

Sandra laughed.

"Don't you think that's gross?" Bob asked her.

"Not as gross as the penis thing..."

"Well, the Mom took the pretzels back to the store where she got them and got a full refund. No damage though. It's a good products liability case if they can show some kind of damage..."

"Do you associate everything with the law?"

"That's my job. I'm a lawyer...Remember?"

"Anything else in the news?"

"A guy in Los Angeles was caught putting razor blades in women's car seat cushions while they shopped at various K-Marts in the area."

"Doesn't he like K-Mart?"

"Either that, or he doesn't like women..."

Sandra laughed.

"Now *that's* gross!" she said.

Bob laughed back at her.

"How is the Mason case coming along?" Sandra asked him.

"You know, in the old days it was a lot easier and a lot simpler to try a case. Now we have to tell the opposition everything we have before the trial. It makes twice as much work...No...It makes four times as much work...And it costs everybody a hell of a lot more money. In the old days we got the case, did the research, lined up our witnesses and evidence and took the case to trial. It was simpler. Sure there were surprises, but justice was not only simpler, it was more affordable. Sometimes I think the state and the deep pockets invented this new system just so the little guy *couldn't* afford his day in court. Of course the lawyers make a lot more because they're doing a lot more work and charging a lot more money for it, so they aren't going to complain...not the new genre of lawyers anyway...I mean I couldn't afford to hire myself if I wasn't me...You know what I mean?"

"It's terrible," Sandra agreed.

"In the old days it was also a lot more fun," Bob said. "It was more exciting and a lot more fun..."

"I can't imagine this ever being a fun business."

"Well, it used to be fun being on the cutting edge of the law, so to speak. These days nobody knows the law and nobody uses common sense. That's why it gets so complex."

"You mean that's why it's so screwed up?"

"Precisely."

"Well, what about Mary Mason??"

"Well, we've waded though all the paperwork. We've exchanged witness lists and evidence. There aren't any surprises coming our way. I

Doors

say we're ready for trial."

"You did that in record time."

"Did I have a choice?"

"Not really."

"How long do you think the trial will take?"

"A week or two..."

"That long?"

"It's a murder case. We have to make it look good."

"What if she's found guilty?"

"She won't be."

"But what if she is found guilty?"

"Then we'll file an appeal?"

"On what basis?"

"Not giving us sufficient time to prepare for trial, for one..."

"Makes sense."

"Why do you think I said it?"

Sandra laughed.

"We're going to win," Bob said. "It's slam dunk on this one. Our police chief was slime...slime from the deep..."

"He *was* a womanizer..."

"To say the least..."

"Anyway, <u>was</u> is the key word here...We're going to have that jury believing that our client did a service to womankind by wiping that slug off the planet...."

Doors

"Sounds good," Sandra said.

"So let's get to work," Bob told her.

"What? No more news stories?"

"No more news stories...."

"Call Mary," Bob told her, "And get her in here. I need to work on her testimony for the trial. We also need appointments with all our other voluntary witnesses, so they know what to expect."

"Are you going to coach them?"

"Why? So they can say, 'yes,' when the prosecution asks them if I told them what so say? You know me better than that. I'm just going to tell them what to expect from the prosecution, and I'm going to tell them to tell the truth...just the standard stuff...just the standard stuff...So get to work!"

"Yes, Boss!" Sandra said saluting him and clicking her heels together.

"Are you saluting me again?" Bob asked.

"How did you know?"

"You're predictable," Bob laughed, "Besides I heard you clicking your heels together.

"A dead give away," Sandra joked with him.

"Precisely," came the reply.

Bob leaned back in his chair and closed his sightless eyes. Duke yawned as he lay at Bob's feet.

"This is a lot of work for a man my age," he thought. "Maybe I need to retire and leave this to the young guys...."

CHAPTER THIRTY-FIVE

TROUBLE AT CENTRAL CITY POLICE

"Did you hear about what's happening at the police station?" Nick's secretary asked him when he came in to work.

"What are you talking about?"

"It's very hush, hush...They're trying to keep it out of the press, but they won't be able to keep it out for long?"

Nick gave her a puzzled gaze.

"The whole thing's about to bust wide open," his secretary told him. "There's a big meeting of all the department heads of this building and with some guys from the police station to discuss how to handle it...that includes you..."

"Will you tell me what you're talking about? And how do you come to have this information before me?"

"They're including the district attorneys' office that handles civil cases, and the secretary for the head of the civil division told me..."

Doors

"Told you what?" Nick asked growing impatient.

"She told me that there's a big shake up down at central city police. You know, cops on the take and all that stuff..."

"Can you be more specific?"

"It appears that there were a couple of divisions down at the station that were skimming off the top of their seizures..."

"What do you mean?"

"It's simple. The cops were taking in the drug money, not reporting the full take, and skimming off the top. Internal investigations found out. They couldn't buy off the guy who blew the whistle, and the rest will soon be history."

"How does that affect the civil division?" Nick asked.

"I'm not sure I should be the one to tell you," came the reply.

"Stop playing games with me! I want to know!" Nick told her.

"All right, but remember you asked for it...It seems your police chief Mason wasn't exactly clean in this thing..."

"Oh God!" Nick said throwing his head back and putting his hands on his forehead. "We're about to go to trial! We can't continue the trial because we forced the judge to fast track the thing..."

"Do you want to know anymore?"

"Go ahead and tell me," Nick said resolved for whatever he might hear.

"Well, there are all sorts of allegations out there. It appears the chief kept a secret bank account, and he'd hidden away about two million dollars in it."

"Two million?" Nick asked incredulously.

"That's what I hear," came the reply.

"How did he ever get that much?"

"Apparently there's a lot of money to be made in drugs," she told Nick.

Nick shook his head. His shoulder still hurt where the bullet had gone through just above his heart. He rubbed the place involuntarily. It seemed to hurt more when he was stressed.

"It appears that civil fears that there may be some serious repercussions if Mary Mason wins at trial. They want you to try a better plea bargain."

"I can't do that," Nick said. "Besides, Grant told me flat out that he would accept nothing short of acquittal or dismissal of the charges."

"Maybe you could sweeten your offer?"

"I don't know," Nick said. His head began to hurt. "Do you have any aspirin?" he asked. "I'm getting a terrible headache."

His secretary took a small bottle of aspirin from her purse and handed it to Nick.

"In this business you need to be prepared," she said.

"Thanks," Nick said taking three aspirins from the bottle and returning it to her.

"The meeting is in fifteen minutes," she said.

Nick shook his head. Here he was ready to go to trial, and this had to happen. He hoped there wouldn't be any more surprises, but he somehow feared there would be. April told him he was going to lose this one, and it looked like she was right. Nick headed for the water cooler and took the aspirins. He hoped they would take the edge off his headache, even if just a little.

"I'm going to give Grant a hell of a fight," Nick thought as he later headed for the meeting.

After the introductions they were all seated at the conference table. No notes were taken.

"We want you to get Mary Mason to accept a plea bargain," he was told by the head of the civil attorneys. "If we lose, this could cost the city a fortune."

"You could take money from the seizure fund," Nick told them.

"We need that money for police enforcement," he was told by someone from the police department, "To buy helicopters and semi-automatic guns and surveillance equipment...."

"It seems like you should be able to get rid of the drug problem with all that money and stuff you're getting if you really wanted to," Nick said.

"We can't do that," came the reply. "Where would we get the money for funding if we didn't have the seizure money? Besides, that would probably put us all out of work and we can't have that now, can we?" he said laughing. "You do like work, Nick, don't you?"

Nick shook his head. Nothing was making any sense anymore. Crime was funding law enforcement, therefore they had to keep up a parasitic existence. It was absurd. It was crazy. Nick decided to go home early that day and bury his head in a pillow. On the way home he thought about getting stinking drunk, but he knew that in the morning that would only make his headache worse.

"Why does April always have to be so dammed right?" he thought.

Nick just didn't know what to do. Maybe he would ask April. It seemed like April always had the right answers. Maybe it came from always representing the underdog. Being a defense attorney and a consumer's rights advocate seemed to somehow give her an edge. At any rate, she had no illusions about the way things were.

CHAPTER THIRTY-SIX
APRIL'S SOLUTION

Nick found April in the back yard when he came home that day sitting on the swing that hung from the big old ash tree.

"Isn't it a beautiful day?" she asked him as her gauze skirt billowed in the wind.

"You're beautiful," Nick told her in return as he gazed upon the silkiness of her long blond hair.

"Your brother called just before you got here."

"What did the bastard want?" Nick asked her.

"Wow! You're in a mood," she said. "Did you have a bad day?"

"You might say that. Now what did the bastard want this time? More free advice?"

"Don't tell me you're still in competition with your brother after all these years?"

"Does he have to do everything I do? I mean first he had to play baseball because I did. Then he had to be better. Then he had to join the science club because I did, and he kissed butt and got all the attention there..."

"You're talking about kid stuff...."

"I know, but did he have to become a lawyer too? Did he have to become a district attorney just like his big brother?"

"He's in another state," April told him. "At least he's not competing now...."

"Like hell he isn't! New Mexico isn't far enough away for me, especially when he keeps calling to tell me his conquests..."

"Then I guess you don't want to know..."

"Want to know what?"

"About his new case..."

"Not really, but tell me anyway."

"Your little brother was assigned to try the eyeball killer case?"

"The what?"

"The eyeball killer case. It seems this deranged individual wanted to make his mark in the art world by painting the perfect eyes. He felt that the only way he could do it was to examine them outside the heads of dead women. So he went hunting on the streets at night for prostitutes, pretended to be a customer, got them in a compromising position, strangled them to death and carefully removed their eyes with the skill of a surgeon. It seems that as a child the deranged man's mother taught him taxidermy on birds and his job was to remove the eyes. He was apparently upset because she used buttons for replacements instead of the more expensive taxidermy eyes. Your brother called to say he was going to be on National TV news tonight if you want to watch...He also said he might need some help and advice on this one..."

"God! He did it again. He gets a serial killer and national media attention. I get an abused woman who kills her husband probably in self defense and..."

"You don't think Mary is guilty?"

"Not anymore."

"What are you going to do?"

"What do you think I should do?"

"Listen," April told him, "You have a job to do. You're representing the State of California. You have to look at it as just a job. What you believe is immaterial. I mean, a defendant is entitled to a defense even if he or she is guilty, right?"

"Right."

"You're supposed to be a vigorous advocate for the rights of your client, right?"

"Right."

"Well, then...it seems to me that the state is entitled to have its position vigorously litigated as well..."

"But I don't believe in the case."

"You aren't listening to me, are you?"

"I'm trying to listen."

"Look. You can't feel guilty about it. Mary Mason deserves her day in court. If you win, you win. If you lose, it was meant to be. You have to do your best no matter what. She'll be vindicated or she won't. It's that simple. You don't make the judgment here. You only present the case. The jury decides her fate, not you."

"They want me to offer a new plea bargain."

"Why?"

"They don't want it to go to trial now."

"You mean because of the funny business down at the police station?"

"How did you know?"

"News travels fast in defense circles."

"You mean the ones involved have already contacted attorneys, even before being charged."

"I mean they contacted me."

"All of them?"

"Two of them."

"What are you going to do?"

"I told them I was retiring. I told them I was just finishing up my outstanding cases and not going to practice for a few years."

"What did they say?"

"The offered me a lot of money up front to take the case. I told them 'no'."

"I thought everyone deserved vigorous representation."

"They do, but not from me. I'm having a baby, remember? I don't need any additional stress."

"Did you refer them to somebody else?"

Doors

"Not yet."

"Why not?"

"They asked me to think about it for twenty-four hours. I told them I wouldn't change my mind, but I finally agreed to think about it."

"It would be a tough defense..."

"The point is, Nick, that even if they are guilty, which they more than likely are, they deserve the best defense possible...just like the state deserves the best advocate possible on their side. It's not personal, Nick. It's just business. It's just business."

"I guess you're right," Nick told her. "What are we having for dinner?"

"Pot roast."

"How did you manage that?"

"I am a woman of many talents. I used the self-timer on the oven and put it all in frozen this morning. Tonight we have pot roast!"

"Very good," Nick said. "I didn't know you could do that!"

"Stick around, Nick. I can teach you a lot."

"I know, April. I know," he said as he kissed her. Then he added, "Let's eat now, so we don't miss my brother's television debut."

"That's sporting of you," April said.

"Maybe," Nick replied, "And maybe I just want to hitch a ride on his star..."

CHAPTER THIRTY-SEVEN
THE PLEA BARGAIN

Bob Grant entered Nick Wilcox's office with his dog, Duke. Duke directed Bob to a chair and he sat down.

"All right. You got us in here. Now do you mind telling me why we're here?"

"I've got an offer to make you," Nick said. "Did you bring your client?"

"She's waiting outside in your lobby..."

"...as I said, I have an offer to make you."

"A plea bargain offer?"

"Yes."

"Isn't this highly irregular? Shouldn't you wait until the time of trial at this point?"

"I wanted to save us all a lot of trouble."

"You mean you wanted to save yourself a lot of trouble!"

"Listen Bob. Let's stop all this posturing, all right? Let's get down to matters at hand. I've been authorized to make your client an offer. Do

Doors

you want to hear it or not?"

"Why not?" came the reply.

"all right, then...Here it is. We're prepared to offer your client involuntary manslaughter in return for a guilty plea."

"Coming down all the time, aren't we Nick? From manslaughter with intent to involuntary manslaughter...Want to try for dismissal?"

"I can't do that, Bob. I don't have the authority to do that...But there's more to the offer...In return for a guilty plea to involuntary manslaughter, the state is willing to recommend probation only, with credit for time served."

"You're kidding me?"

"I'm quite serious. Will you take it?"

"I have to talk to my client, of course. It's up to Mary, of course. I must say that I've never received such a lucrative offer in all my years of practicing law, Nick."

"So will you recommend the deal to her, Bob?"

"No."

"Why not?"

"Well, for one thing, there's no guarantee that the judge will accept your recommendation of probation only. For another thing, my client would still have a record that she does not want to have. For a third thing, I must have a hell of a case if you're making me an offer like this."

"Be practical, Bob. A bird in the hand..."

"I know...I know..., but I've never been the practical sort, Nick. You should know that by now. I have a good record, Nick; and I intend to lose this one and then really stick it to this city and possibly the state."

"You wouldn't sue the state for malicious prosecution, would you?"

"Try me, Nick."

"On what basis?"

"On the basis that the state knew Mary Mason suffered severe physical abuse at the hands of her husband and knew there was a domestic violence restraining order issued against him, and the state knew that the order of the court was not enforced and left Mary Mason no choice but to defend herself and her child..."

"...I see your point," Nick said. "But why not take the conservative, safe approach?"

"Look, Nick, I understand your position. I'm not saying 'no' to you right now. I will take the offer to my client, and I'll let you know. I promise we will consider it. I just won't recommend the offer, that's all. The final decision is Mary's. She may say, 'Yes'. I have no way of knowing."

"How soon can you let me know."

"How long is the offer open?"

"You're putting me in a spot, Bob."

"I know. I intend to make you squirm a little."

"You can have up until the time of trial. The offer will remain open until the time of trial. Is that enough time for you?"

"Sounds fine, Nick. If you consider dismissal as an option, let me know. I'd have to recommend that."

"I told you, I don't have the authority for that!"

"I understand, Nick, but let me tell you this...that would probably all but eliminate any case we would have against the state. You'd have a good argument, anyway."

"What about your possible suit against the city?"

"I'd have to think about that."

"Could you enter into some kind of an agreement with us?"

"A secret agreement?"

"Perhaps."

"I don't play the game that way, Nick. Any agreement we reach has to be up front. The judge has to approve it."

"I understand."

"Do you think you may be able to swing a dismissal on those terms?"

"You aren't threatening me, are you, Bob?"

"I don't play that way. Let's just say I'm making an inquiry as to a possible resolve of these matters and settlement of matters yet to be resolved."

"You present my offer, and I'll present yours."

"I'm not making an offer, Nick. That's up to you. I'm making an inquiry. That's all. I'm just making an inquiry."

"I do have a question for you, Bob. It's off the record of course..."

"...of course..."

"Why are you calling the child to the stand as a defense witness?"

"It's your worst nightmare, Nick. That's all I can tell you."

Doors

Nick shook his head. Could it be true? Could the rumors be true that the politically correct police chief everyone had admired for all those years was not only a womanizer, and an embezzler, but also a child rapist...someone who had molested and raped his own three year old daughter?

"Will you get back to me, Nick?" Bob asked interrupting Nick's thoughts.

"Sure. Sure," Nick mumbled as Bob left the room with Duke. "...And you talk to your client, all right?" he called after Bob.

"I promise," Bob said as he left the room smiling.

Bob left the door open, so Nick got up and shut it. When he returned to his desk he called to his secretary on the intercom.

"Call another meeting," he told her. "Get everybody in here who was here the other day. I have something to discuss with them. Tell them it's a first priority. It's number one."

"It's done," came the reply. "Shall I set it up for tomorrow morning?"

"Set it up for this afternoon," Nick told her, "And make sure everyone will be here."

"That's impossible," came the reply over the intercom.

"Why?"

"I happen to know that the head of civil division is out today on personal leave."

"All right. Make it first thing tomorrow," Nick directed her, knowing he would get no sleep tonight. ""Set it up for eight in the morning."

"Civil doesn't come in until nine..."

Doors

"All right...Nine in the morning then...Make it nine," Nick said growing impatient. "Make sure everyone knows it's important. We only have a couple of weeks until the Mason trial, so get them in here now!" Nick said.

"It's done," came the reply.

Nick fidgeted in his chair. He started to look at some files on his desk, but found he couldn't concentrate.

"This is a hell of a job," he thought.

CHAPTER THIRTY-EIGHT
THE BIG MEETING

"Look," Nick said as all the department heads sat down for the big meeting he had called, "I made the offer. I offered them a deal I thought they couldn't refuse."

"What was the offer?" the head of the civil division asked him.

"I offered involuntary manslaughter with a sentence recommendation of probation."

"They should take that," the head of civil told him.

"You haven't had many cases against Bob Grant, have you?"

"No."

"Well, if you had," Nick told the head from the civil department, "Then you'd know better than to say that?"

"What more could the guy want?" someone from police headquarters asked.

"He wants an acquittal," Nick explained. "And in return he may and I repeat, he may agree not to pursue a case against the state for malicious prosecution; and he may agree not to bring an action against the city for negligence in not enforcing the restraining order obtained by Mrs. Mason against her husband."

"What do you mean may?" the head of civil asked.

"It's simple," Nick told them. "The offer has to come from us."

"Are you sure he won't accept the offer already on the table?" someone from the police department asked.

"Yes," Nick said.

"How can you be so sure?" the head of the civil department asked him.

"I told you," Nick said. "I know Bob Grant, and he knows we have a shitty case..."

"What are we going to do?" the head of the civil department asked him.

"That's why I called this meeting. I thought we should take a consensus."

"We'll look weak if we give in now," someone from Nick's prosecution staff said.

"Better to look weak than stupid," someone in the room added.

"Can we keep this thing quiet?" another voice asked.

"No," Nick said. "That's part of the deal. The offer we make has to be an up front kind of thing. It has to be approved by the judge."

"If we lose this thing at trial," someone from Nick's department added, "It's going to open up a floodgate of litigation. Abused women are going to start popping off their husbands and use the abusive defense. Then they'll sue the state fro not protecting them."

"The problem is," Nick said, "That in this case it's probably true. Bob

Grant has a hell of a case, especially in light of the recent developments down at city hall...which brings me to another point...I may be prosecuting some of your people on that," Nick said turning to the acting police chief. "It may create a conflict situation..."

"...anyway we can keep this thing quiet?" the police chief asked.

"I hear it's going to be turned over to the grand jury," Nick said. "We won't be able to keep it quiet if they send down indictments."

"Maybe you could leave out some of the evidence," the acting police chief said.

"That wouldn't be ethical," Nick said.

"It also wouldn't be the first time," came the reply. "Besides, we're the guys who give you the testimony and evidence that helps you prove your cases."

"Are you saying you won't cooperate with the investigation?"

"You know what I'm saying," came the reply.

"Too bad we're not in Idaho," someone else from the police department said. "The federal prosecutor can't convict any police there."

Nick stared at the policeman.

"A police chief in Boise was caught on video tape by the FBI carrying a safe out of a drug house. It went to trial and the defense was that the police chief was taking the safe for evidence. Despite evidence to the contrary, the jury acquitted him. Then in another Idaho town the police chief was taped tipping off a whorehouse where there was also illegal gambling that a federal raid was about to occur. The jury found that gaming and prostitution were a part of the fabric and history of the state and that on that basis the police chief did nothing wrong."

"That's a strange way of looking at law and order," Nick said.

"Maybe," came the reply, "But at least they respect their law enforcement personnel."

Nick shook his head. He wondered what the world was becoming that those in whom people placed their trust somehow could be above the law.

"This is California," Nick said. "This is not Idaho. I don't think the jury will be so easily persuaded in this case. Look what we have. We have a dead police chief who was killed by his estranged wife who had obtained a domestic violence restraining order against him that she couldn't get enforced. The same guy has turned out to be a known womanizer, probably molested or raped his own three-year-old daughter, and has embezzled two million dollars out of the drug forfeiture program; and he placed the embezzled funds in a secret account. If we go to the jury with this, we lose. It's simple. We lose."

"Make Mary Mason the offer," the head of civil said. "We'll take the embarrassment. Maybe we can keep some of this from hitting the fan. Maybe we can salvage a little respect for our law enforcement officers out of this."

"Be serious," Nick said. "You're only worried about the civil suit and the money out of city coffers."

"Well," another person from the civil division added, "Maybe we can let the jury know that if we lose this and a suit follows, then taxes will go up to pay for it. We can hit them on their selfish side."

"Grant will object. I would be found in contempt of court," Nick said.

"So? The jury would still hear it...even if it was stricken from the record and they were told not to pay attention to it, they would still hear it."

"I won't do that," Nick said. "I have standards."

"To hell with standards," the head of the civil department said.

"Look," Nick told them, "Let's do a blind vote. We'll vote by ballot," he said as he tore paper from his yellow legal pad and passed it out. "Write 'yes' for making the offer, 'no' for not making the offer."

Each person took the piece of yellow paper and wrote in their votes. It was almost unanimous. Everyone had voted 'yes', except Nick who had abstained. Somehow voting 'yes' seemed like the same thing as losing. Nick didn't like losing, even if he deserved to lose. It was further agreed that the offer should be made the day of trial. A hope was still held by some that Bob Grant might just accept the offer of involuntary manslaughter and not hold out for dismissal, but Nick knew better. Bob Grant was no fool. He was just about the sharpest guy Nick had ever come across in a courtroom, and he was honest and ethical; and that made Bob Grant all the more dangerous.

That night Nick went home and made love to April in front of the fireplace with complete and open abandon. He thought if he could lose himself in her, the ache inside of him would somehow disappear. Nick didn't know exactly why he was bothered by all of this. He wasn't born

yesterday. Nick knew the ways of the world. He thought he'd seen it all.
It just made him sick, that's all. It just made him sick inside. Maybe it was
because he was entering the realm of fatherhood, and that meant his future
would not end with just him. His future would now be unending.

CHAPTER THIRTY-NINE
BOB'S MEETING WITH MARY

Bob reached down and patted Duke. Duke was a good dog, but he was still a dog. Sometimes he got into mischief just like any other dog, but as far as Bob was concerned, Duke was the best. Duke was his eyes. Early this morning when he was petting Duke he noticed a growth on the back of Duke's neck. He took Duke to the veterinarian and was told that a biopsy had to be taken. Bob didn't know what he would do if it was cancer. If it was cancer that would mean Duke didn't have much time left. Bob would have to think about getting another dog. That meant getting on a waiting list. There was a shortage of good seeing eye dogs, and what made it more difficult was that the dog you got had to be compatible with your personality. Bob didn't know if he could handle a young dog again. He liked Duke. Duke was old like he was.

"Well, Mary," Bob said as Mary entered his office. "I have some good news for you."

"You do?"

"Yup."

"Well, just don't sit there," Mary told him. "Tell me! I could use some good news."

"We have an offer, Mary, but before you get too excited, I want to tell you that we shouldn't accept it, because I think the offer is going to get even better."

"I don't understand."

"They offered us involuntary manslaughter with a sentence recommendation of probation."

"That's good, isn't it?"

"It's good, but if we don't jump the gun I think we can go one better. I think they'll offer to dismiss."

"Why would they do that?"

"They have a bad case, Mary; and they know they have a bad case. They also know that when we win...and we will win...that I'm going to bring legal actions against both the state and the city and then they'll have to pay for it big...real big..."

"So?"

"So, the point is, they will offer to dismiss providing I agree not to bring any further civil actions against them."

"But isn't that how you're going to make your money on this thing?" Mary asked him. "I know Mom and Dad haven't paid you much...not enough for all this, anyway."

"I'm not in this thing for the money, Mary. If I was in this business for the money I would have been rich by now. I'm not a fool, Mary. I'm not in this for either the money or the politics. If I were in it for the politics I'd be a judge by now...I'm just not interested in things like that. That's why I can't be bought."

"What are you talking about?"

"Guys get bought, Mary. They sell out their clients. It's simple. No one hardly ever figures it out. It may even be subtle, like not asking for sanctions because you may want a favor in the future from a powerful, political law firm."

"What are sanctions?"

"Sanctions are given when the other attorney does something that he shouldn't do...maybe to slow up the legal process or something like that. The court says that the wrongdoer attorney has to pay for the time of the attorney that didn't do anything wrong and had to respond to something that the other guy did that he shouldn't have done. It's a punishment for attorneys for doing the wrong thing."

"I get it," Mary said.

"Anyway, Mary, I think they're going to dismiss you, and that would be good."

"How soon will we know?"

"You can't rush these things. It's my hunch that they won't come forward with the offer until the morning of the trial."

"Why so far away?"

"It's not as far away as you think, Mary. It's only a couple of weeks away now."

"But why so far away?" Mary repeated the question.

"They're hoping we'll go for the involuntary manslaughter offer."

"That's a good offer, too, isn't it?"

"It's a good offer, but it still leaves you with a record, and no guarantee the judge will accept the sentencing recommendation...not to mention the inconvenience of having to report your every move to a probation officer and the threat hanging over you of maybe having to go back to jail if you make a mistake."

"What do you mean?"

"Well, in probation the judge gives a sentence and suspends it subject to a certain amount of time in probation. The probation order says you may stay on probation so long as you are law abiding. The term 'law abiding' can mean anything in this town. You could get a traffic ticket and with the wrong judge end up in prison completing your suspended term. Under the circumstances, it's better to be completely clear of this thing."

"I see," Mary said simply.

"In spite of the fact your husband was a royal pain in the ass, he had a long line of political friends, Mary. Amoral people have a different way of looking at things. It's something those of us with morality could never understand."

"I think I understand," Mary said. "Unless the charges are dismissed, that son of a bitch will have a choke hold around my throat, even from the grave..."

"That about sums it up, Mary."

"What about the insurance money?"

Doors

"As soon as the dismissal comes through, everything will be freed up...the house, the insurance...everything."

"I'm going to demolish that house," Mary said.

"Why not sell it?" Bob asked her.

"Who would buy such a place?"

"I would."

"You could live somewhere where a murder took place?"

"I could live somewhere where justice was done."

"You want my place?"

"How much do you want for it?"

"I'll give it to you."

"You can't afford that, Mary. I'll pay fair market value. You get an appraiser in, and I'll pay the fair market value."

"Only if you let me pay your regular fees."

"That sound's fair, Mary."

"How much will that be? Can I discount the house for you?"

"No. You pay me. I'll pay you. I want to avoid any appearance of impropriety."

"What are your fees then?"

"I discount my fees, Mary, because I'm blind."

"You shouldn't do that."

"I do it because I figure it takes me longer to do things because of my blindness."

"No, it doesn't."

"Yes, it does."

"So what are your fees?"

"I don't know. You'll have to check with Sandra. Ask her for a copy of the bill."

"All right."

"It's not over until the fat lady sings," Bob told her, "So don't jump the gun. There's always the infinitesimal possibility this entire thing could simply unravel. The law is full of contradictions. Things could still unravel."

"Then where would that put us?"

"It would put us back in court at trial. We still have to prepare for this thing as though we're going to trial."

"That makes sense."

"Of course it does."

"I hope nothing unravels."

"So do I. Trials are a lot of strain. They're no fun."

"I'll pray about it," Mary said.

"Didn't I tell you that I don't believe in that stuff?"

"Yes. I'm going to pray anyway, Bob."

"One more thing, Mary,' Bob said, "Don't tell anyone about what we talked about today...especially not the press. We want the favorable publicity on you to keep flowing up until the day of trial...so don't tell a soul. We can't risk this getting out."

"Can I talk to my priest?"

Doors

"You can talk to your priest. He knows that what you tell him is privileged and he can't tell anyone else, but you can't tell anyone other than your priest...not even your mother and father?"

"Can I tell my therapist?"

"Your therapist is all right too. Your therapist holds privileged information also, but nobody else. You can talk to your doctors, your therapist, your priest...but nobody else except me. Is that understood?"

"Yes."

"If you have any questions, you can call me. Just act as though you're planning on going to trial. I want you to come in soon so we can talk about your testimony and what to expect at trial. Bring Quinn. I want to prepare her also."

"Does Quinn have to be a part of all this?

"If we end up in trial, I'm afraid so, but I'll request to have the courtroom cleared except for the jury, judge, DA, you and me, when she testifies. I'll make it as easy as possible for her. I don't want to scare her at all. I'll make it as easy as possible, I promise."

"I know you will, Bob. I trust you completely."

"It's almost over, Mary..."

"No, Bob...It's just beginning...."

CHAPTER FORTY

MARY TALKS TO HER PRIEST

Mary went to the mission early that night and waited nervously for Father Donovan. Without realizing it, she found herself pacing up and down the kitchen. She didn't know exactly what she was going to tell him; therefore, she promised herself she would deal with him only in generalities.

"Hi, Mary," he said as he came into the kitchen area.

"I see you're still wearing your clerical collar."

"I'm wearing it for you," he said. "I've sent in my resignation. It's only a matter of time before it's accepted. The bishop asked if I'd stay on as priest until they found another father to fill in here. There's a shortage of priests, you know. It's because of the celibacy thing."

"Are you sure you should stop being a priest?"

"That's sort of what the bishop asked me, but the answer is 'yes', Mary. The answer is 'yes'. It's pure and simple. I no longer desire to be a priest."

"How will your family take it?"

Doors

"Badly," came the reply. "My mother promised me to the priesthood before I was born. She considers me her ticket into heaven."

Mary smiled.

"You look nervous, Mary."

"I have something to tell you."

"Spit it out, then..."

"I'm not sure I know where to begin."

"Begin at the beginning."

"They offered me involuntary manslaughter with a sentence recommendation of probation."

"That's wonderful..."

"...There's more."

"More?"

"Bob thinks he can get the charges dismissed in exchange for us not bring civil suits against the city and state."

"That's even better."

"I'm nervous about it."

"Why?"

"Bob doesn't think they'll offer dismissal until the day of trial. I don't know if I can stand it until then."

"What does your lawyer want you to do."

"He wants be to wait for a dismissal offer. He's pretty confident I'll get it. What do you think I should do?"

"I'm not exactly an impartial observer, Mary."

Doors

"You're still my priest."

"Even as a priest I can only advise you to follow your conscious and the tenements of God's laws, Mary."

"All right, then...tell me as a friend..."

"As a friend I say trust your attorney."

"You think so?"

"I think so."

"If the charges are dismissed, where will that put us, Mary?"

"I don't know."

"Will you agree to marry me?"

"I told you, I don't know. It's all happening too fast. I don't want to be pressured right now. I need some time to think about everything that's happened. I need to spend some time with Quinn. You need some time too. We're both facing a new way of life now. I've never been alone and on my own before. I got married right out of high school. I've never gone to college. I've never held a job outside the home."

"You're still very young, Mary. You have time for all that."

"Will I?" Mary asked. "Will I have time for that if I get married right away?"

"We don't have to get married right away."

"You won't pressure me?"

"No."

"I would like to at least start seeing you, though, once our new lives begin. Can we at least see each other?"

Doors

"I suppose so."

"I have a job offer at the university to teach..."

"Already?"

"Actually, I've been thinking about this for a long time...even before I met you. You mustn't blame yourself for me leaving the priesthood. It just happened that you came along; and I fell in love with you, that's all."

"Are you sure?"

"Do you want me to prove it?"

"Could you?"

"Could I what? Prove I love you or prove that I thought about leaving the priesthood before I met you?"

"Prove that you were thinking about the priesthood before I met you, of course."

"Look at this, Mary," Father Donovan said as he pulled an envelope out of his pocket. Inside was a letter. He read it to Mary and it said, "This is in response to your recent inquiry about a position with our university staff..." It was dated a full year before Father Donovan had met Mary.

"I feel rather foolish," she said. "I guess I'm not quite the temptress I thought I was..."

"Does that bother you?"

"Not really. It makes me feel a lot better about things."

"About what things?"

"About my attraction to you."

"Are you saying it was my fault," father Donovan asked her.

Doors

"Maybe. Maybe you were flirting with me just a little."

"I probably was. I confess. I probably was flirting with you just a little. The point is that I am not going to be a priest for much longer; and it looks like you won't be going to prison, so we can see each other and be together if we want to see each other and be together."

"That's true."

"I understand that you want your time and space. I understand that, and I'll try to respect that."

"And what about your time and space?"

"I've been alone for a long time now. I don't want to be alone too much longer. Do you understand that?"

"Yes."

"Then maybe we can figure out a compromise when all of this is over," Father Donovan told her.

"Maybe," came the reply.

"Then let's not talk about this any longer," he said. "We have a lot of work to do before everyone starts arriving."

"That's true," Mary said as she reached for a hook on the wall and took down her apron from it.

"Let's get cooking," he said.

"Let's cook," came the reply.

Mary smiled at Father Donovan and knew he would wait for her until she was ready. A love and understanding like theirs came along once in a lifetime and only if the recipient was very, very lucky.

CHAPTER FORTY-ONE

THINKING IT ALL OVER

Nick and April finished dinner and went outside to sit in the lounge chairs on the patio. Neither of them had talked much at dinner.

"You're terribly quiet," April told him as she tossed back her long blond hair. "Is something wrong? Are you sick or something?"

"I've been thinking it over, April," Nick said somewhat resolutely, "And I've come to the conclusion that our legal system is screwed up...It's completely off the track..."

"Haven't we had this conversation before, Nick? Isn't it usually me who feels that way?"

"Yeah, but I'm really feeling it now."

"Why?"

"Because I'm under pressure. I'm forced to do things I don't want to do. I'm forced to file charges I don't want to file. Then I'm forced to offer a dismissal of charges in exchange for wiping somebody else's butt clean. It stinks."

"I thought we weren't going to talk about Mary Mason anymore," April said.

"Who said I was talking about Mary Mason? I was only being hypothetical."

"Hypothetical, my ass! You were talking about the Mason case again, and I don't want to hear you whine about it anymore. You win some and you lose some in this business. This time you lose. So what? You're just used to being on the prosecution side where the cards are stacked in your favor. What do you want? A kangaroo court? I say the system worked this time, Nick. I say it worked!"

"It was manipulated, April. It was manipulated."

"So it was manipulated. Manipulation is part of the system. It's a given. It's built into the system, Nick. This time it just worked against you, that's all. You don't mind it when it works in your favor, so don't be such a damned hypocrite!"

"What's your definition of a hypocrite, April?"

"I'll tell you my definition of hypocrite," April told him after thinking for only a moment. "You know the judge in Sacramento who let the air out of the tire of a handicapped van because it was parked in his reserved space at the courthouse?"

"Yeah?"

"Well, that's my definition of a hypocrite. Someone who's supposed to be thinking about the greater good of the people and then childishly lets the air out of someone's tires because they parked in his space. I mean it smacks of judicial impropriety, that's all..."

Doors

"What does that have to do with me?"

"What does it have to do with you? Nick, you talk about justice all the time. You talk about getting criminals off the street. Mary Mason is not a criminal. She's getting a little back door justice, that's all. What's the matter with a little back door justice so long as the result is the right one."

"Police Chief Mason is turning out to be quite an ass hole," Nick said.

"So what's new? What about that doctor who was extradited from Mexico and then tortured by American police in Los Angeles? They wanted him to admit administering some kind of a truth drug or something to a federal agent who was later found dead. There's crap all over, Nick. As far as I'm concerned, Mary Mason did this city a service when she plunged that butcher knife into her husband's heart," April told him. "The guy was more than an ass hole, Nick. The guy was corrupt and evil beyond mere words."

"Are you advocating murder?"

"I'm advocating justice. I'm advocating blind justice. I don't care much how it works. This time it worked. That's all. This time it really worked."

"It's not over yet," April.

"It will be."

"How can you be so sure?"

"I know Bob Grant. He knows exactly how to play this game."

Nick thought for a while. He decided April was probably right, but he still didn't like losing. He couldn't seem to get past the point that this was not a game about winning and losing. It was a game about how to best obtain justice, and it all depended on one's perspective. It all depended on how you looked at it. Actually, it all depended on your definition of what exactly justice was supposed to be. Nick supposed the African Americans might even be right in their theory that the drug laws were castrating to their males because of the fact that more of them got arrested and were put in jails and prison as a result of those laws than their white counterparts. He supposed that all crimes were somehow equal. Why should white-collar crime be treated less seriously than blue-collar crime, anyway? The result was basically the same. Didn't God intend for all sins to be treated equally with no single sin greater than any other except for the great unforgivable sin that He had never defined for mankind? Yet Nick still didn't want drugs brought into this white neighborhood, and he supposed if blacks and browns moved in that that was exactly what would happen. Was he a racist because he was afraid, or what? Why should his children have to be subjects of the result of any supposed oppression of the minorities, whether real or not? Theoretically, he believed all men were created equal. He couldn't help what those people did. He couldn't be his brother's keeper, after all. He had to think about himself. He had a family now. Nick's head began to hurt. He didn't want to think anymore. He was tired of it all.

"Let's go to the movies," Nick said quite suddenly. "I need some relaxation. I don't want to watch anything I have to think about, though. I don't want to see anything serious. Let's see a comedy, all right?"

"Only if you'll buy me bonbons, soda and popcorn," April told him laughing and immediately changing the subject as one would change the channel on a television set by remote control.

"We just ate dinner," came the protesting reply.

April smiled at Nick.

"I'm eating for two now, Nick. I deserve it!" she argued, joking with him.

Nick smiled. He wondered at the wisdom of this woman he's married. He wondered how he'd ever gotten so very lucky.

CHAPTER FORTY-TWO

ADVICE FROM MOM

Mary and her mother sat on Mary's bed. It was the same bed that Mary had slept in as a child. In fact, her mother had always kept the room the same as Mary had left it on her wedding day. Mary squeezed her old teddy bear in her arms. Quinn was in the backyard playing in her sandbox with the neighbor kids.

"Bob wants to buy my house when this is all over."

"Any idea when that will be?"

"Soon, I hope. Bob doesn't want me to discuss it with anyone."

"But I'm your mother..."

"It's not that I don't want to discuss it with you, it's that I can't discuss it with you, but I want you to know that when I sell the house I'm going to pay you back every cent you put out for me."

"I don't expect that. You have to get back on your feet, you know."

"I know you don't expect it, Mom, but I'm a big girl now and I expect to pay my own way in life. I have to grow up sometime."

"I guess so."

"What do you mean 'You guess so'?"

Doors

"It's just that you've been through so much, and I blame myself for a lot of it. If only I had listened to you sooner, maybe there was something I could have done to help."

"I went to April, Mom. I tried to stop him. There was nothing anyone could do. I guess what I ended up doing was the only way I could stop him."

"But I'm your mother..."

"Mothers can't fix everything, Mom."

"My mother always did."

"You were never in a situation like mine."

"That's true."

"So don't blame yourself. You don't owe me anything. I owe you, and I'm going to pay you back. I know I can't pay you back for the grief this has given you, but I can pay you back for the second mortgage you had to take on your house."

"What will you and Quinn live on when this is all over if you do that?"

"I'm not going to think about it in those terms. I'm in therapy, remember? I'm learning to take things one day at a time now."

"But you have to consider the future..."

Mary looked away.

"What's wrong?" her mother asked. "What aren't you telling me?"

"Father Donovan is leaving the priesthood," Mary told her mother.

Mary's mother crossed herself.

"So what does that have to do with you?" she asked Mary.

Doors

"He wants to marry me."

"He what!?!" her mother asked incredulously.

"You heard me," Mary said looking back at her mother again.

"Why would he want to marry you?"

"He says he loves me."

"Did he leave the priesthood because of you, Mary?" her mother asked sternly.

Mary shook her head to say no.

"He's been thinking about it for a long time," Mary explained. "He applied for a teaching job at the university over a year ago. He gave his resignation to the church and everything. He says he's leaving the priesthood even if I don't marry him."

"What does your lawyer say about all of this?"

"I didn't tell Bob."

"Why not? What do you think people will think, anyway?"

"They'll probably think I seduced a priest, but nothing could be farther from the truth. He hasn't even touched me. Besides, I don't want to mix the two things. One thing has absolutely nothing to do with the other. I told Father Donovan that I wouldn't even think about it until this mess was all over and finished."

"Do you think it can ever be finished?" Mary's mother asked.

"I'm going to see to it that it's finished. I know it won't be easy. Quinn and I are going to need a lot of therapy to get through this."

"Then maybe you should marry your priest."

Doors

"I don't know if marriage is the answer. I don't even know him. Why I don't even know his first name. I should at least know his first name, don't you think?"

"Do you love him?"

"Yes."

"Love is never wrong, Mary. Love is always good."

"I don't want it to seem sordid."

"It's not sordid. You two have found one another under perhaps the worst of circumstances. Things can only get better and sweeter from this time forward."

"I don't know, Mom. Maybe I'm rushing into something. I don't want to rush into something..."

"Is he pressuring you?"

"No."

"Then go ahead and take your time. Mary, you deserve to be loved. You really deserve it. You deserve a good and kind man to love you and take care of you."

"I can take care of myself, Mom."

"I know that, Mary. That's not what I meant. You need to know what love is, that's all. Everyone needs to know that. The caring I'm talking about is a mutual thing that two people give one another, a loving, caring and sharing kind of thing."

"Is that what you and Dad have?"

"Yes. That's exactly what your father and I have together, and I wish it for you more than anything else in this world."

"Do you really think I could be that lucky?"

"The opportunity is knocking at your door, Mary. You only need to open up to it."

"I don't know. I'm so mixed up right now."

"Mary, you have to do what is best for you and Quinn. I can't tell you what to do. I won't tell you what to do. This has to be a decision that comes from your heart, not mine. You have to decide what it is that will make you happy. I only know that I believe true love only comes along once in a lifetime, and then you have to be very, very lucky to recognize it and take advantage of it. Oh, I'm not saying that you can only love once. Love is all encompassing, but there's a certain kind of love that is extremely rare and quite special. It goes beyond physical attraction, far beyond that..."

"I think I know what you mean..."

"Is it that kind of love, Mary?"

Mary thought for a moment.

"I think so, Mom. I really think so. This man really loves me. He really does."

"Then don't let that love get away, Mary. You deserve that in your life, believe me, you won't regret it."

Mary began to cry.

"I've never felt this way before," Mary said, "Not even when I look at Quinn; and I thought I could never love anybody as much as I love Quinn."

Doors

"This is a different kind of love," Mary's mother explained, "It's the kind of love a woman dreams of...the fairytale princess kind of love."

"You mean fairytales can come true, Mom?"

"With the right man in your bed, they can," her mother told her.

Mary and her mother hugged each other and laughed. Then they cried. Then they laughed some more. Mary made her decision and kept it hidden in her heart.

CHAPTER FORTY-THREE

COUNTDOWN TO TRIAL

"I'm glad you brought Quinn in with you today," Bob Grant told Mary as Sandra showed them into Bob's office. "Did you tell her about me?"

"I told her you were Mommy's lawyer, and that you were going to help explain to the people in the courthouse why Mommy killed Daddy so that Mommy wouldn't have to go away for awhile."

"Did she understand that?"

"I don't know."

"Is she acting afraid of me?"

"Why would she be afraid of you? I told her you were a very good friend."

"Does she know I'm blind?"

"Ask her."

"Honey, do you know Mr. Bob is blind?"

"What does that mean?" Quinn asked him.

"It means that I can't see you, honey. Did you know that?"

"Can you see Mommy?" Quinn asked innocently.

"No, honey, Mr. Bob can't see anything, not even your Mommy."

"How can you help my Mommy if you can't see her?"

"Well, Quinn, Mr. Bob knows all about the law; and he can help Mommy prove that she didn't do anything bad," Bob explained to the child.

"Are you doing this because Mommy killed Daddy?"

"Yes, sweetheart."

"I'm glad Mommy killed Daddy," Quinn said. "Daddy hurt Mommy and Daddy hurt me real bad also."

"Quinn, honey, do you know what it means to tell the truth?"

"Yes."

"Then tell Mr. Bob what it means to tell the truth, all right?"

"All right. It means that you don't tell any fibs. That's what it means."

"Is it bad to tell a fib?"

"Yes."

"What happens if you tell a fib, Quinn?"

"Jesus doesn't like it when you tell a fib, and Mommy gets angry because little girls are not supposed to tell fibs. Good little girls only tell the truth."

"Can you tell the judge the truth when you go to court?"

"Is that the man in the black robe Mommy told me was going to ask me some questions?"

"Yes. The judge will ask you some questions, and a nice man named Nick is going to ask you some questions, and I'm going to ask you some questions; and some people will be listening carefully for your answers."

"I'm real scared," Quinn told Bob burying her head against her mother's

Doors

skirt.

"Don't be afraid, honey," Bob told her. "It's very important that you be very brave for your Mommy and help her. Can you do that sweetheart?"

Quinn puffed out her chest like a little peacock.

"I can do that!" she said. "I like helping Mommy. I'm a very good helper," she said, her big blue eyes opened wide.

"That's good, Quinn. That's real good. Now all you have to do is tell the truth. Just answer the questions, and tell everybody how Daddy hurt you and Mommy."

"You mean how Daddy hurt me in my private place?"

"Yes, sweetheart," Bob said as he took two anatomically correct dolls from his desk. "Have you ever seen dolls like this before?" he asked.

"My doctor has some," Quinn said excitedly. "Those are just like Dr. Lori's dolls!"

"Show Mr. Bob how Daddy hurt you," Bob said.

"I thought you couldn't see?" Quinn protested.

"That's all right. Mommy can explain it to me later. Go ahead now and show Mr. Bob."

"All right," Quinn said as she demonstrated what had happened to her.

"Did she do it?" Bob asked Mary.

"Yes," Mary replied.

"Good, Quinn," Bob told her. "Now when you see the judge in the courtroom somebody will use some words to explain what you are doing with the dolls, so don't be afraid. All right? Don't worry either because Mr.

Bob is going to make sure Mommy and Dr. Lori are there with you. All right?"

"All right," Quinn told him.

Bob turned his chair toward Mary.

"I don't want you to talk about this at home. Don't make a big deal out of this. Chances are we are going to have this thing dismissed, and she won't even have to testify. I just want her to be ready. That's all. What I told her goes the same for you. All I want you to do is tell the truth. I'll ask the questions and you just tell the truth. When they asked you what your attorney told you about testifying, simply tell them I told you to tell the truth. They aren't supposed to ask that question because what I tell you and what we talk about is privileged, but they always ask the question anyway. That's why I never coach my clients. Besides, if I object too much, the jury will think we have something to hide, so I want to use my objections sparingly."

"Is that all?" Mary asked. "I mean this is my life here."

"Try to get a lot of rest for the next few days. You need to look relaxed and not harried. Harried looks guilty. Go to the beach. Get a little tan. Spend time with Quinn. Get lots of sleep."

"Sleep won't be easy."

"Then go to the doctor and get some sleeping pills. I mean it! You have to look rested."

"Anything else?"

"Wear something soft and pink...wear a single strand of pearls, white gloves, matching shoes and purse. If you don't have anything like that go out and buy it. Make the skirt soft and flowing. I want you to look sweet and helpless."

"Aren't woman supposed to be self-sufficient these days?" Mary asked.

"Maybe, but not you. You are the victim, not the victorious. Do you understand?"

"I understand."

"You are just a sweet old fashioned girl. You're the kind of girl every mother dreams her son will bring home. That's your image."

"But I am that kind of girl," Mary protested.

"Then you won't have any trouble playing the part," Bob said as Quinn sat down on the floor and played with Duke.

"Leave the doggy alone," Mary told Quinn.

"Let her play with him," Bob told her. "Duke loves the attention. It keeps them both busy. Duke gets so bored sitting in here with me all day."

"How did his tests come out?" Mary asked. "Sandra said he had a lump or something."

"It's cancer," Bob said. "We'll have it out right after we're done with your case. I probably lose him, though. I probably won't have him much longer. He's twelve, you know. He's had a long life for a Seeing Eye dog...but he doesn't deserve to suffer. If we can't get it all I'll probably put him down."

"What a shame," Mary said.

"Well, you don't worry about that. I want you to take Quinn out for an ice-cream cone right now. I want you to start relaxing this very minute. Is that clear?"

"That's clear!" Mary said. "Come on Quinn," Mary called to her daughter, "Mr. Bob says we need to go get some ice-cream right now!"

"Oh boy!" Quinn squealed with delight, jumping up and down with excitement as they left. "Ice-cream! ice-cream! We all scream for ice-cream!"

CHAPTER FORTY-FOUR

THE DAY OF TRIAL

Bob and Mary stood outside the courtroom door. Sandra was there, Quinn, Mary's mother and, of course, Bob's dog Duke. Mary's mother held Quinn's hand. Mary wore a pink dress with a flowing skirt. She was glad it was spring, otherwise she never would have found the kind of dress Bob had wanted her to wear. Bob gave her a single long stemmed pink rose tied with a pink ribbon. Mary looked like a schoolgirl.

"I feel like I'm going to a prom instead of my trial," she told Bob when he handed her the rose. "It's lovely," she said.

"It smelled pretty," Bob told her. "I had Sandra pick it out for you. It's for luck?"

"Do we need luck?" Mary asked.

Sandra laughed.

"Luck is always good," Bob said. "It can't hurt."

Nick Wilcox came up toward the courtroom with his legal aids.

"Here comes Mr. Prosecutor," Sandra told Bob.

Bob smiled.

"Smile pretty," he told Mary. "The show is about to begin."

Mary didn't understand.

Behind Nick Wilcox came a procession of the press.

"Do you have a comment?" one of them asked Mary.

"No comment right now," Mary told them as Bob directed her. "I'm sorry," she said smiling sweetly.

"Who gave you the pink rose?" someone asked her.

"My lawyer," she told them.

"Why pink?"

"It's my favorite color," she said because it was the truth.

Flashbulbs went off and the video cameras rolled.

"You look lovely," a male reporter told her.

"Thank-you," Mary replied.

Meanwhile, Mary's mother hustled Quinn away from the crowd.

"Is Mommy famous, Grandma?" the little blond haired girl asked.

"Sort of," Mary's mother replied. Let's go inside and sit down," she said as the courtroom doors opened and as they walked toward them.

"Bob says there's a children's waiting room," Sandra told them as she approached. "He wants you to take her there for now."

"Where is it?" Mary's mother asked.

"It's right down the end of this long hall," Sandra said pointing. "Bob said to take you there, so let's go...all right?"

"I think it's an excellent idea," Mary's mother said.

"Can I play with Duke?" Quinn asked Sandra.

Doors

"You can do that later," Sandra told her as she took Quinn's other hand. "We're going to go to a room where you and your Grandma can color and read books and play with lots of toys. How does that sound to you?"

"It sounds like fun!" Quinn said as she walked down the hall.

Mary's mother thought it was considerate that the press had sense enough to leave Quinn alone and not expose her to any unnecessary stress. She didn't know that Bob had called everyone on the press list and asked them very specifically not to bother the child. He more specifically let them know that there would be legal action against them if they bothered the child and upset her prior to trial. He also promised them good coverage and a statement from his client when it was all over if they followed his directive. It seemed to work. No one bothered the little girl. No one dared bother the little girl!

"This is going to be fun," Quinn said as they walked down the hall.

Meanwhile, Nick Wilcox approached Bob Grant and removed him from the throng of reporters.

"Have you thought about our offer?" Nick asked Bob.

"You mean involuntary manslaughter with sentence recommendation of probation?" he asked.

"Yes," came the reply. "What is your answer?"

"Can I take care of my client?" Bob asked. "We can talk later," he said as Duke directed him through the crowd to Mary.

Bob escorted Mary into the courtroom and sat her at the defendant's table. The reporters went in and sat in the courtroom also, but they stopped flashing their cameras and taking video. It was forbidden by local court rules to take any kind of pictures in the courtroom.

Bob opened his briefcase and took out his files.

"Sandra will help me with the exhibits when she gets back," he said.

Mary said nothing.

"Are you all right?" he asked.

"I'm fine," Mary said taking a deep breath.

Nick Wilcox came into the courtroom and put his briefcase on the prosecution's table. Two assistants came in with him and sat down also.

"Three attorneys to one doesn't seem fair," Mary told Bob.

Bob laughed.

Nick was irritated. He walked over to the defense table.

"Let's talk," Nick said to Bob.

"Conference?" Bob asked.

"With the judge," came the reply.

"We're going to get our dismissal offer now," Bob whispered to Mary as he leaned over and patted Duke, then and he and Duke followed Nick up to where the bailiff stood.

"We want to see the judge," Nick told the bailiff.

"Go to the conference room," the bailiff directed. "I get the judge for you.

They went to the conference room with Nick leading the way. After they got there they sat down at the long table across from one another as was the custom among opposition counsel.

"Are you going to accept my offer?" Nick asked impatiently.

"No," came the reply.

"Then you want to go to trial on this thing?" Nick said posturing himself.

"Nobody wants to go to trial," Bob said.

"What do you want?"

"I already told you what we wanted," Bob said.

"You're nuts!" Nick said throwing up a smoke screen. "Why do you insist on playing hardball?" he asked. "It's not in the best interests of your client," Nick shouted at him growing agitated. Nick began to pace around the room.

"I think it is in my client's best interests," Bob said calmly.

"So...you want dismissal?" Nick asked as he sat down again.

"Yes," came the reply.

"And in return we get...?"

"What do you want?" Bob asked wryly.

"You know what we want," Nick answered with a sarcastic tone. He was growing impatient again. "We want a deal that you will agree to release the State of California and Central City from any and all liability."

"Up front?" Bob asked. "Before the court?"

"Up front and before the court," came the reply.

Shortly thereafter the judge came into the room.

"We have a deal," Bob told him smiling.

"And the deal is?" Judge Ramsey asked.

"The deal is dismissal with releases by Mary Mason from any and all civil liability as against the State of California and as against the City of Central," Nick said.

Judge Ramsey smiled at Nick.

"I don't like playing politics," he said, "But I do like this deal. This case was really smelling bad, son," he said. "You can be proud of yourself. You did the right thing."

"Shall we put it on the record then?" Bob Grant asked.

"Let's do it," Judge Ramsey said as he shook the hands of both attorneys. "A job well done, gentlemen!" he said.

"Thank-you," came the replies from each of them.

As Nick walked back out to the courtroom he felt relieved. He also felt like something else had happened to him. He didn't know why, but somehow he felt like he had turned out to be a winner in this case after all. Maybe it was because justice had prevailed for a change. He didn't really know. But as he saw Mary holding her pink rose, he knew in his heart that he had done the right thing. For once in his life he had done the right thing, and it felt good. It felt really good. Nick decided that some back door justice was all right after all.

As the judge approached the bench, Bob gave a thumbs up signal to Mary. Sandra smiled at her.

"Congratulations!" Sandra whispered.

"Shhh!" Bob warned.

The court was called to order and the dismissal with conjunctive agreements read into the record as the court reporter took careful notes on her machine. The judge dismissed the jury and thanked them for their trouble, expressing his satisfaction at the result of not having to move forward with this trial. Then the judge ordered that the courtroom be cleared.

"It's too bad we had to go to all the trouble of jury selection last week," Bob whispered to Mary.

As everyone left the courtroom, the news reporters gathered around Mary.

"How do you feel?" they asked her.

"I feel like justice has been done," she told them, "And I am extremely grateful to my attorney, Robert Donald Grant. I couldn't have gotten through this without him," she said smiling.

"Do you have the statement you promised us?" someone asked.

"I have an exclusive for you," he said laughing. "Tonight I'm flying off to Las Vegas to marry my long lost childhood sweetheart!"

"Can you afford the time off?" another reporter asked.

"Sure," he said, "I cleared my calendar for a two week trial!"

Nick Wilcox overheard him and wondered if Bob had bluffed him, but he really didn't care. All Mary could think about was getting to her little girl and kissing her and hugging her.

"Where's Quinn?" she asked Sandra.

"I'll take you to her," Sandra said. Then she went and told Bob where she was going.

"I'll see you back at the office," he said. "I'll need to have you order up some airline tickets for tonight..."

Sandra smiled.

"I love happy endings!" she said as Mary smiled.

When they got to the children's waiting room, Mary ran to Quinn and kissed her and hugged her.

"You're the best little girl in the whole world!" Mary told Quinn.

"And you're the best Mommy in the whole world," Quinn said hugging and Kissing Mary back.

Mary's mother smiled at Mary and then gave her a big hug as tears streamed down both of their faces.

"Why are you so said?" asked Quinn. "Why are you crying?"

"Mommy and Grandma aren't crying," Mary explained, "These are tears of happiness."

"Then I should cry too," said Quinn, "Because I am very happy. Does this mean we all get to go home now?" Quinn asked.

"Yes, it does!" replied Mary.

"Except for me," interjected Sandra, "I'm going back to the office now," Sandra said as she hugged Mary good-bye. "Keep in touch," she said as she left the room.

Mary's mother smiled.

"Do we have to come back here again?" Quinn asked.

"We never have to come back here again," Mary said. "In fact, let's celebrate! Let's go get some ice-cream!"

"Ice-cream! Ice-cream!" Quinn shouted. "Oh Boy!" she said jumping up and down as predictably she would. "I love ice-cream!" she squealed. "I scream! You scream! We all scream for Ice-cream!" she chanted as they walked out the door with Quinn skipping between them.

"You know," Mary said to her mother, "Sandra said she loved happy endings. I think I love happy endings too!"

"I'm with you," her mother said. "What about your priest?"

Mary smiled at her mother.

"I'll see him later," she said. "Then we'll see."

Then Mary shut the door behind them.

what's eating you?

a workbook for teens with **anorexia, bulimia** & other **eating disorders**

TAMMY NELSON, MS

Instant Help Books

A Division of New Harbinger Publications, Inc.

Publisher's Note

This publication is designed to provide accurate and authoritative information in regard to the subject matter covered. It is sold with the understanding that the publisher is not engaged in rendering psychological, financial, legal, or other professional services. If expert assistance or counseling is needed, the services of a competent professional should be sought.

Distributed in Canada by Raincoast Books

Copyright © 2008 by Tammy Nelson
Instant Help Books
A Division of New Harbinger Publications, Inc.
5674 Shattuck Avenue
Oakland, CA 94609
www.newharbinger.com

Cover design by Amy Shoup

Printed in the United States of America

Library of Congress Cataloging-in-Publication Data

Nelson, Tammy.
 What's eating you : a workbook for teens with anorexia, bulimia, and other eating disorders / Tammy Nelson.
   p. cm.
 Includes bibliographical references and index.
 ISBN-13: 978-1-57224-607-2 (pbk. : alk. paper)
 ISBN-10: 1-57224-607-3 (pbk. : alk. paper)   1.   Eating disorders in adolescence--Popular works.   I. Title.
 RJ506.E18N45 2008
 618.92'8526--dc22

                                2008003617

10   09   08

10   9   8   7   6   5   4   3

table of contents

introduction

This book is about the prevention and treatment of eating disorders in teenagers. Every year, thousands of young girls develop eating disorders and eating disorder behaviors. Why? Because our culture holds standards of perfection that most of us will never achieve. We live in a very competitive society. We all want to be perfect. Some of us work harder at it than others, and some of us kill ourselves trying to get there.

Our media portrays a visual ideal of women that has nothing to do with what the average woman looks like. Yet girls as young as ten are trying to look like supermodels, actresses, and pop stars. No matter what the ideal in our culture is, girls will try to meet it, and the ways they choose—dieting, overexercising, purging, and other behaviors—are often self-destructive. Girls who are still growing have nutritional needs that dieting deprives them of. They need food, and lots of it, to be healthy and emotionally happy. When they deny themselves adequate amounts of food, their minds and their muscles starve, sometimes with devastating results.

Overeating, or compulsive eating and obesity, is another problem in our culture today. Eating too much food when you are not hungry is an emotional issue, not a hunger issue. People may eat simply because it tastes good, and in our society that's okay sometimes. Everyone uses food to celebrate holidays, birthdays, and other special occasions. But using food to take care of their need for love, attention, and affection puts people's physical and emotional health at risk; they need to find other ways to care for themselves.

Bingeing, or eating an extreme amount of food in a short period of time, is one type of overeating. People who binge may then purge, or try to get rid of the food they've eaten. There are different ways to purge; all are dangerous and unhealthy and can lead to self-destructive eating patterns.

Using this book, you will work on how to eat in healthy ways and how to stay in balance, physically and emotionally. You'll learn about eating behaviors that are dysfunctional, and you'll learn how to deal with stress and frustration that might otherwise lead to eating disorders. Feeling good about your body is also an important part of your health, and many of the worksheets deal with improving your body image.

Each worksheet includes these sections:

Focus
This section lets you know the issues the worksheet will address.

Exercise
Each exercise is organized in easy-to-follow steps. You can complete many of them right in this book, or you may want to copy them so that you can do them more than once. You'll also find a list of special materials, such as drawing paper or glue sticks, needed for the exercise.

Follow-Up
After each exercise, there are questions or points to help you think about what you've just learned. If you need additional space, you can use the pages provided for notes at the end of this book, or you may want to write your answers in a separate journal.

More to Think About
Here you'll find additional exercises to do after you finish a worksheet, or further ideas to think about. There may also be additional questions you can answer in a journal.

Many of these exercises may bring up a mix of emotions. You might feel sad, mad, or scared.   You may react physically, feeling nauseated, jumpy, nervous, or tense. One good thing to do is to write about these feelings, using your journal or the space provided for notes. Remember, also, to tell someone else how you feel. Talk to your therapist, your parents, or a trusted friend. Your school counselor, social worker, or principal may also be able to help. There are also many websites where you can get information about eating disorders, depression, and anxiety.

The goal of this book is to help you be balanced and happy, and ultimately, to love and accept yourself exactly as you are.

eating disorders and body image

Did you know that if the typical mannequins you see in store windows were real women, they would be too thin to menstruate, or that if Barbie dolls were real, they would have to walk on all fours because of their physical proportions? Are you aware that twenty years ago, models weighed 8 percent less than the average woman, while today they weigh 23 percent less?

According to a recent National Women's Health Report, seven million American women have eating disorders. The facts and figures below, published by the Council on Size & Weight Discrimination, illustrate how widespread eating disorder behaviors have become and how great a gap there is between reality and the body types idealized by the media:

- The average American woman is 5'4", weighs 140 pounds, and wears a size 14 dress.

- The "ideal" woman—portrayed by models, Miss America, Barbie dolls, and screen actresses—is 5'7", weighs 100 pounds, and wears a size 2.

- One-third of all American women wear a size 16 or larger.

- 75 percent of American women are dissatisfied with their appearance.

- 50 percent of American women are on a diet at any one time.

- Between 90 percent and 99 percent of reducing diets fail to produce permanent weight loss.

- Two-thirds of dieters regain the weight within one year. Virtually all regain it within five years.

- The diet industry (diet foods, diet programs, diet drugs, etc.) takes in over $40 billion each year and is still growing.

- Quick weight-loss schemes are among the most common consumer frauds, and diet programs have the highest consumer dissatisfaction of any service industry.

- Young girls are more afraid of becoming fat than they are of nuclear war, cancer, or losing their parents.

- 50 percent of 9-year-old girls and 80 percent of 10-year-old girls have dieted.

- 90 percent of high school junior and senior women diet regularly, even though only between 10 percent and 15 percent are over the weight recommended by the standard height-weight charts.

- Girls develop eating and self-image problems before drug or alcohol problems; there are drug and alcohol programs in almost every school, but no eating disorder programs.

This exercise will help you understand healthy eating and a healthy body image. You'll learn about behaviors that may lead to eating disorders, and you'll look at your own eating behavior.

Healthy eating is eating what you want when you are hungry and stopping when you are full. You recognize what you crave and let your body have what it needs, including a balance of fruits, vegetables, protein, dairy products, and carbohydrates. You allow yourself treats for special occasions or just because you feel like it sometimes. You don't deprive yourself of any food group or particular food because you think it is "bad." You look at food primarily as a pleasant way to fill your body with fuel so it can function at its highest capacity.

You have a healthy body image when you are comfortable with your size, shape, and body parts. You wear clothes that flatter your shape, and you are relaxed about how you move. You don't compete with other women or feel bad about yourself when you think you are less attractive than another woman or than the cultural stereotype. You have few, or no, negative thoughts about your body.

Some of the more common eating disorder behaviors are listed below. As you read the list, think about your own eating behavior. On a scale of 1 to 10 (1 = not at all, 5 = often, and 10 = always), circle the number that best describes you.

I have excessive control over the way I eat.

    1   2   3   4   5   6   7   8   9   10

I ignore my body's signals of hunger or fullness.

    1   2   3   4   5   6   7   8   9   10

I eat when I feel strong emotion instead of when I am hungry.

    1   2   3   4   5   6   7   8   9   10

I focus totally on food and eating.

    1   2   3   4   5   6   7   8   9   10

Food and eating take up all my time.

    1   2   3   4   5   6   7   8   9   10

My daily living activities are affected by either eating or restricting food.

    1   2   3   4   5   6   7   8   9   10

I allow my weight and body image to interfere with my relationships.

    1   2   3   4   5   6   7   8   9   10

I allow thinking about eating or not eating to interfere with my relationships.

    1   2   3   4   5   6   7   8   9   10

My weight and body image interfere with my taking part in normal activities.

    1   2   3   4   5   6   7   8   9   10

I struggle constantly for perfection in dieting, body image, or weight.

    1   2   3   4   5   6   7   8   9   10

I have lost or gained a large amount of weight in a short period of time.

    1   2   3   4   5   6   7   8   9   10

I am overly concerned with weight loss.

    1   2   3   4   5   6   7   8   9   10

I weigh myself on a scale more than once a week.

    1   2   3   4   5   6   7   8   9   10

I have strict rules about how much food I eat.

    1   2   3   4   5   6   7   8   9   10

I have food taboos, such as, "I shouldn't let foods from different food groups touch each other on my plate."

    1   2   3   4   5   6   7   8   9   10

For a long time, I have been strict about what foods I eat.

    1   2   3   4   5   6   7   8   9   10

I compensate for taking in too many calories by exercising.

    1   2   3   4   5   6   7   8   9   10

I vomit or use laxatives to help me lose weight.

    1   2   3   4   5   6   7   8   9   10

I eat large amounts of food in a short period of time without wanting to.

    1   2   3   4   5   6   7   8   9   10

I do not realize when I have eaten too much.

    1   2   3   4   5   6   7   8   9   10

When I binge, I lose track of how much I've eaten.

    1   2   3   4   5   6   7   8   9   10

I forget to eat for days at a time.

    1   2   3   4   5   6   7   8   9   10

I eat only diet foods and diet drinks for days at a time.

    1   2   3   4   5   6   7   8   9   10

I am usually dissatisfied with my appearance.

    1   2   3   4   5   6   7   8   9   10

I am always dieting.

    1   2   3   4   5   6   7   8   9   10

I use diet drugs and herbal supplements to help me lose weight.

    1   2   3   4   5   6   7   8   9   10

I think about having gastric bypass surgery or liposuction.

    1   2   3   4   5   6   7   8   9   10

I lie about my weight to my friends and parents.

    1   2   3   4   5   6   7   8   9   10

I have at least three different sizes of clothes in my wardrobe.

    1   2   3   4   5   6   7   8   9   10

Even at my lowest weight, I am not satisfied with what I weigh.

    1   2   3   4   5   6   7   8   9   10

follow-up

Look over your responses to this exercise and consider these suggestions:

- If you circled 5 or higher for more than two statements, you may be on your way to developing an eating disorder. You may need help and should learn more about eating disorders.

- If you circled 5 or higher for more than four statements, you are definitely at risk of developing an eating disorder. Talk to an adult—parent, teacher, counselor, or doctor—right away.

- If you circled 5 or higher for more than five statements, your health may be in danger. You should seek medical attention.

more to think about

- ◆ What eating disorder behavior on this list can you change?

- ◆ How will you change that behavior in a healthy way?

- ◆ Which behavior do you think you will have a difficult time changing? Why?

your past and future   2

focus

This exercise will make you aware of when your eating disorder behaviors began and help you plan for a healthier future.

At ten years of age or older, girls enter a stage called puberty and begin to develop into young women. Puberty brings a lot of emotional and physical changes that sometimes trigger eating disorder behaviors. Thinking back to your past, can you identify the first time you recognized some of the signs of an eating disorder?

When was the first time you were embarrassed about your body?

_____

When did you first restrict the type of food you ate because you were aware of how it might affect your body?

_____

When did you first weigh yourself without a parent or doctor present?

_____

Do you remember the first time you controlled your portion size?

_____

When was the first time you tried a diet food, including soda?

_____

When was the first time you binged? What did you binge on?

_____

When was the first time you purged after a binge? How did you do it?

_____

Now that you are older, look at what you can change that may help you in your growth over the next ten years. Choose one or more of the commitments below and decide on a period of time for which you will keep that commitment, no matter what.

I will not weigh myself for _____.
Instead, I will judge the size of my body by how I feel in it.

I will not drink diet soda for _____.
Instead, I will drink water or other healthy beverages.

I will not eat diet foods or go on a diet for _____.
Instead, I will listen to my body and eat in a way that is healthy for me.

I will not overexercise to get rid of calories for _____.
Instead, I will exercise for health and relaxation.

I will not binge for _____.
Instead, I will talk about or write about my feelings first.

I will not purge for _____.
Instead, I will tell someone that I have overeaten and feel scared and anxious.

follow-up

Share your commitment with someone you know, making that person aware that you may want to talk about your feelings.

I will share this commitment with _____.

more to think about

- How do you think you have changed since your eating disorder behaviors began?

- How do you feel about keeping this commitment?

draw your feelings 3

focus

This exercise will help you deal with stress. It will help you be more creative about looking at your problems and more realistic about how you see yourself.

Most people don't think in words; they think in images. As a human being, your mind is a collection of pictures and memories, storing images like a camera. Those images are connected to the part of your brain that collects smells, tastes, and sounds. When you smell fresh bread, for example, you may see a picture of your grandmother baking. Emotions work the same way, attached to an image in your mind. For example, if you feel angry, what mental picture do you see?

Sometimes, expressing your feelings in images can be easier than describing them in words. In this exercise, you are going to draw how you feel. The exercise is not about creating beautiful art; it is about communicating how you feel.

what you'll need

Colored pencils or thin markers
Two large sheets of drawing paper

Think about your mood for a moment. Do you feel like drawing in dark, bold colors or soft, pastel colors? Choose colors that you are drawn to, and make lines and shapes that seem to match your feelings. Are you feeling open? Boxed in? Sharp and edgy? Soft and mushy?

1. Using only lines, shapes, and colors, draw how you are feeling. As you draw, don't think about what you are drawing—let your feelings take over.

2. Using a new sheet of paper, draw how you would like to feel, again using lines, shapes, and colors.

follow-up

Answer the following questions:

How are your drawings similar? _____

_____

_____

How are they different? _____

_____

_____

Do you notice anything about the drawings that surprises you? _____

_____

_____

What did you learn about your feelings in this exercise? _____

_____

_____

How did drawing these pictures make you feel? _____

_____

_____

more to think about

Every day this week, take a few moments to draw how you feel. Notice what your choice of colors, shapes, and lines says about the day-to-day similarities and differences in your feelings. Pay attention to your eating disorder behaviors too. As you become aware of your behavior, look at your drawing. Can you make a connection between your feelings and your eating disorder behaviors?

boundaries and barriers 4

focus

This exercise will help you understand the difference between boundaries and barriers, and how they affect your relationships with others.

Your personal boundary is an imaginary line you draw around yourself to protect you from something you feel threatened by. If the threat is real, that boundary is important for your self-protection. But what if the threat is imagined or left over from the past? Then your boundary becomes a barrier, and it is probably harmful, rather than helpful.

The emotional distance you keep between yourself and other people is an indication of how safe you feel with them. The people closest to you are the ones you feel least threatened by, and you can let them into your inner thoughts and feelings. With other people, you may need to set better boundaries. Do you ignore your own needs to help others? Are you constantly focused on helping other people with their problems instead of working on your own? Do people take advantage of you?

Can you identify your boundaries? Do you put actual space between yourself and others? Do you withdraw from your friends and family, keeping your opinions and thoughts to yourself? Do you barricade yourself in your room? Do you hide behind alcohol or drugs?

And what about food? Or extra weight? Extra weight can sometimes be a barrier that we think we need in order to protect ourselves against something we perceive as a threat. Without that weight, we might be afraid of being too vulnerable to the dangers we see around us.

As you do the following exercises, keep in mind the difference between a barrier and a boundary.

1. Around this outline, draw a line that indicates a boundary that is a comfortable personal space for you. Indicate the thickness of that boundary and its shape and texture. Next, around the line you have drawn, use a different color to draw a boundary that indicates where you want to keep your peers and others that you are not sure you trust. Finally, draw a boundary that shows where you want to keep people you don't trust. Make sure you indicate the thickness or texture of that line.

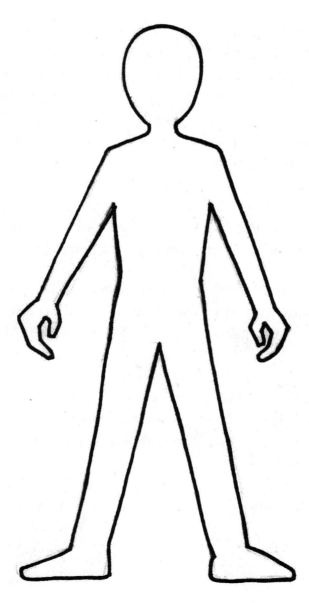

2. Using the space below, draw where you feel safest. Then, indicate where you feel safe having other people who are in your life. Who is in your inner circle? Who is in the next circle of your life? Which people do you keep in the outer circles of your life?

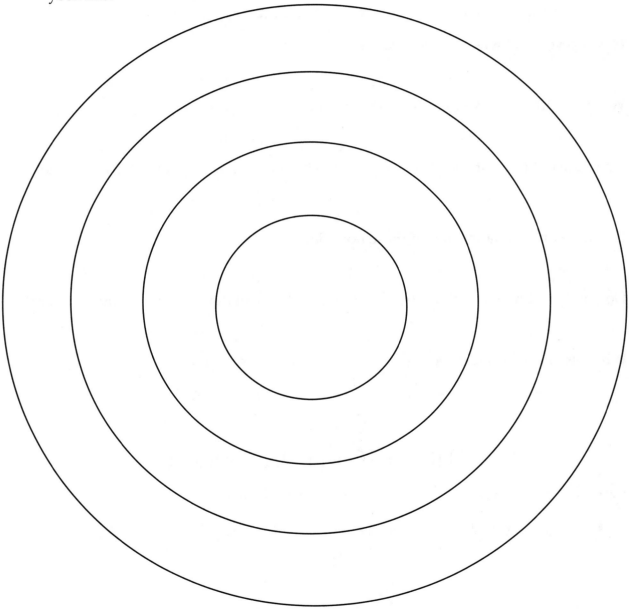

Indicate with colored arrows where you would *like* to move each of these people if you were feeling more comfortable with your own boundaries and safer in your body.

follow-up

Are you surprised by any of the boundaries you have drawn? _____
_____

How do you feel when you see yourself in the middle? _____
_____

Whom would you like to pull into your inner circle with you? _____
_____

Do you want to create healthier boundaries by moving some people farther away?
_____

Do you want to change any of these boundaries? _____
_____

Do you have any ideas about how you might like to let down some of your barriers?
_____

What else have you learned about yourself from this exercise? _____
_____

more to think about

◆ What can you share with your parents from this exercise?

◆ What can you share with your friends from this exercise?

---

focus

This exercise will help you understand your personal myths and how they relate to your life.

In many stories, children read about the prince who saves the helpless princess. This recurring theme has created generations of girls, and perhaps boys, who believe that we all need someone to rescue us. The theme of "happily ever after" is another fairy-tale idea that has influenced how we view our relationships and has made us wish for happy endings.

1. Write a fairy tale about your idealized life. Before you start, think about these questions:

    *   What will your happy ending be?
    *   Who is going to rescue you?
    *   What will happen to cause a conflict in your life?
    *   Who is your archenemy?
    *   Who will magically be there to support you?
    *   What do you need to survive the conflict?
    *   What will happen to you after you have everything you want?

My Fairy Tale

Title _____

There once was a _____

who lived _____.

And she felt _____.

Sometimes she liked to _____.

Then _____.

And next she met _____.

Something terrible happened: _____.

And her archenemy _____.

Then an amazing magical thing occurred: _____.

And she was rescued by_____.

A secret was revealed: _____.

In the end, _____.

And *after* the "happily ever after":_____.

2. Think about the fairy tale that was your favorite when you were growing up.

- What fairy tale was it? _____

   _____

- What did you like about it? _____

   _____

   _____

- How did that story help you create the fairy tale you just wrote? _____

   _____

- What character do you most relate to in your fairy tale, and why? _____

   _____

   _____

- What would be an alternative ending for your fairy tale? _____

   _____

   _____

follow-up

How do myths in our culture help us, and how do they hurt us? _____
_____
_____

What fairy-tale character do you most relate to? _____
_____
_____

Why is it important to think about what follows the happily-ever-after ending of fairy tales?
_____
_____
_____

How do you think these ideas apply to your eating disorder behavior? _____
_____
_____
_____

more to think about

◆ Can you write a new fairy tale that focuses on you as a different character?

◆ Who do you want to be?

focus

This exercise will show you how what happens during family meals can affect your eating disorder behaviors.

While the dinner table can be a warm and comfortable place where your family gathers and talks about their day, it can also be a place for a quick, and possibly stressful, meal. The dinner table offers a window into the dynamics in your family and how they affect you.

How your family deals with food is an important part of exploring eating disorder behaviors. One way to examine your family members' attitudes about food and eating is by drawing your family dinner table. This drawing can also help you look at issues between you and other members of your family.

what you'll need

Colored pencils or thin markers
Two large sheets of drawing paper

Draw a picture of your family at the dinner table. Take as much time as you need and include as much detail as possible about the table, the people, yourself, and the background.

When you have finished your drawing, answer the questions below. Keep in mind that there are many different ways to talk about your drawing, and there are no right or wrong answers.

Who is sitting at the table with you? _____

Where are you in relation to other family members? _____

What are the spaces like between family members? _____

Who is hidden by the table or chairs? _____

Is anyone missing from the table who should be there? _____

What are you doing? _____

What is everyone else doing? _____

Is there food on the table? _____

What are the family members eating? _____

Are you eating? _____

What do the colors suggest to you? _____

Which people are drawn in similar colors? _____

Which people are similar in size or shape? _____

Looking at this drawing, what are your feelings? _____

_____

What would you change about this table? _____

_____

follow-up

What do you think your observations about your family dinner table mean?

_____

_____

What do you think your drawing says about how you developed your eating disorder behaviors?

_____

_____

What would you like to change about the way you interact with your family?

_____

_____

more to think about

- ◆ Can you draw a picture of your family at the breakfast table? Is it different? How?

- ◆ Can you draw a picture of how you would like your family to be at the dinner table? How is it different?

- ◆ Can you share your drawing with someone in your family?

- ◆ Can you ask members of your family to draw their own pictures of the family dinner table?

7 healing overeating

focus

This exercise will help you understand compulsive overeating and find other behaviors you can substitute.

For many people, overeating is a comfort that helps them feel less anxious. Finding other ways to cope with anxious feelings is an important part of recovering from compulsive overeating.

The questions below explore what you might feel like if you stopped overeating. Answering them can help you understand why you overeat and how you can stop. It can also tell you what to do as an alternative, to prevent overeating in the future.

If I can't eat whatever I want whenever I want it, I will feel:

1. _____   3. _____

2. _____   4. _____

If I can't eat whatever I want whenever I want it, here's what I will probably do instead:

1. _____   3. _____

2. _____   4. _____

If I can't eat whatever I want whenever I want it, I will probably look:

1. _____   3. _____

2. _____   4. _____

If I can't eat whatever I want whenever I want it, I'll probably have to change:

1. _____   3. _____

2. _____   4. _____

If I can't eat whatever I want whenever I want it, these things will not change:

1. _____   3. _____

2. _____   4. _____

I wish I could eat whatever I want whenever I want it because:

1. _____   3. _____

2. _____   4. _____

If I can't eat whatever I want whenever I want it, I will miss:

1. _____   3. _____

2. _____   4. _____

follow-up

What seems to be the common theme among all your answers? _____

_____

_____

Do you see a pattern in your feelings about overeating? _____

_____

_____

more to think about

◆ How do you feel about depriving yourself of what you want?

◆ What do you think you can do to help you feel like you are giving yourself a gift instead of depriving yourself?

8 body image scale

focus

The Body Image Scale can help you understand how you are feeling at any given time about your body and about yourself.

Sometimes we blame the way our bodies look for how we feel about our lives. It is important to be aware of what we feel, not just what we look like. What we feel is not always connected to how we look.

The Body Image Scale is an important tool to determine what you are feeling and what you are at risk of doing to your body. If you score high on the Body Image Scale, congratulations! You are probably doing pretty well in your life and taking good care of yourself. If you score low on the Body Image Scale, you need to seek help because you may be in danger of harming yourself.

This scale can show you the progress you are making. Make a copy and keep it in your journal or hang it in your room or locker. Use it often to check where you are. If you are sinking low on the scale, ask yourself why and talk with someone.

Body Image Scale

Circle the number of the sentence that describes how you are feeling about yourself at this moment.

1. I have very extreme dislike for my body.

2. I have extreme dislike for my body.

3. I dislike my body.

4. I occasionally dislike my body.

5. I have average feelings about my body.

6. I am comfortable with my body sometimes.

7. I am usually comfortable with my body.

8. I am almost always comfortable with my body.

9. I like my physical appearance.

10. I am totally accepting of my body.

follow-up

Use the Body Image Scale only as a suggestion of how you feel about your body. It's a tool to help you become more self-aware, but it won't tell you how you are doing in your recovery from eating disorder behaviors.

When you are at different places on the Body Image Scale, try to identify what you feel about your life and your relationships—not about your body. You may notice that what you feel about your body changes depending on what's going on in your life. You'll learn to deal with your feelings rather than turning them into negative thoughts about your body.

more to think about

◆ How do you think your feelings about your body affect your eating disorder behaviors?

◆ When you are feeling better about your body, what is usually the reason? If your reason is related to your weight, think of five alternative reasons that have nothing to do with how much you weigh or what you look like.

if my body parts were colors

focus

This is an exercise to get you to think about your body. Sometimes art activities can give you a new way of looking at yourself.

Having an eating disorder can make you feel like you are living your life from the neck up. You may never want to be in your body at all. Yet your body can be a very colorful and amazing place to live. Can you look at your body as separate parts, each with a different color? Taking the time to focus thoughtfully on your body in this way will help increase your awareness of how you feel about it

Color this outline as if it were a picture of you. Use a different color for each body part. Then fill in the blanks on the following pages, indicating what color you chose for each body part and why. Think about what the colors mean to you.

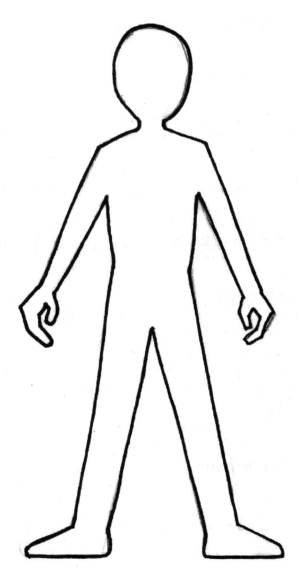

activity 9 ✳ if my body parts were colors

My face is _____ because _____

_____.

My neck is _____ because _____

_____.

My arms are_____ because _____

_____.

My hands are_____ because _____

_____.

My breasts are_____ because _____

_____.

My stomach is_____ because _____

_____.

My back is_____ because _____

_____.

My buttocks are_____ because _____

_____.

My thighs are_____ because _____

_____.

My calves are_____ because _____

_____.

My feet are_____ because _____

_____.

My toes are_____ because _____

_____.

follow-up

How do you feel about your body parts, now that they are colors? Go back and write a feeling next to each description.

more to think about

- Without focusing on your weight, what would it take to get your body parts to be the colors you'd like them to be?

- What attitudes would you have to change in order for it to happen?

10 kickback effect

focus

This exercise will teach you ways to change your eating patterns and make it easier for you to control your behaviors.

Most people can stick to a weight-loss plan or a diet for about three weeks. After the first three weeks of giving up unhealthy eating, most people experience what can be called the "kickback effect." They decide that their plan is no longer going to work; their willpower runs out, and they return to their previous eating habits. Dieting is a temporary solution to a long-term problem. To make changes that are permanent and healthy, you can't depend on willpower alone. You also have to understand your feelings, and this understanding can prevent the kickback effect.

Change works on the three-step rule:

- It takes three days for your body's cravings to end when you stop doing something addictive.

- It takes three weeks to start a new routine and determine if you like it.

- It takes three months to break a habit.

If you regularly eat processed sugars, simple carbohydrates, and junk foods, your body is used to the spike in your blood sugar level that takes place when you digest large amounts of sugar or simple carbohydrates. You actually crave sugar and the "high" it gives you; this craving is the number one symptom of an addiction.

It takes three days of no sugar and regular amounts of protein, which regulates your blood sugar, for your body to stop craving sugar highs. After three weeks, you can get used to a new food plan. By eating healthy amounts of food every few hours, you'll stabilize your blood sugar and protein levels, allowing your body to feel content. At the end of three months, healthy eating patterns will become a habit, and occasional treats of sweet desserts or snacks can be added into the food plan. Food will no longer be used as a way to deal with emotions.

Keeping the three-step rule in mind, answer the questions below:

What unhealthy eating behavior am I willing to give up for *three days?* _____

How do I feel about giving that up for three days? _____

What new routine will I commit to for *three weeks*, to see if I like it? _____

How will that new routine affect my life, and how will I feel about that change? _____

_____

What habit do I hope to break over the next *three months*? _____

How will I know I have broken that habit? _____

follow-up

After three days, record what you are feeling and what changes you have made:

_____

After three weeks, record what you are feeling and what changes you have made:

_____

After three months, record what you are feeling and what changes you have made:

_____

more to think about

◆ What will be different in your life?

◆ How will you feel different about yourself?

◆ Without your earlier habits to lean on, what feelings might come up in you?

11 perfectionism

focus

This exercise will help you be more reasonable in what you expect of yourself.

Perfection: Do you know anyone who is perfect? Is there anything in the world that is perfect? When you try to be perfect, you set up expectations that can never be reached, which leads you to a constant feeling of disappointment. Striving for a perfect weight, a perfect body, or a perfect anything will only lead to feeling bad about yourself. It can start a spiral into eating disorder behaviors.

In the space below, draw a perfect circle.

What do you notice about how hard it is to draw something perfectly? _____

_____

Even beautiful flowers are not perfectly shaped. In the space below, draw a flower, making sure that it is not perfect.

What do you like about the flower with all its imperfections? _____

_____

follow-up

Twelve-step recovery programs use slogans that help addicts and alcoholics be realistic in their expectations and feel less anxious. These slogans can help you, too. Choose one or two from the examples below and write them down where you can see them every day. Repeat them to yourself whenever you find yourself thinking you need to be perfect.

- Easy does it.
- One day at a time.

- Keep it simple.
- First things first.

more to think about

- Think about your expectations for yourself. If you get a B instead of an A as a school grade, are you happy?

- What about your expectations for other people?

12 your food plan

> ## focus
>
> This exercise will help you make a plan for healthy eating. It will also help you see how your eating habits can affect you emotionally.

Sometimes we become so out of touch with what our bodies need that we don't even know when we are hungry or full. Eating too many or too few calories throws your body out of balance and can lead to emotional and physical illness. Letting go of unhealthy food patterns and adding healthy foods is important for eating disorder recovery and prevention. A nutritionist or registered dietitian can help you understand what a balanced meal plan is and how many calories you should be eating each day.

Your food intake affects how you feel emotionally. Make copies of this worksheet and record what you eat and how you feel every day for three weeks.

Date	What I ate	How I felt emotionally
Breakfast		
Lunch		
Snack		
Dinner		
Snack		

What do you notice about the connection between what you eat and your emotions?

_____

_____

With whom can you share this activity to see if you are on a healthy food plan?

_____

_____

follow-up

The third week of a new food plan is crucial, and you may feel like giving up. At the third week, ask yourself:

What should I change at this point? _____

_____

What should I give up because it isn't working? _____

_____

Why do I feel these things are not working? _____

_____

What should I keep that is working for me? _____

_____

What can I do to make the things that are working for me continue in the next three months?

_____

_____

more to think about

In three months, look at this worksheet again and record your thoughts and feelings.

your family portrait 13

focus

This exercise will help you see that what happens between members of your family can affect your eating disorder behaviors.

Let's take a look at your current family structure. It is likely that stress generated within your family contributes to your eating disorder behaviors. If you can better identify what is happening, you will have a clearer language to communicate your feelings to your family. One way to do this is to draw a family portrait.

what you'll need

Colored pencils or thin markers
Two large sheets of drawing paper

Draw a picture that includes you and all the people in your immediate family. Show each person in your drawing doing something.

Answer the following questions about your family portrait:

Where are you in the family portrait? _____

Where are your family members in relation to you? _____

Who is grouped with whom? _____

Is there anyone who seems cut off or separated from everyone else? _____

Who has their eyes open? Closed? _____

Who has hands? Who has feet? _____

Does everyone have a mouth? Ears? _____

Is anyone blocked by an object? _____

Where are the kids in relation to the parents? _____

Where are the food-related objects: stove, table, food, and so on? _____

Where are they on the page in relation to you? To other family members? _____

Which people are drawn in the same colors? _____

What do you think the colors mean? _____

How are you different from everyone else? _____

Who is nearest you? Farthest from you? _____

Is everyone the same size? Who is largest? Smallest? _____

What interests you the most about your family portrait? _____

What would you like to change about your drawing? _____

What do you think the portrait says about your eating disorder behaviors? _____

_____

_____

follow-up

Looking at your drawing, what can you say about how your family interacts?

_____

If you changed yourself, what would change in your family portrait?

_____

more to think about

Here are some common interpretations that might interest you:

- Mouths can represent having a voice. Who has a voice in your family and who is not speaking?

- Ears can represent the ability to hear what is going on. Who is listening and who is not listening?

- Closed eyes can mean that someone is trying to ignore what is happening.

- Having no hands can mean a feeling of no control.

- Having no feet can mean feeling stuck, with no control over moving in one's life.

Can you think of other things in your drawing that might represent what is going on in your family?

14 abstract self-portrait

focus

This exercise will help you become more aware of your individuality and understand that who you are inside is the real you.

Every day, we are bombarded with television, radio, and magazine ads that focus on plastic surgery, dieting, clothes, and make-up. The media focus on appearance is so strong that many of us fall into the trap of identifying our outside appearances as the "real" us and forgetting who we really are on the inside.

So how do you focus more on who you are inside? How are you different from everyone else? How do you find the real you? One way is to remember that you are more than your appearance.

what you'll need

Colored pencils or thin markers
Two large sheets of drawing paper

Using only lines, shapes, and colors, draw an abstract portrait of yourself. Do not include your eyes, hair, legs, arms, or other parts of your body. Instead, your drawing should represent who you are on the inside—how you feel, what you think, what you are made up of—but not what you look like. Fill up the entire page.

On a second sheet of paper, draw another abstract self-portrait. This time, draw what you want to be like inside. Remember, this is not a drawing of your body or your face.

Then answer the following questions:

What do you like about your first drawing? _____

_____

What did you find hardest about drawing yourself abstractly? _____

_____

What colors did you use most often in your first drawing? _____

_____

What do you think those colors mean? _____

_____

How do you feel about your second drawing? _____

_____

How do the shapes, lines, and colors differ in both drawings? Why are they different?

_____

_____

What would you have to change about yourself to get from the first drawing to the
second?

_____

_____

What do you think these drawings have to do with your eating issues?

_____

follow-up

If you drew an abstract self-portrait every day, what do you think you would see?

_____

_____

Whom can you share your drawings with? _____

more to think about

- ◆ How does this drawing help you more clearly identify who you are as a person?

- ◆ If you were to draw another abstract self-portrait in a few hours, it would be different. What does that tell you about the nature of who you really are?

what I want to tell my parents 15
(if only they would listen)

focus

This exercise can help you work toward an open and honest relationship with your parents. You'll learn to communicate your feelings and be more accepting of their feelings.

If you could tell your parents how you really felt, what would you say? You can use this exercise to express your feelings and share what you've written with your parents.

Using the letter on the following page, write to your mom, your dad, or both, telling them how you really feel. Find a time when your parent(s) can listen and talk without interruption, and read your letter out loud. Be willing to listen to feedback. If the feelings get too intense, take a break and come back later.

Dear _____,

Sometimes I find it hard to tell you how I feel. I know you want to help me, and you may not be sure about how to do that. This letter can be our first step in understanding each other.

When I say something, can you please repeat it back to me so I know you got it? I will then tell you either, "Yes, you got it" or "No, that's not quite it," and repeat what I said until I've made myself clear. It will mean so much to me if I can tell that you are really listening, instead of rushing to give me advice.

Lately, I have been feeling _____. When you _____, it makes me feel _____.
And I know that when I _____, it makes you feel _____. Some things I need you to know about what I am going through right now are _____
_____.
I really need some help with _____.
Some ways that you can help me are _____
_____. Some things I think we need to change are _____.
If there are things you think need to change, I am open to listening.

I really need to know that you hear my feelings and I want to hear yours. I know that may be hard for both of us and I am committed to having an open and honest relationship. Can we do that together?

Thanks for listening.

Love,

_____

follow-up

Talking to your parents can be hard and frustrating, both for you and for your parents. Having a format for expressing your feelings, like the letter you wrote above, sometimes makes it easier to say what you need to.

What was it like to write your letter? _____

_____

_____

What was it like to talk to your parent about your letter? _____

_____

more to think about

- ◆ Who else do you need to write a letter to?

- ◆ Can you use this format to write a letter to someone else?

16 negative self-talk

focus

This exercise will help you turn negative thoughts into positive ones. When you learn how to do that, you will feel better about yourself.

We can't always be positive. Sometimes we say negative things about other people and the way they look; sometimes others say negative things about the way we look. These messages become part of our self-talk, or the words we use in our own minds when we talk to ourselves about the way we look.

Self-talk can be either positive or negative. "I look good today" is a positive message; "I look fat and ugly today" is a negative message. Self-talk can influence how our day is going, what our mood is, and even how we act toward other people.

Our feelings about our bodies can change drastically every second of the day. For example, imagine how you feel standing next to someone who is short and petite in comparison to you. Now picture yourself standing next to someone who is twice your size. Although your body size hasn't changed, chances are you have a totally different feeling about yourself. By changing our negative thoughts, we can change how we feel about our bodies.

1. Write any negative thoughts you have about any part of your body or your body as a whole.

    _____

    _____

2. Write any messages, good or bad, you have heard about your body. If possible, list the people you heard these messages from.

    _____

    _____

3. Write any messages you heard as a child about other people's bodies.

    _____

    _____

4. How did these messages make you feel about yourself?

    _____

    _____

5. For each negative thought you wrote in response to the first question, write one positive thought. Try to pick messages that you really believe are true. For example, "I hate my hair" could be "My hair has a nice natural wave."

    _____

    _____

follow-up

Are there people you would like to talk to about the messages you heard about your body? You may want to say something like:

> "I have been working hard on my self-esteem. I realize that some of the negative thoughts I have about my body come from my past. Will you talk about that with me?"

During and after the conversation, remember to maintain positive thoughts about your body.

more to think about

Positive self-talk is the beginning of a positive body image. Learning to see yourself realistically, and not how others see you, is an important part of learning to rid yourself of negative body thoughts and change the way you judge your body.

about food and weight loss 17

---

focus

This exercise will help you understand your ideas about food and weight loss, if compulsive overeating is a problem for you.

Answer each question as honestly as you can. You can complete the worksheet in one sitting or take your time and answer one question a day.

To me, food represents _____.

All my life, I've used food as _____.

What will help me lose weight is _____.

Looking at my body makes me feel _____.

I am angry at _____.

The feelings I use food to bury are _____.

Food helps me avoid _____.

I love food because it _____.

Sometimes I am afraid to eat because _____.

Parts of my body that I love are _____.

To lose weight, I am willing to sacrifice _____.

Strengths that will help me lose weight are _____.

What has helped me in the past is _____.

follow-up

I realize now that food has been a way for me to _____

_____.

Being more aware of how I have used food to avoid my feelings has helped me because

_____

_____.

more to think about

◆ Draw what you think being healthy would feel like, not what it would look like.

relaxing your body 18

---

focus

In this exercise, you'll learn different ways to relax your body. Learning how to relax will help you when you feel stressed.

Can you tell when you are stressed? Do you know what your body feels like when it is tense? When it is relaxed? Studies have shown that we can actually decrease our blood pressure, slow down our pulses, and lower our heart rates by relaxing. Relaxation techniques can actually change what happens in our minds and bodies and ultimately, can even change what our bodies look like! Knowing how to control stress in our bodies helps us to be physically and emotionally healthier, and it can prevent us from using self-destructive eating and purging habits to deal with our uncomfortable feelings.

Practice these exercises once a day. You can record them on a tape player, have someone read them to you from this page, or read the worksheet carefully and practice what you remember.

Exercise One

1. Find a comfortable place to sit or lie down and focus all your attention on your body.

2. Slowly breathe in through your nose and out through your mouth, ten times.

3. Focus all your attention on your feet. Imagine the bottoms of your feet open like trap doors. Picture all the stress in your body flowing out from the bottoms of your feet and into the floor.

4. Imagine stress flowing out from the bottoms of your feet, into the floor, and down into the earth. The stress flows like water into the dirt, through the mud and rocks, and into the molten lava at the center of the earth, dissipating like steam into the Earth's core.

5. Focus on your calves, letting go of all stress.

6. Focus on your shins, relaxing, letting go of all tension, and feeling it drain out through your feet and into the floor.

7. Relax your knees and your thighs. Feel the muscles in the back of your thighs and the front of your thighs, the muscles that carry you around all day, as they relax. Feel the flow of relaxation all the way down to your feet.

8. Feel the base of your spine as it settles into the surface beneath you. As you are pulled down by gravity, feel how relaxing that is.

Exercise Two

1. Breathe into your belly, filling it with air. Relax it fully as you exhale.

2. Relax your lower back. Moving up your spine, relax the rest of your back.

3. Feel your shoulders relax. Feel them pull down toward the Earth. Let all the tension roll off them and flow into the ground.

4. Breathe in and exhale. Let all the tension from your shoulders and your back flow down into the Earth, letting it all go and feeling what it is like to relax.

5. Relax your arms—your upper arms, your biceps and triceps, your forearms; relax your hands and all your fingers. Feel the stress flow down your arms and hands, flowing out of your fingers and down into the ground.

6. Relax the back of your neck where it meets your spine. Relax your jaw. Relax your tongue. Take a deep breath, feeling all the tension flow out of your jaw muscles.

7. Relax your forehead. Feel the tension smooth out of your forehead. Let all the worry lines smooth out of your face, feeling the stress and tension leave your face and neck, flow down your shoulders, and over your arms, leaving your body and flowing down into the ground as you exhale.

Exercise Three

1. Take a deep breath. Exhale. Relax.

2. Take another deep breath. Let the feeling of relaxation smooth over your entire body, soothing your muscles, relaxing your joints.

3. Feel light and warmth soothe and cover your entire body and flow into the floor.

4. Breathe and relax; feel your body. Think of your sore, stuck places, and breathe warmth and light into those stuck places. Relax and let go.

5. Feel the tension drain through your body and into the floor.

6. Take a deep breath into your core. Relax and let go.

7. Fall into a relaxed state of consciousness; sleep if appropriate.

8. Come to, fully relaxed and aware and comforted in your body.

activity 18 ✳ relaxing your body

follow-up

What were some things you noticed that made you realize your body was tense?

_____

_____

Which relaxation exercise worked the best for you? Explain why.

_____

_____

What part of this exercise can you practice at home? At school?

_____

_____

Which parts can you teach your friends? Your siblings? Your parents?

_____

_____

How can relaxation help you with healthy eating?

_____

_____

more to think about

- You can relax your body throughout the day, as you need to.

- The signal to your body will be a deep breath in and out, letting go of all the stress of the day.

- How often can you commit to practicing these exercises each week?

What happened to the little kid you used to be? You had total control over that person's body. You could run and jump and play with other kids, and your body did exactly what you told it to. When you wanted to run, it ran. If you wanted to rest, it stopped. With all the hormonal changes of adolescence, your body may seem to have a mind of its own. Sometimes it responds in ways you feel totally powerless over. You can feel great in your body one day and terrible the next; it is all part of growing up.

Feeling unhappy in your body can lead to negative thoughts that make you feel even worse about yourself. These thoughts can cause you to feel depressed, afraid, or exhausted, and they can lead to self-destructive behaviors. Repeated often enough, these thoughts become part of your consciousness. They replay in your mind even when you are not aware of them and affect your physical, emotional, and spiritual health.

1. Complete the following sentences with the first responses that come to your mind:

   The worst thing about my body is _____.

   The best thing about my body is _____.

   What I don't like about my body is _____.

   What I appreciate about my body is _____.

   My body is not cooperating, because it _____.

   My body has always been _____.

   What I have come to accept about my body is _____.

   I feel the following about my body:

   My body is _____.

   My body is _____.

   My body is _____.

   My body is _____.

   My body is _____.

   My body is _____.

   My body is _____.

   My body is _____.

   My body is _____.

   My body is _____.

2. Positive affirmations are statements written in the present that can help you change your thoughts about yourself. If you said, "My body is fat and ugly," a positive affirmation to correct that message would be, "My body is beautiful and perfect." You may not believe an affirmation at first, but by repeating it and focusing on it, you can turn your negative thoughts into positive ones.

Looking at the comments you wrote about your body, notice how many negative messages are running through your mind. Go back and rewrite these messages, turning them into positive affirmations.

My body is _____.

My body is _____.

My body is _____.

My body is _____.

My body is _____.

My body is _____.

My body is _____.

My body is _____.

My body is _____.

My body is _____.

3. Writing affirmations and reading them is an important part of "rewiring" your mind to eliminate the negative messages you have been feeding yourself. Pick out one affirmation from the list above, and write it out ten times.

My body is _____.

My body is _____.

My body is _____.

My body is _____.

My body is _____.

My body is _____.

My body is _____.

My body is _____.

My body is _____.

My body is _____.

4. Post several affirmations—either your own or ones from the list below—where you will see them often: on your bathroom mirror, in your locker at school, over your desk. Let them sink in and begin to change the way you think about yourself. Remember, you don't have to believe them at first. Eventually your subconscious will teach itself to like you and be gentler with you!

AFFIRMATIONS

✔ I approve of my body exactly the way it is.
✔ I love my body and all its parts.
✔ My body is healthy and strong.
✔ I am loving and gentle with my body.
✔ I am grateful for my healthy and happy body.
✔ I am happy to be good to my body.
✔ My body is wonderful just the way it is.
✔ I love my figure and accept its changes.
✔ My body is beautiful in its uniqueness.
✔ I love the way my body works.
✔ I am happy with my looks.
✔ My body is perfect just the way it is.
✔ My body is the perfect container for me.
✔ My body is healthy and beautiful.

---

follow-up

Put your sheet of affirmations on the wall above your bed or in your bathroom so you can look at it every day. Each morning, choose an affirmation that works for you. Throughout the day, read it aloud, write it down, and say it to yourself.

more to think about

Look back at some of the negative messages you have been telling yourself. It's not likely you would ever say those things to your best friend or to your sister, so why would you say them to yourself? The next time you find yourself playing negative messages in your head, be as gentle and loving with yourself as you would be with your best friend.

I am ... 20

> ## focus
> This exercise will help you understand what is special and unique about you.

As teenagers, we often want to be just like everyone else. To become healthy adults, we must first look at how we are similar to, and different from, others. Then, we can begin to shape ourselves as individuals.

1. Fill in the blanks after the words, "I am...." It is important that you do it quickly and without a lot of thought so that your answers are spontaneous.

I am _____

I am _____

I am _____

I am _____

I am _____

I am _____

I am _____

I am _____

I am _____

I am _____

I am _____

I am _____

I am _____

I am _____

2. Read your answers aloud, as if you were reading a poem. Record or videotape yourself as you read. As you replay it, notice how it describes you as a unique person.

3. Notice which statements were negative messages and which ones were positive. Mark each negative message with a minus sign and each positive message with a plus sign.

4. For each statement, ask yourself:

   • Has someone else told me this message about myself? Who was it?

   • How have these messages affected my body image?

5. Look at the first five statements you wrote. If they are negative, can you change them?

6. Notice your last five statements. These are ones you may have had to really search for. Are they more real than the first five? Why?

7. Choose five positive messages and write them as affirmations. For example, if the statement is, "I am nice to my younger sisters," the affirmation might be, "I am a nurturing, caring person, and I am good with children."

   I am _____

   I am _____

   I am _____

   I am _____

   I am _____

follow-up

Share your "poem" with a person you feel close to. Try this exercise again in several weeks or months and see how you have changed. It is amazing how we can grow in short periods of time!

more to think about

- As you grow stronger in your sense of self, your "I am" messages may grow more positive.

- Notice that the more positive and supportive your messages to yourself are, the more positive and supportive your messages to those around you become.

- We all need affirmation to grow, and we have to give it to ourselves first.

21 family patterns

focus

This exercise will help you look at how members of your family handle conflict and how family conflicts affect your eating behavior.

Think back to the worksheet 6, "Family Dinner Table", earlier in this book. All families have their own ways of relating to each other. The way your family handles conflict can also affect you, and you may react to conflict with self-destructive eating patterns.

The questions below will help you see how your family may have affected your eating patterns.

What are some of your dysfunctional eating patterns? _____
_____

What would happen to the rest of your family if your eating behavior became more stable?

_____

_____

What emotions are most commonly expressed in your family? How are they expressed?

_____

_____

How do you resolve conflict in your family? _____
_____

How would you describe the energy in your house at mealtime? _____
_____

When you are in a conflict with a family member, how does that affect your eating patterns?

_____

_____

When there is conflict in the family, how does that affect the family's eating pattern?

_____

When you are upset or angry, how do you express yourself?

_____

follow-up

Look at the answers you gave above. What patterns do you notice at home?

_____

Are there ways your family deals with conflict that make it hard for you to have a healthy emotional balance? _____

_____

How can you handle conflict without turning to dysfunctional eating patterns?

_____

_____

more to think about

◆ Can you share any or all of your answers with your family?

◆ If you do share and there is conflict as a result, how will you handle it?

22 pop star

focus

This exercise will help you realize that you are an individual and do not have to conform to society's idea of the ideal body.

Several years ago, magazines portrayed women in popular situation comedies as having tiny, extremely underweight bodies, with large and seemingly overdeveloped heads precariously balanced on their frames. These women were nicknamed "lollipops." We know now that being so underweight is not only unattractive, it is a warning sign that a young woman is in serious physical danger. But women are still in competition to maintain the "ideal" body, whether it is the lollipop body or the curvier body of some of today's pop stars. Our media continues to foster the idea that happiness depends on having the body they deem ideal.

Think about the stars in music, the models in magazines, and the actresses in movies and television. In the space on the left, draw the body that you think is the ideal portrayed in the media. On the right, draw what you think your body looks like.

How is your body different from the cultural ideal of today? _____
_____

How is your body the same as or close to the cultural ideal of today? _____
_____

What do you do to try to force your body to be like the ideal of today? _____
_____

How does that hurt you physically, emotionally, and spiritually? _____
_____

What might be unattractive about the cultural ideal of today? What don't you like
about it?
_____
_____

List ten things you like about your body. Don't think too hard; just write!

1. _____   6. _____

2. _____   7. _____

3. _____   8. _____

4. _____   9. _____

5. _____   10. _____

follow-up

What problems do you think pop stars idealized by the media might have?

_____

_____

What do pop stars have to do to stay popular?

_____

_____

_____

more to think about

◆ How is your life easier than the life of a TV sitcom character?

23 be a tree

focus

This exercise will help you understand that people are unique and do not have to compete.

No two trees in the forest look alike. If we expect that they will all be different and don't see one as better than another, why do we compare our bodies to someone else's?

Find a comfortable place to sit or lie down. Read this exercise and practice as you read it. Then try it with your eyes closed.

Be a tree.

Feel your roots.

Spread your branches.

Feel the wind in your branches.

Know that you are grounded in the earth and nothing can tip you over.

You can sway with the storms and grow toward the sun.

You have an endless supply of energy coming up from the ground. Whenever you need it, you can send your roots down and feel that energy coming up into your trunk and spreading out into your branches and leaves.

When the world feels tough, let your branches absorb the light from the sun. Know that you can be a tree among trees.

Appreciate for a moment that no two trees are alike. Every tree in the forest is different, and yet without every tree, there would be no forest.

Do trees compete to look the same?

follow-up

How does competing to look like everyone else work for you? _____

_____

How does competing to look like everyone else work against you? _____

_____

Who told you that you had to look like everyone else? _____

_____

How would it feel to look like you do and know that that was good enough? _____

_____

more to think about

- ◆ Practice being a tree whenever you feel competitive around your friends or in school. Spread your branches and be you. Remember, no two trees are alike.

24 "I'm not good enough" thoughts and how to stop them

focus

This exercise will help you cope when you start to have negative thoughts about yourself.

Do you ever have "I'm not good enough" thoughts? You may have those thoughts when you feel lonely or when you compare yourself to others. You may have them when you feel like your body should look different than it does.

If your "I'm not good enough" thoughts had a face, what would it look like? Draw the face below.

If it had a voice, what would that voice sound like? _____

_____

Does it speak about your body? If so, what does it say? _____

_____

What would you like to say back to the "I'm not good enough" voice? _____

_____

What is it like inside your head when that voice is ruling your day? Draw what it feels like, using lines, shapes, and colors.

Draw what it would feel like inside your head if that voice were quiet.

Imagine you could tell that voice to stop talking. Would you yell, "STOP"? Would you shout? Describe how you would tell the voice to stop. _____

_____

What can you picture in your mind to help you stop your "I'm not good enough" thoughts? It might be a stop sign or a soundproof wall or a police officer blowing a whistle. Draw that picture below.

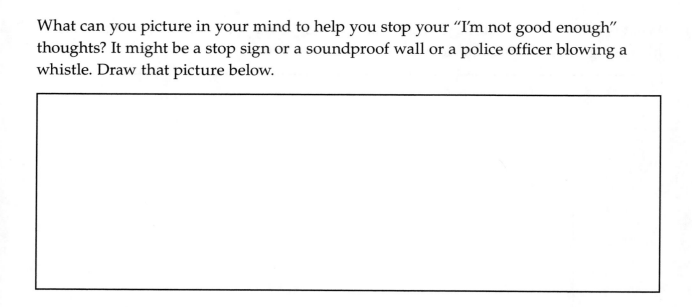

follow-up

Your "I'm not good enough" thoughts can lead to self-destructive behaviors, like bingeing, purging, or restricting food. Learning to recognize these thoughts is an important step in gaining a sense of control over your patterns of self-destruction. When you have an "I'm not good enough" thought, you can do the following:

- Recognize it.

- Tell it to stop.

- Picture something that will stop it.

- Write or draw about it.

- Talk about it.

more to think about

These steps will help you to get past your old behavior and move on to using new, healthy coping skills. You can take control of your recovery and move into the life you want to live!

whose body is this? 25
part I: I am unique

focus

focus

This exercise will help you accept the type of body you have and recognize your similarities to family members who came before you.

No two bodies in this world have the same shape. Even identical twins have slight differences between them. Our unique shapes—the gentle slope of our shoulders, the broad, strong expanse of our hips, the roundness of our bellies—are all a result of the families we come from.

The cultural ideals in our society determine what we hold to be attractive. If you are growing up at a time when being tall and thin is the ideal, and your ancestors were short and stocky, you may feel uncomfortable with the short, stocky body you inherited. Looking at the models in magazines, you may feel hopelessly out of fashion. Realizing that no amount of dieting, plastic surgery, or magical thinking can change your heritage, can you love and accept yourself exactly as you are? Whether your relationship with your mother and other female relatives has been smooth or problematic, can you acknowledge the strength of the women in your family who came before you? Can you feel the connection your body gives you to them?

In this visualization exercise, you will get in touch with all of your female ancestors. Let yourself experience the feeling of connection you have to all the women before you!

1. Close your eyes and take several deep breaths into the center of your body. Relax into your chair, grounding your feet on the floor and letting gravity pull you into the Earth.

2. Imagine yourself in a safe and relaxing place in nature. There is beauty and tranquility all around you, as far as your inner eye can see.

3. Now imagine that your mother stands behind you, supporting you, holding you up. You lean on her slightly.

4. Behind her stands her mother. You both lean back on her, and she supports you both gently. You relax. Breathe.

75

5. Imagine the three of you relaxing against your great-grandmother, as she stands behind you. You are all in a line, one behind the other.

6. Now imagine the four of you relaxing against your great-great-grandmother standing behind you.

7. Slowly picture all the women in your ancestral line standing behind each other, all holding you up. Visualize these women, reaching back in time to the first woman you can imagine.

8. See these women as strong, capable, beautiful, and unique. Feel what that feels like. Breathe.

9. Open your eyes. Write down any thoughts or feelings you may have in your journal or the Notes pages at the end of this workbook.

Think about the countries your ancestors came from. Then focus on your body and its separate parts. Part by part, identify whom you most closely resemble in your family. For example write, "My legs are most like my mother's. She came from Poland."

My hair is most like my _____'s. She came from _____.

My face is most like my _____'s. She came from _____.

My eyes are most like my _____'s. She came from _____.

My mouth is most like my _____'s. She came from _____.

My shoulders are most like my _____'s. She came from _____.

My arms are most like my _____'s. She came from _____.

My breasts are most like my _____'s. She came from _____.

My belly is most like my _____'s. She came from _____.

My hips are most like my _____'s. She came from _____.

My legs are most like my _____'s. She came from _____.

My ankles are most like my _____'s. She came from _____.

My feet are most like my _____'s. She came from _____.

I am also like my female ancestors in these other ways:

_____

_____

_____

_____

follow-up

Were you able to see all the women in your ancestral line? _____

How did it feel to lean against them as they supported you? _____

Can you draw a picture of what this visualization was like for you?

```
┌─────────────────────────────────────────────┐
│                                               │
│                                               │
│                                               │
│                                               │
│                                               │
│                                               │
│                                               │
│                                               │
│                                               │
│                                               │
└─────────────────────────────────────────────┘
```

more to think about

After you complete these exercises, say the following affirmations aloud:

- ◆ I am powerless to change some things about my body.

- ◆ I appreciate the parts of me that resemble my ancestors and make me unique.

- ◆ I honor my relatives, living and dead.

- ◆ The way I look is special and connects me to the women in my family lineage.

Add further affirmations if you can. Remember, affirmations are positive and in the present. For example, "I am beautiful like my Aunt Jeanne" or "I love my Native American heritage."

whose body is this? 26
part II: interview

---

focus

This exercise will help you see how your family history has influenced your eating behavior and body type.

In Worksheet 25, we began to explore the connection between heritage and body make-up. How our bodies look is not only a result of how we eat and exercise, but also a result of what we inherit. To continue, you'll interview female family members to learn about their body images.

You can use the introduction below to explain to your relatives that you are learning about women in your family and their body images. If you prefer, you can introduce the interview in your own words. Bring a notebook; you may also want to record the interviews on audiotape or have someone videotape them.

Body Image Interview

Thank you so much for taking the time to let me interview you. I am interested in hearing about the women in our family and how they have felt about their bodies. I realize you may not know much about our family several generations back, and that's okay; please just answer my questions the best you can. If you have any pictures of you now or when you were younger that you could share with me, I can make copies and return the originals. When I've finished collecting information, I'll share what I've learned with you.

1. How do you feel about your body today?

2. How did you feel about it when you were my age?

3. Where were you born? In what year?

4. What was it like growing up as a girl where you lived?

5. What was the ideal body when you were a teenager?

79

6. How closely did you feel you fit that ideal?

7. Did you feel pretty when you were a teenager?

8. Did you feel like you fit in?

9. How did your mother feel about her body when you were growing up? How did you know?

10. What do you think the ideal body was when she was a teenager? Was she like that or unlike that?

11. Where did your mother grow up?

12. Where did your grandmother grow up?

13. What was the ideal body when she was growing up? Was she like that or unlike that?

14. Who do you think you most resemble, and why?

15. Who do you think I most resemble, and why?

follow-up

Write up the interviews and put them into a binder, with pictures or drawings of all of your female relatives. Share these stories with your relatives. Someday, you may even have your own daughter to share them with!

more to think about

◆ Adapt this interview form and use it to learn about your friends, your teachers, and other people you know. You can interview the men in your family as well to learn about their body images.

◆ Ask all of your friends to answer some of these questions and bring the forms home to their own relatives. Meet to discuss the results.

focus

This exercise will help you recognize your connection to your family and realize that eating disorder behaviors are often rooted in family history.

Each of us has an effect on our appearance, but we have also inherited a set of unchangeable factors from our parents and their parents before them. These factors influence what we look like. By looking at your family tree, you can begin to understand the impact of those who came before you.

Before you can create a family tree, you'll need to gather information by talking with relatives, both men and women, about their recollections of your family. Start by asking your parent, grandparent, aunt, or uncle to sit down with you and make a list of as many relatives as they can think of. Put lists together for both sides of your family.

You can use the questions below as a guide and also ask for other information you are interested in knowing about your family and its history.

- How old are these relatives or how old were they when they died?

- What did they die of?

- What country were they born in, and what country are they in now?

- Did anyone in our family have anorexia or bulimia? Was anyone obese?

Here are some additional questions you may be curious about:

- Who were the athletes in the family? What sports did they play?

- Who played an instrument?

- Were there any artists in our family? Doctors? Farmers?

- Did anyone serve in the military? Where and when?

- Are there any feuds between family members?

- Were there any divorces? Stepfamilies?

- Are there any stories in our family of quirky or interesting relatives?

Think of other questions you may be curious about. Remember to be patient and give people time to think and go back into their memories. Finally, ask for family pictures that you can copy and return.

When you have compiled as much information as possible, you are ready to begin creating your family tree.

what you'll need

Colored pencils or thin markers
#2 pencils with erasers
A large sheet of oak tag
A glue stick
A photo of yourself
Photos of relatives
Small stickers

1. Draw a tree with the base of the trunk at the bottom of the paper. Add branches stretching up to the top and corners of the page.

2. Find a baby picture of yourself, or draw one based on your parent's recollections, and glue it on the trunk of the tree.

3. Fill in the names of your parents above you on the trunk, just where the branches begin. Include their names and current ages. Add pictures of them if you have them.

4. On a branch to the left above your parents, add your mother's parents' names with their ages or the ages that they were when they died. If they have passed away, indicate that with a thin root to the ground or up to a cloud in the sky

above your tree. Include anything you have that reminds you of them: pictures, flags of their country of origin, medals, and so on.

5.   On a branch to the right of your parents, repeat step 4 for your father's parents.

6.   If you have brothers or sisters, write in their names and ages to the left and right of your picture. Include pictures.

7.   If you have nieces or nephews, include them below their parents. Write their ages as well.

8.   Beneath your grandparents on both sides, include any children they had and their ages. These people are your aunts and uncles, your parents' brothers and sisters.

9.   Beneath or next to your aunts and uncles, include the names and ages of your cousins.

10.   Now continue up the tree and out, adding your great-grandparents on both sides with whatever information you have about them.

11.   Expand with any great-aunts, great-uncles, and second cousins.

12.   If you have further information, continue up and out, adding great-great-grandparents and more.

Note: If there have been divorces and remarriages in your family, show couples who are together now. Connect children to their biological parents with a green line and to their stepparents with a blue line. Possibly confusing, but it is common!

Now that you have compiled an actual picture version of your family tree, you are ready to look at eating disorder patterns. Place a sticker next to the name of any relative who has had an eating disorder issue, including anorexia, bulimia, or obesity.

Using colored pencils or markers, color your family tree. Hang it up on a wall or mount it on a wooden board or foam core.

follow-up

How did it feel to interview your relatives for your family tree? _____

_____

What were some things you noticed about your family when you began compiling notes from your interview? _____

_____

What did you learn about your similarities to many of your family members? Your differences? _____

_____

How many people in your family tree did you discover had eating disorder issues?

_____

_____

Do you think that your family's history is unique or that most families have similar issues in their background? _____

_____

Are there any family members or situations that you feel embarrassed about? _____

_____

Which part of your family tree do you feel particularly connected to? Are they relatives who are alive today, or are they ancestors? _____

_____

more to think about

Invite your relatives to a Family Tree party to share the family tree you have created. Take pictures of them as they enjoy it, and send copies to family members who can't be there.

from mother to daughter 28

focus

This exercise will help you communicate with your mother and become aware of ways that you are alike.

In every generation, there is a body shape considered to be ideal. Some years, it is fashionable to be thin; some years, it's the style to have curves. And in every generation, many are not going to fit the standard of perfection. A mother who has a problem with her own body image is more likely to have a daughter with eating disorder behaviors. And that mother's problem may have come from her mother.

Ask your mother the following questions:

1. If you had to describe how you feel about your body in a few words, what would you say?

    _____

2. What do you want to pass on to me about how I should feel about my body?

    _____

3. What issues about your own body do you need to work on?

    _____

4. What did your mother value about women's bodies?

    _____

5. How did your mother feel about dieting?

    _____

6. What messages did your mother pass down to you about women's bodies?

    _____

Now, imagine your mother looking at herself in a mirror. What is she saying?

_____

_____

What is her body language saying? _____

_____

follow-up

How do you think the answers your mother has given affect you? _____

_____

What messages have you learned from your mother about how to feel about your body?

_____

_____

_____

more to think about

◆ Can you share what you learned in this worksheet with your mother?

◆ If you have a daughter someday, what would you like her to know about your feelings about your body and about how she should feel about her own body?

frustration scale 29

focus

This exercise will help you cope with frustration and stress. You can use the techniques you'll learn to avoid eating disorder behaviors.

Tension is the building up of energy that leads to stress. Stress is the uncomfortable feeling we have when things feel out of our control. When we feel powerless to change the things that create our stress, frustration results. Sometimes we deal with frustration by relying on temporary, and often unhealthy, coping mechanisms.

Using the Frustration Scale, you can learn to delay acting out with self-destructive behaviors and to use positive coping skills instead. When you notice signs of tension or stress, use this scale to determine your frustration level. At certain points on the scale, you'll find suggestions for positive coping skills and, at the end, an explanation of how to use those skills. With practice, you will automatically know what to do when you recognize where you are on this scale!

Frustration Scale

Circle the number that corresponds to how you are feeling at the moment.

1. **Calm**
   Your body is relaxed; your breathing is slow.

2. **Slightly tense, but feeling good**
   Your body is slightly tense and your breathing a little more rapid than usual, but you basically feel relaxed and happy.

3. **Somewhat tenser, but in a good way**
   Your breath is slightly rapid, and your muscles are tense.

4. **Tense and feeling some stress**
   You may be tapping your finger or shaking your foot.

   ✔ Find a stress reducer.

5. **Somewhat stressed**
   Your shoulders, stomach, or lower back may feel tight.

   ✔ Find a stress reducer.

6. **Really stressed and getting frustrated**
   You are thinking more unhealthy thoughts and feeling more uncomfortable in your body.

   ✔ Take a time-out.

7. **Feeling pretty frustrated**
   Everything is bothering you. Your body is feeling tight and uncomfortable. You may feel pain and find it hard to relax or slow down your breathing.

   ✔ Take a time-out.

8. **Growing more frustrated**
   Your body is very uncomfortable. You may feel tension in your chest and find it hard to catch your breath, or your breathing may be rapid. You may be clenching your fists or your jaw. You may have a headache or backache. Your shoulders may be hunched or sore.

   ✔ Talk with someone.

9. **Really stressed**
   You are fighting with everyone around you. You feel like—or may even be—throwing things or punching walls. You want to do something self-destructive. You might feel like yelling or blowing up.

   ✔ Use your tools.

10. **Stressed to the max**
    Your frustration has affected your health, and you have gotten sick or acted out. You are feeling over the edge and may feel shame or remorse for some self-destructive act.

    ✔ Use your tools.

Positive Coping Skills

Positive coping skills are behaviors that can help you deal with uncomfortable feelings in a healthy way.

Find a Stress Reducer

To reduce stress, try meditating or doing a visualization. Work on a journal entry, draw a picture, or call a friend. You can also use positive affirmations.

Take a Time-Out

Time-outs are important stress reducers for everyone. They are a good way for you to relax for a few moments and reduce your own frustration.

Outside is a good place to take time-outs, if possible. Give yourself a limit—two minutes? Five? Ten? Sit and do nothing but focus on your breath, the sky, or a tree for a specified period of time. When your time-out is over, reevaluate where you are on the Frustration Scale.

Talk with Someone

If you are at a crucial point, find someone to talk with. Are your parents around? Can you tell someone how you are feeling? Pick up the phone and call a friend. Call your therapist. If you can't find someone to talk with right away, open your journal and write down how you feel. Write a letter or an e-mail to someone, even someone imaginary, like your future self. Telling someone how you are feeling will help you reduce your stress; then go back and see where you are on the scale.

Use Your Tools

At the end of this workbook, you will find additional tools you can use to keep yourself from acting out self-destructively.

follow-up

After you have practiced using positive coping skills, reevaluate where you are on the Frustration Scale. How has your frustration level improved? _____

_____

When you are more frustrated, are you also more likely to use eating disorder behaviors? _____

_____

Where on the Frustration Scale are you when you start thinking about acting out your eating disorder behaviors: 5, 6, 7? What can you do to decrease your frustration when it approaches that level? _____

_____

Can you spot different levels of frustration in the people around you? What are your family members like at a 6 or 7? Do they ever get to 8, 9, or 10? Can you talk with them about how that makes you feel? _____

_____

more to think about

Share this scale with your family so that they know the language you are using when you talk about the Frustration Scale. Let them know that when you get to a 6 or 7, it is time for you to take a time-out.

focus

This exercise will help you think about the positive aspects of being a woman.

You cannot be creative and self-destructive at the same time. Creating something new shows your intention to move forward and expresses your need to grow. Creativity and self-destruction are two opposing forces, which is why art is so healing.

what you'll need

A large, sturdy piece of paper or cardboard
(or a piece of wood is okay if it is sanded and smooth)
A glue stick or white glue
Scissors
Magazines, photos, and other print materials
Natural materials like shells, leaves, flowers, twigs, sand, and so on
Fabric scraps, buttons, beads, and so on
Shellac

Make a collage that shows what makes you feel alive. Include images, words, and materials that represent what gives you hope and makes life worth living.

Glue what you have chosen onto your paper, filling the entire surface, even overlapping some materials. When the collage is entirely dry, spread a thin layer of shellac or white glue over the surface of the collage images. White glue, if thin enough, will dry clear and create a hard and clear surface for your collage that will protect the art and keep the edges from curling up. Display your collage where you will see it every day.

follow-up

Is there a central theme that seems to appear in your collage, showing what makes life worth living for you? _____

Did anything that appears self-destructive find its way into your collage? _____
_____

How can you change it? _____
_____

How did you feel while you were making your collage? _____
_____

Did you lose track of time or forget about your problems for a short time? _____
_____

With whom can you share your collage? _____

more to think about

◆ Remember, you cannot be creative and self-destructive at the same time.

◆ When you feel like doing something harmful to yourself, like bingeing or purging, do something creative. Make a collage!

focus

This exercise will give you more practice in expressing yourself creatively. It will help you think about the type of person you would like to be and the type of world you would like to live in.

Long ago, people thought the world was flat, and they were afraid they would fall off if they went too close to its edge. They could not imagine Earth as we know it. Today we see the world quite differently, and we are all influenced by our worldviews. We create our environment and our reality by believing in the vision we hold to be true.

What vision do you hold to be true about your world? Do you believe it is a gentle, nurturing place that cares for you and that you can count on? Do you believe that you are alone and on your own? How do you see the world around you? And do you believe you can change it?

what you'll need

A sturdy box like a shoebox, of any size
A glue stick or white glue
Scissors
Magazines, photos, and other print materials
Natural materials like shells, leaves, flowers, twigs, sand, and so on
Fabric scraps, buttons, beads, and so on
Shellac

Create a collage that shows your vision of the world. Use the inside of the box to show your ideal self and the outside to show your ideal world. You can make your box as realistic or as whimsical as you like.

Here are some questions for you to think about in creating your vision box:

- What is your vision of an ideal world?

- What is important to you for your personal future?

- Focusing on the type of person you want to be rather than on your appearance, how do you see yourself in the future?

follow-up

What did it feel like to create your vision box? _____
_____

What do you notice about your vision box as a whole?_____
_____

How is the inside different from the outside? _____
_____

What are three things you notice about the inside? _____
_____

What are three things you notice about the outside? _____
_____

When you look at your vision box, what do you feel? _____
_____

more to think about

- What do you need to change in your life right now to create the ideal world on the outside of your box?

- How much of what is in your ideal world is within your control?

- How much of your ideal self is already part of you? What do you need to do to appreciate that?

- With whom can you share your box?

- What do you want to say about your vision?

focus

This exercise will make you more aware of your true self. It will help you understand whether you show your true self to the world or hide behind a mask.

We all wear masks. We put on a face for the outside world, depending on where we are and whom we are with. Sometimes we wear the mask of a grownup or the mask of a student or the mask of a child. We may wear so many masks that it becomes hard to remember who we really are! Only by discovering the masks that you wear can you begin to take them off. Who is your true self? Sometimes there are layers of masks, and it takes time to dig down to the true you.

Sometimes it's good to put on a mask and have a dialogue with yourself. When we truly look at all our different "faces," we can begin to understand what parts of us are real and what parts of us are only a defense against letting people get to know us. In this exercise, you will make masks that show your true self and the self you hide behind.

what you'll need

Cardboard, at least 8" x 11"
Popsicle stick or tongue depressor
A glue stick or white glue
Scissors or a craft knife
Thin markers
Decorative materials

1. Cut the cardboard into the shape of a face. Glue the stick to the bottom of the shape, or pierce the cardboard and insert the stick into the mask. Using scissors or a knife, make holes in the cardboard for eyes and mouth. If you prefer, you can draw the features.

2. Your creation should represent one of the masks you present to the world. Glue on any decorative materials that help portray this self.

3. Repeat the last activity, but this time, make a mask of your true self. Who have you been hiding? Can you show her in a mask?

4. Now put the first mask up to your face and look in a mirror, as you think about the answers to these questions:

    • What do you see?

    • If that mask were to say something, what would it be?

    • If that mask had a name, what would it be?

    • How has that mask helped you to protect yourself up until now?

    • How is the second mask different from the first?

follow-up

If the person each mask represents were to talk with you, what would she say? Talk with the mask on, and then take it off and talk back to her. Write down your conversation.

more to think about

◆ How can you use this worksheet to remind you that you don't always need to wear a mask?

◆ Notice when you are wearing your first mask out in the world. What can you do to make the situation safe enough for you to take the mask off?

focus

This exercise will help you become more aware of your feelings and how they affect you. Being aware of your feelings can help you avoid self-destructive eating behaviors.

We can react to our feelings in many different ways. We may communicate them appropriately, responding directly to others or to ourselves through creative expression. But when our feelings are too overwhelming, painful, or anxiety provoking, we may react by:

- Burying our feelings

- Focusing excessively on our bodies–counting calories, having negative body image thoughts, or having "fat" thoughts, and so on—to distract ourselves

- Acting out with self-destructive behaviors, such as purging

Being able to identify your feelings and recognize your way of reacting toward them is important in working toward a balanced and focused life. Many different emotions fall into the categories of mad, sad, glad, or afraid. Sarcasm, jealousy, and irritability are all "mad" emotions. "Sad" emotions include loneliness, grief, and regret, while contentment, peace, and cheerfulness are in the "glad" category. "Afraid" feelings include anxiety, nervousness, or panic. We all experience so many different emotions that sometimes it's hard to recognize what we are feeling!

Write down as many "mad" feelings as you can think of: _____

_____

Write down as many "sad" feelings as you can think of: _____

_____

Write down as many "glad" feelings as you can think of: _____

_____

Write down as many "afraid" feelings as you can think of: _____

_____

Having an idea of how you feel in any given moment is important to avoid acting out your feelings or burying them. Being aware of your emotions can help you express them in healthy ways. Take a moment to listen to your inner emotional state. How are you feeling right at this moment? Check all that apply:

❏ Afraid	❏ Content	❏ Hurt	❏ Perplexed
❏ Aggressive	❏ Curious	❏ Incredulous	❏ Prayerful
❏ Amazed	❏ Depressed	❏ Indifferent	❏ Regretful
❏ Ambitious	❏ Determined	❏ Innocent	❏ Relieved
❏ Angry	❏ Disappointed	❏ Intuitive	❏ Sad
❏ Annoyed	❏ Ecstatic	❏ Irritable	❏ Sarcastic
❏ Anxious	❏ Enlightened	❏ Jealous	❏ Shocked
❏ Apologetic	❏ Enraged	❏ Joyful	❏ Shy
❏ Aroused	❏ Envious	❏ Lonely	❏ Smug
❏ Arrogant	❏ Exasperated	❏ Loving	❏ Stoic
❏ Ashamed	❏ Excited	❏ Mad	❏ Stubborn
❏ Aware	❏ Focused	❏ Meditative	❏ Surprised
❏ Bold	❏ Frustrated	❏ Mischievous	❏ Sympathetic
❏ Bored	❏ Glad	❏ Moody	❏ Thoughtful
❏ Brash	❏ Grateful	❏ Nervous	❏ Thrilled
❏ Cautious	❏ Grieving	❏ Obsessive	❏ Uncomfortable
❏ Cheerful	❏ Guilty	❏ Obstinate	❏ Withdrawn
❏ Confident	❏ Happy	❏ Panicked	
❏ Confused	❏ Hopeful	❏ Peaceful	

follow-up

Each day, using the list above, choose five emotions you have felt. Write down those feelings in your journal or the Notes section at the end of this workbook. When you have an intense feeling, try to use the list to start a dialogue with the person your feelings are directed toward. Notice how that helps you avoid self-destructive behaviors. Write down any progress you think you have made by choosing to identify, feel, and express your feelings instead of burying them, avoiding them, or acting them out.

more to think about

- Checking your feelings regularly will help make you more aware of when you are most likely to turn to dysfunctional eating behaviors to avoid your emotions.

34 body image poetry

focus

This exercise will help you think about the positive aspects of being a woman.

In her poem *Phenomenal Woman*, Maya Angelou wrote about uniqueness of women and the beauty of their bodies. The poem opens with these lines:

Pretty women wonder where my secret lies.

I'm not cute or built to suit a fashion model's size....

Throughout the poem, Angelou refers to different qualities of women: the "span of my hips," "the joy in my feet," "the sun of my smile," "the need for my care." Her message is that women—women of all sizes and shapes—are phenomenal. Think about the words Maya Angelou has written. You many want to read the entire poem.

How does her message make you feel about being a girl? A woman? _____

_____

How does this message relate to your body image? To your self-esteem? _____

_____

In your journal or on the Notes pages at the end of this book, write a poem that shares your personal message about self-acceptance.

follow-up

Look for more poems that speak about women and body image. You can visit your library, find poems online, go to poetry readings, or browse in local bookstores. Find poets whose work you like, and read—get inspired!

more to think about

- Start a collection of poems that have an important message for you. They may be poems you've written or poems by others.

- Share your collection with someone close to you.

35 taking a time-out

focus

This exercise will help you build your self-control. When you are in control of yourself, you are less likely to turn to eating disorder behaviors.

Have you ever been so frustrated that you felt like you were going to explode? When we don't let ourselves take the time we need to regroup, our feelings can escalate and become overwhelming. At times, they may be too difficult to handle.

When you were a small child, your parents may have put you in time-out when you misbehaved. Time-out was a good way for you to relax for a few moments and reduce your own frustration. Now that you're older, time-out can still help when you reach the point where you don't know how to cope with your feelings. Time-out can give you the moments you need to experience your feelings, without worrying about how they affect others. Instead of burying your feelings or acting them out by reaching for eating disorder behaviors, you can give them a chance to pass.

Time-outs are an important way to reduce your stress, and they can be an alternative to overeating, undereating, or purging. If you practice this technique before you really need it, it will be easier to use when you do.

1. Remove yourself from a frustrating situation. Sit and do nothing but focus on your breath for a specified period of time. Try ten minutes at first. If you can't do ten minutes, try five. After your time is up, go back to the situation and see if your frustration level has decreased.

2. Writing during a time-out can help you get control of your feelings. While you are in time-out, write down everything you are feeling and thinking during that time. Try to write down everything you can, without worrying that someone else will read it or talk to you about it. Keep this thought in mind as you write: you can throw it all away when you are done.

Wait until twenty-four hours have passed before reading what you have written. Waiting may help you gain insight into your emotions and your urge to act out. And if at any time you want to throw out what you wrote, do it!

follow-up

Describe how you feel when you need a time-out. _____

_____

Are there situations when it may be difficult for you to take a time-out? _____

_____

How can you make time-outs easier and more natural for you when you are upset?

_____

_____

more to think about

- ◆ How can you tell the people you are with that you need a time-out?

36 recognizing what you need

Is it hard for you to ask for what you need because you are afraid you won't get it? It may feel so much easier just to say, "I don't need anything!" But that can translate into a downward spiral affecting all your relationships. "I don't need anything" turns into "I don't need anything from you." Even your body gets involved in proving that you don't need anything from anyone, sending the message, "I don't even need food!"

Yet we all need food. And we all need other people. What else are you trying to prove that you don't need? It's likely that you do have needs that you have been afraid to tell others about. People can't read your mind. It's okay to tell them what you need. There's no guarantee that they will give it to you, but if you don't tell them, they don't even have a chance to meet your needs.

What are you trying to deprive yourself of? First, identify what you are denying:

1. I deny that I need _____

2. I deny that I need _____

3. I deny that I need _____

4. I deny that I need _____

5. I deny that I need _____

6. I deny that I need _____

7. I deny that I need _____

8. I deny that I need _____

9. I deny that I need _____

10. I deny that I need _____

Now name ten needs. They can be physical, emotional, or spiritual.

1. I need _____

2. I need _____

3. I need _____

4. I need _____

5. I need _____

6. I need _____

7. I need _____

8. I need _____

9. I need _____

10. I need _____

follow-up

Every day this week in your journal or in the Notes section at the end of this workbook, write down one thing that you need and one person who you think could help you meet that need. Each day, decide if you will ask that person to help or if you will try to meet the need yourself.

more to think about

◆ Do you normally focus on other people's needs?

◆ What is it like to think about your needs?

◆ Do you usually consider yourself weak if you ask for what you need?

◆ What might it feel like to be strong and still need things and people?

37 draw a bridge

focus

This exercise will help you move toward positive ways to cope. It will give you a healthy vision of your recovery.

Getting from one place to another is simple if we are talking about crossing a quiet neighborhood street. If we are talking about getting from dysfunctional eating patterns to healthy, balanced body image thoughts, getting from one place to another is much more complicated.

what you'll need

Colored pencils or thin markers
A large sheet of drawing paper

Draw a bridge from one side of the paper to the other. Add as many people or details as you like.

- Imagine that the left side of the bridge is your past, and draw where you are now.

- Imagine that the right side of the bridge is your future, and draw where you want to be.

- Underneath your bridge, draw what you are afraid of or what you are trying to conquer.

- Above your bridge, draw your image of the support and help you get from people in your life.

When you have finished your drawing, answer the questions that follow.

1. Describe what you see on the left side of your bridge. _____
_____

2. Describe what you see on the right side of your bridge. _____
_____

3. What is underneath your bridge? _____
_____

4. What is above your bridge? _____
_____

5. Is there anyone or anything on the bridge? _____
_____

6. If you could put yourself on the bridge, how far across would you be? _____
_____

7. How does this drawing apply to your eating disorder behaviors? _____
_____

follow-up

In a few weeks, look at your bridge again. Where would you be on it now?

_____

_____

In a month or two, draw another bridge. What is on either side? What is above and below? Where are you?

_____

_____

_____

more to think about

◆ Share the insights you gained with friends and family members. Then ask them to draw their own bridges and share their insights with you.

your emotional toolbox

At this point, you have many tools to keep you from relying on your past eating disorder behaviors. Instead of acting out self-destructively, you can pick a positive coping skill to help you to deal with uncomfortable feelings. This section reviews these tools in detail. On the next page, you'll find a handy list you can post to remind you of all the healthier solutions available to you.

Keep a Journal

A journal can be a safe place to write your thoughts and feelings. Sitting in a comfortable place, write down everything you are feeling. Begin with any emotions you notice and move on to any physical sensations you are aware of. Describe your surroundings in detail and move on to describing the relationships in your life.

Draw Your Feelings

Think about how you are feeling at the moment. If you were made up of lines, shapes, and colors, what would they be? Are you feeling soft and pastel? Are you more earth-colored right now? Do you take up the whole page or are you crouched in a corner? Your edges may be sharp and spiky or fuzzy, with smeared edges that you've rubbed with a tissue or cotton ball. Draw your feelings at this moment, feeling yourself relax as you express the moment on paper.

Create a Collage

You'll need a glue stick or white glue, scissors, and a large piece of construction paper, cardboard, or smooth wood. Using old magazines, find pictures and words to describe how you feel at that moment or how you would like to feel. Cut out the pictures and words or tear them, leaving the edges fuzzy. Glue the images onto your surface in a way that reflects your feelings. Fill the entire surface, even overlapping some images. When your collage is dry, paint a thin layer of white glue (or shellac) across the surface. If thin enough, the glue will dry clear and create a hard surface that will protect your collage and keep the edges from curling. On the back of your collage or in your journal, write about what you have done.

Use Relaxed Breathing

Slowly breathing in through your nose and out through your mouth, take five deep breaths. As you inhale, concentrate on filling your belly with air like a balloon. Then exhale, deflating the balloon, letting all the air out of your body. As you inhale, imagine breathing in peace and tranquility; as you exhale, imagine breathing out stress, tension, and anxiety.

Use Guided Imagery

Find a comfortable place to sit or lie down, and focus all your attention on your body. Slowly breathe in through your nose and out through your mouth, ten times. Focus all your attention on your feet. Imagine the bottoms of your feet open like trap doors. Picture all the stress in your body flowing out from the bottoms of your feet, into the floor, and down into the earth. The stress flows like water into the dirt, through the mud and rocks, and into the molten lava at the center of the earth, dissipating like steam into the Earth's core. Focus on your calves, letting go of all stress. Focus on your shins, relaxing, letting go of all tension, and feeling it drain out through your feet and into the floor. Relax your knees and your thighs. Feel the muscles in the back of your thighs and the front of your thighs, the muscles that carry you around all day, as they relax. Feel the flow of relaxation all the way down to your feet. Feel the base of your spine as it settles into the surface beneath you. As you are pulled down by gravity, feel how relaxing that is.

Talk with Someone

Can you tell someone how you are feeling? Talk to your parents or pick up the phone and call a friend. Call your therapist. Call a hotline. There are many hotlines that can help you in the middle of the night if you are awake and need to talk with someone. You can find their phone numbers in your phone directory or by calling information.

Write

Write a letter or an e-mail to a person you trust with your thoughts or with whom you'd like to share your feelings. Even if you never send it, tell that person what you are feeling and describe your life at this moment. You can also write to a person you make up, like an imaginary guide. What will you say about what you are going through? What questions will you ask? Imagine you get a response to your letter. What does it say? Or imagine you are your future self. Write a letter telling that future self how you are feeling. Ask your self where she is now and how she is doing. Can she give you any advice about getting through this time in your life? Can she reassure you that you will get through this time?

Take a Time-Out

Outside is a good place to take time-outs, if possible. Can you sit and do nothing but focus on your breath or the sky for a specified period of time? Try ten minutes at first. If you can't do ten minutes, try five. At the end of your time-out, see if your frustration level has decreased. Make sure you tell the people you are with that you are taking a time-out and will be back at the end of your specified time.

Use Positive Affirmations

Remember, positive affirmations are always in the present, not the future: "I am better," not "I will be better." You can use an affirmation like a key to turn off negative thoughts that are getting you down, but you don't actually have to believe it at the moment. What positive affirmation can you use right now? Can you tell yourself that you are okay right at this moment? Can you tell yourself, "I love and accept myself exactly as I am"? Repeat one positive affirmation twenty times and see how you feel.

YOUR EMOTIONAL TOOLBOX

Pick a tool that you think will work, and if it doesn't work, try another. Something in this toolbox will certainly work for you; it's just a matter of finding the right one for the situation you're in!

✔ Keep a journal.

✔ Draw your feelings.

✔ Create a collage.

✔ Use relaxed breathing.

✔ Use guided imagery.

✔ Talk with someone.

✔ Write.

✔ Take a time-out.

✔ Use positive affirmations.

NOTES

NOTES

NOTES

NOTES

NOTES

NOTES

NOTES

NOTES

Tammy Nelson, MS, has worked as a psychotherapist for over fifteen years. She is executive director and co-founder of the Center for Healing and Recovery in Norwalk, CT, and co-director and co-founder of the Ridgefield Center for Families & Children in Ridgefield, CT. Nelson is a licensed professional counselor, a registered art therapist, a licensed alcohol and drug counselor, and a certified Imago Relationships therapist. She resides in the New York City area, where she works in her private practice treating anorexia, bulimia, and other eating disorders using group and expressive therapy.

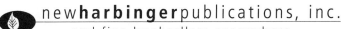